PRAISE FOR
MICHELLE DE KRETSER'S

THE LOST DOG

Finalist for the Commonwealth Writers' Prize
Longlisted for the Man Booker Prize
Longlisted for the Orange Broadband Prize

"Engrossing.... De Kretser confidently marshals her reader back and forth through the book's complex flashback structure, keeping us in suspense even as we read simply for the pleasure of her prose.... De Kretser knows when to explain, and when to leave us deliciously wondering." —Moira Macdonald, *Seattle Times*

"Uncannily compelling. At the end, it suddenly becomes clear that every seemingly gratuitous observation in the book was leading us toward a very particular conclusion not only about these characters but also about how our lives are defined by the cruelties and kindnesses of those who precede us.... De Kretser's daring willingness to let suspense accrue without promising resolution is a worthy echo of Henry James's brilliance." —Dara Horn, *Washington Post*

"More often than not, de Kretser nails some situation or foible in twenty words or less.... There is much here that dazzles.... De Kretser's writing is as boldly beautiful as ever."
—Alison McCulloch, *New York Times Book Review*

"*The Lost Dog* is an uncompromisingly literary (and literate) book: ferociously intelligent, highbrow, allusive, and unflinching.... There are all kinds of terrors lurking within the heart of the book — these are for the reader to discover — but the one that is most palpable is the undeniable fact that this book is touched, like Rilke's 'terrible angel,' by the terror of greatness."

— Neel Mukherjee, *Time*

"De Kretser is as piercing in her observations of a city as Don DeLillo is at his best — naming and thus celebrating the kitsch and the familiar....A delight to read, revealing itself in small gemlike scenes."

— Tina Shaw, *Listener*

"A persuasive vitality and an ethical alertness that give keen observation relevance and wit....De Kretser's displaced and subtle characters are genuinely interesting, and her writing is emotionally accurate....A fine novel."

— Ursula K. Le Guin, *Guardian*

"The Booker judges have saluted the awesomely smart and agile writing of Sri Lankan–born Australian Michelle de Kretser in *The Lost Dog*....In trendy downtown Melbourne and the bush beyond, a lonely Indian-born academic searches for his beloved dog, for his childhood in Asia and Australia, and for the secrets of a mysterious artist whose vision of mixed-up urban life matches his own fragile sense of self."

— *Independent* (Editor's Choice)

"This is my favorite kind of novel. It is full of incident and character, tells a gripping story, has many touches of brilliance, and can make you laugh and wonder....The language is full of light, color, and precise observation, and better still, the author can handle ethical and political concerns with a light touch."

— Carmen Callil, *Guardian*

"Rich, beautiful, shocking, affecting." — Clare Press, *Vogue*

"This book is so engaging and thought-provoking and its subject matter so substantial that the reader notices only in passing how funny it is.... Michelle de Kretser is one of those rare writers whose work balances substance with style. Her writing is very witty, but it also goes deep, informed at every point by a benign and far-reaching intelligence."   — Kerryn Goldsworthy, *Sydney Morning Herald*

"A wonderful tale of obsession, art, death, loss, human failure, and past and present loves. One of Australia's best contemporary writers."   — *Harper's Bazaar* (Australia)

"Stunningly beautiful.... Michelle de Kretser is the fastest rising star in Australia's literary firmament."   — *Metro* (Australia)

"*The Lost Dog* is written in a devastatingly pointed style, with not a hint of Jamesian circumlocution. De Kretser has a talent for sizing up a character, at once bringing them to life and puncturing their pretensions. Her hard-boiled sentences invariably hit their mark. 'Seeing through' is one of her strongest suits....A wonderfully written novel that is often funny but, despite its sharp critical intelligence, not at all cynical."   — James Ley, *Age* (Australia)

"A nuanced portrait of a man in his time. The novel, like Tom, is multicultural, intelligent, challenging, and, ultimately, rewarding."   — Andrea Kempf, *Library Journal*

"This is the best novel I have read for a long time. The writing is elegant and subtle, and Michelle de Kretser knows how to construct a gripping story.... This writing is new and constantly surprising, without being showy or quirky. It is exact, like Penelope Fitzgerald's; it is strange, like Patrick White's. When I finished, I immediately started on her previous book, *The Hamilton Case*, which is equally extraordinary."   — A. S. Byatt, *Financial Times*

THE
LOST
DOG

ALSO BY MICHELLE DE KRETSER

The Rose Grower
The Hamilton Case

THE LOST DOG

A Novel

MICHELLE DE KRETSER

BACK BAY BOOKS
LITTLE, BROWN AND COMPANY
NEW YORK   BOSTON   LONDON

Back Bay Books / Little, Brown and Company
Hachette Book Group
237 Park Avenue, New York, NY 10017
Visit our website at www.HachetteBookGroup.com

First published in North America in hardcover by Little, Brown and Company, April 2008
First Back Bay paperback edition, August 2009
Originally published in Australia by Allen & Unwin in 2007

Back Bay Books is an imprint of Little, Brown and Company. The Back Bay Books name and logo are trademarks of Hachette Book Group, Inc.

Boyd Tonkin's profile of Michelle de Kretser, which appears in the reading group guide at the back of this book, was originally published in *The Independent* on June 20, 2008. Copyright © 2008 by Independent News and Media Limited. Reprinted with permission.

Library of Congress Cataloging-in-Publication Data
de Kretser, Michelle.
 The lost dog : a novel/Michelle de Kretser. — 1st ed.
   p. cm.
  ISBN 978-0-316-00183-0 (hc) / 978-0-316-00184-7 (pb)
 1. Authors — Fiction.   2. Australia — Fiction.   3. India — Fiction.
I. Title.
 PR9619.4.D4L67 2008
 823'.92 — dc22   2007043331

10 9 8 7 6 5 4 3 2 1

RRD-IN

Printed in the United States of America

FOR GUS, OF COURSE

The whole of anything can never be told.

—HENRY JAMES, *Notebooks*

Yes this is my album
But learn ere you look
That you are expected
To add to my book

Iris de Souza
Holy Redeemer Convent, 1931

TUESDAY

Afterward, Tom would remember paddocks stroked with light. He would remember the spotted trunks of gum trees, the dog arching past to sniff along the fence.

He cleaned his teeth at the tap on the water tank. The house in the bush had no running water, no electricity. It was only sporadically inhabited and had grown grimy with neglect. But Tom, spitting into the luxuriant weeds by the tap that November morning, thought, Light, air, space, silence. The Benedictine luxuries.

He placed his toothpaste and brush on a log at the foot of the steps; and later forgot where he had left them. Night would send him blundering about a room where his flashlight swung across the wall, and what he could find and what he needed were not the same thing.

On the kitchen table, beside Tom's laptop, was the printout of his book, *Meddlesome Ghosts: Henry James and the Uncanny*. He remembered the elation he had felt the previous evening, drafting the final paragraph; the impression that he had nailed it all down at last. It was to this end that he had rented Nelly Zhang's house for four days, days in which he had written fluently and with conviction, to his surprise, because he was in the habit of proceeding hesitantly, and the book had been years in the making.

He owed this small triumph to Nelly, who had said, "It's what you need. No distractions, and you won't have to worry about kennels."

This evidence of her concern had moved Tom. At the same time, he thought, She wants the money. The web of their relations was shot through with these ambivalences, shade and bright twined with such cunning that their pattern never settled.

His jacket hung on the back of a chair. He put it on, then paused: shuffled pages, squared off the stack of paper, touched what he had accomplished. James's dictum caught his eye: *Experience is never limited, and it is never complete.*

When Tom called, raising his voice, the dog went on nosing through leaves and damp grass. It was their last morning there; the territory was no longer new. Yet whenever the dog was allowed outside, he would race to the far end of the yard and start working his way along the fence. Instinct, deepened over centuries, compelled him to check boundaries, drew him to the edges of knowledge.

Afterward, Tom would remember the dog ignoring him and the spurt of impatience he had felt. The dog had to be walked and the house packed up before the long drive back to the city. He was keen to get moving while the weather held. So he didn't pat the dog's soft head when he strode to the fence and reached for him.

The dog was standing still, one forepaw raised, listening.

Tea-colored puddles sprawled on the track. A cockatoo flying up from a sapling dislodged a rhinestone spray. It was a wet spring even in the city, and in these green hills, it rained and rained.

The dog's paw-pads were shining jet. He sniffed, and sneezed, and plunged into dithering grass. A twenty-foot rope kept him from farmland and forest while affording him greater freedom than his lead.

The man picking his way through rutted mud at the other end

of the rope disliked the cold. Tom Loxley had spent two-thirds of his life in a cool southern city. But his childhood had been measured in monsoons, and the first windows he knew had contained the Arabian Sea. Free hand shoved deep in his pocket, he held himself tight against the morning.

Light rubbed itself over the paddocks. It struck silver from the cockatoo and splintered the windshield of a toy truck threading up the mountain where trees went down to steel. But what Tom took from the scene was the thrust and weight of leaves, the season's green upswinging. Over time, his eye had grown accustomed to the bleached pigments of the continent where he had made his life. But love takes shape before we know it. On a damp, plumed coast in India, Tom's first encounter with landscape had been dense with leaves. A faultless place for him would always be a green one.

He glanced back at Nelly's house. Afterward, he would remember his sense that everything — the pepper tree by the gate, the sloping driveway, the broad blue sky itself — was holding its breath, gathered to the moment. The impression was forceful, but Tom's thoughts were busy with Nelly as he had once seen her: astride a sunny wall in the suburb where they both lived, a striped cat pouring himself through her arms.

In the corner of his eye, something blurred. At the same time, the rope skidded through his fingers. His head snapped around to see gray fur moving fast, and the dog in pursuit, the end to which sinew and nerve and tissue had always been building.

Tom swooped for the rope and clawed at air. On the hillside above the track, the dog was swallowed by leaves.

Birdsong and eucalyptus air.

A lean white dog, rust-splotched, springing up a bank.

Things Tom Loxley would remember.

IT HAD BEGUN, seven months earlier, with a painting.

April becalmed in hazy, slanted light. Tom clipped on the dog's lead, and they left his flat to walk in streets where houses were packed like wheat. Windows were turning yellow. Dahlias showed off like sunsets. On an autumn evening in the city, Tom looked sideways at other people's lives.

At a gallery he hadn't entered in the four years since his wife left, long sash windows had been pushed up; there were smokers on the terraces with glasses in their hands. Tom tied the dog to the garden side of the ornate iron railings and went up the steps.

A group show: four young artists. Their friends and relatives were congratulatory and numerous in the two rooms on the ground floor. Tom drank cold wine and looked at paintings. They seemed unremarkable, but he knew enough to know he couldn't tell.

From the street it had seemed that there were fewer people upstairs. He had his glass refilled by a pierced girl with ruffles of hair parted low on the side, and started up the stairs. But something made him glance back. She was looking up at him, her face gleaming and amused; and he realized, with a little lurch of perception, that she was a boy.

The second-floor room that ran the width of the building contained work unrelated to the exhibition below. A well-fleshed man stood in front of a painting, blocking it from view.

"Eddie's still channeling Peter, it seems." He had a thin, carrying voice. A dark boy standing beside him snickered.

On the short wall opposite the door was an almost abstract landscape at which Tom looked for four or five minutes, a long time. Then he went out onto the balcony and saw a couple leaving the gallery stop to fondle the dog's floppy ears. The word *Beefmaster* passed on the side of a van.

When Tom stepped back through the floor-length window, the large man was in the center of the room. More people had attached themselves to his group. He gazed out over their heads; his face was round and turnip-white. The pallor made his eyes, which were very dark, appear hollow. He murmured as Tom passed. There was a small explosion of laughter.

Tom gulped wine in front of the picture opposite the door. His scalp hummed. He thought, I am the wrong kind of thing. He thought, I don't belong here. The adverb having a wide application.

By an act of will, he directed his attention to the landscape in front of him. His formal training in Art History was limited to two undergraduate years. They had left him a vocabulary, formal strategies for thinking about images. He believed himself to possess a set of basic analytical tools for operating upon a work of art.

Faced with this picture, he thought only, How beautiful. And relived, at once, the frustration that had edged his youthful efforts, shadowing the pleasure he took in looking at art. Pictures belong to the world of things. They cannot be contained in language. Tom was still susceptible to their immanent hostility. It had persuaded him, as a student, to concentrate on literature.

There he was at home in the medium. For all their shifting play, narratives did not exceed his grasp. He paid them the tribute of lucid investigation, and they unfolded before him.

An English voice said, "Isn't it *completely* wonderful?"

A milky woman with crimson pigtails was smiling down at him. "I was *sure* it was you." She went up on her toes; she was wearing beaded mesh slippers. Up and down she went again, holding out her hand.

The rocking was a boon. It identified a party in the summer; a long woman rising and falling. "We met at Esther's, didn't we?" Tom took her cool, boneless fingers. "I'm sorry, I don't remember...?"

"Imogen Halliday. But everyone just says 'Mogs.'"

Mogs was wearing a kimono fashioned from what might have been burlap, slashed here and there to show a silky green undergarment. She said, "How is Esther? I've been simply *swamped*."

"I've been out of touch myself."

Two years earlier, Tom Loxley and Esther Kade had been deputed by their respective university departments, Textual Studies and Art History, to attend a weekend conference on Multimedia and Interactive Teaching Strategies. Under the circumstances, alcohol and sex had seemed no more than survival mechanisms. Later both regretted the affair, which outlived the conference by only an awkward encounter or two. But Esther now felt obliged to invite Tom to her parties to show there were no hard feelings; for the same reason, he felt obliged to go.

Interactive strategies, he thought.

"Isn't life mad? But I *adore* working here." Mogs swayed above him, waving a hand on which a green jewel shone.

Christ, thought Tom. It's *real*.

Mogs was, in her own way, catching.

"I was looking at you: you were transfixed. *Isn't* she a marvel?" The slippers rose and fell. "Nelly *Zhang*," said Mogs's soft English voice.

Tom nodded. He had read the name, which meant nothing to him, on the list he had picked up at the door. And noted that the picture was not for sale.

"Carson's known her forever. Since before ... you know, *everything*. She's over there with him, actually. In the black ... tunic, I think you'd say."

Tom turned his head and saw a woman in a loose, dark dress that fell to midcalf. Red beads about her neck, her twisted hair secured with a scarlet crayon.

"Really exciting. A *painting*. An early work, of course. She was barely out of art school. From Carson's own collection. Such a privilege just to *see* it now that Nelly only shows photographs of her work."

Mogs was all right. But Tom wished she would go away. He wanted to be left alone with the picture.

Outside the gallery, a spotlight fell across a strip of grass where Nelly Zhang squatted, scratching the dog's chest.

"Hail, dog," she said. "You speckled beast." She peered at his name tag. Her sooty fringe made an almost shocking line against her powdered skin.

The dog wagged his tail. His good looks habitually elicited caresses, tidbits. Experience had taught him confidence in his ability to charm.

Nelly stood up. Tom was not a tall man, but her head was scarcely higher than his shoulder.

She said, "Lovely dog."

He remembered that his wife used to refer to the dog as a chick magnet.

Nelly was lighting a thin cigarette. The pungency of cloves and behind it — Tom's sense of smell was acute — a bodily aroma.

The dog tilted his spotted muzzle and sniffed. Tom bent to untie his leash.

"That looks professional."

"Just a quick-release tie."

"A man who knows his knots. So much rarer than one who knows the ropes."

He didn't say, I was lonely growing up.

He didn't say, String is cheap.

BUT IT MIGHT HAVE BEGUN long, long before that evening in Carson Posner's gallery. It might have been historical.

War took an Englishman called Arthur Loxley to the East and in time returned him with two medals and a shattered knee to ruined Coventry. His mother had been killed in the first raid; to his father he had never had much to say. A trio of sisters inspected him as if their free trial period might expire and leave them stuck with him forever. At some point each took him aside to ask what he had brought her from the Orient. Their blue eyes glittered with the understanding that the world had been made safe for the business of acquisition.

He was twenty-six, and his knee ached all through the winter. But the map was still stained pink. Pink people could move about it as they pleased, could rule a line on it and bring nations into being. Arthur returned to India, where that kind of thing was causing a commotion. He paid no attention to it, having had his fill of history. What he was after, then and for the rest of his life, was a bolt-hole, with drink thrown in. There was also the memory of a twenty-four-hour leave he had spent in the whorehouses of Bombay. A Javanese half-caste with spongy golden thighs was instructing him in the art of cunnilingus when boots thundered past in the street and a Glaswegian voice bellowed that Rangoon had fallen. Thereafter, news of defeat would always induce in him a mild erotic stir.

Having drifted down the Malabar Coast, he fetched up in Mangalore, where he was taken on as an inventory clerk by Mr. Ashok Lal, an exporter of cashew nuts with a godown in the port. When Arthur looked up from his ledger, boats rocked on green water.

He rediscovered, with gratitude, the room India granted to casual human theater. It was there, on every street: in garlanded Ganesh affixed to a radiator grille, in a scabby, naked toddler with liquid jewels at his nostrils, in the man who, possessing no legs, propelled himself on a wheeled plank, advancing on Arthur with a terrible smile. It was not that Arthur idealized the place, for he was a kind man and the daily spectacle was often cruel. But he relished the friendly attention paid here to comedy and tragedy alike, a willingness to be entertained, amused, horrified, that he recognized as a form of thanksgiving for the faceted world.

And so, from modest pleasures, Arthur fashioned a happy life.

The locally distilled whiskey was cheap, the beer cheaper. He ate deviled prawns every Sunday. Once a month he visited a former maharani who had a house with turquoise shutters in the shadow of the cathedral, and five exquisitely skilled girls.

An Indian who had been with the firm for eighteen months was promoted over Arthur, whose congratulations were sincere. He was as indifferent to distinctions of race as to his own advancement. He drank steadily, sometimes fabulously, but always arrived at his desk sober.

Contentment, being rare, never fails to attract attention. Arthur Loxley, with his veined cheeks and drunkard's careful gait, was increasingly in the thoughts of a beautiful woman. Iris de Souza's father had informed her at the age of six that she was to marry an Englishman, and neither of them had ever lost sight of that goal. Iris's skin was fair, her face ravishing; many a pretty Eurasian was let down by toothpick legs, but Iris's calves were shapely. Her mother, a handsome crow, had had the good sense to die young. Her father . . . But it would take a separate volume to explore the intricate self-loathing of this man, who despised in others the inadequacies that crawled in his own murk. He was an umbrella, tightly furled. Springing open, he might gouge flesh from your fingers. His rages were unpredictable and inconsistent. Iris acquired early the important female attribute of fear.

Fear, crouched always like an imp under her ribs, leaped out on her thirty-third birthday. She remained in front of the mirror, fingering the treacherous silver thread coiling through her hair. She could still pass for twenty-four, but that was hardly the point.

Next door the Ho baby was crying.

It was the war, thought Iris, the war had ruined everything, mixed everything up. It was the mixing she had loved, at the time. In the WVS she had rolled bandages and mixed with English people. A girl called Babs — a new style of girl, fresh from England — was kind to the Eurasian volunteers. It was rumored that Babs was a Communist. Iris was able to overlook this — also the way Babs wasted time conversing with tonga drivers, also Babs's blond mustache — because Babs took a shine to her. There were invitations to tea, the loan of a monograph on shanty dwellers.

In April Babs was offered the use, for a week, of a tin-roofed out-bungalow on a tea garden in the Nilgiris. It stood on the far side of the valley from the manager's house; his assistants had gone to the war and left their bungalow vacant. Unfortunately, Babs had seen fit to invite two Indian sisters as well, the up-to-date kind who had opinions. Even the discovery that the Guptas were connoisseurs of detective fiction could not redeem them in Iris's view. With their homespun saris and dog-eared Agatha Christies, they had a disturbingly ambiguous air.

All was righted by the advent of Captain Lawrence Fitch, Babs's brother. He brought with him one of his fellow officers in the Hussars, a beanpole he addressed as Saunders; but for Iris, this second young Englishman remained purely notional. There was only Lawrence: attentive to her every whim, always at hand with a shawl or a fish-paste sandwich, his honey-brown eyes sticky with appreciation. He had a scar just below the hollow at the base of his throat. More than anything in the world Iris wished to press her mouth to it. He gave off a powerful odor of tobacco and leather mingled, mysteriously, with burning sugar.

Ponies were hired. As Lawrence helped Iris mount, his fingers grazed her thigh.

There were mornings on the spines of ridges clad with rhododendron, a picnic in spotty light by a stream. There were cards and Charades. One evening, with an extravagant sunset spreading itself between mountains, Ayushi, the younger Gupta girl, who wore a diamond nose stud, was persuaded to tell their fortunes. Smoothing Iris's palm with a firm, flexible thumb, she offered her a journey over water. The tiny diamond winked like a code.

Iris was a good dancer. Lawrence enfolded her in his smell and hummed along to "Embraceable You" as he steered her through the French doors onto the verandah. On their last evening he wore his dress uniform of scarlet, dark blue, and gold. Iris got her wish; and much more besides.

It was clear to Iris that she was engaged to Lawrence. Only nothing was said for the moment. Discretion was her personal sacrifice to the war; she spent twenty months feeling exalted.

In that time he wrote to her twice; the second time, three scrawled lines stating what he would like to do to her when they next met.

In the last December of the war, she went into the WVS canteen and was greeted with the news that Babs's brother was dead. In Babs's sitting room, on an ugly blond-wood settee, Iris poured out her own sorrow.

Babs stared at her. Then said, in a thick voice, "How dare you claim a connection."

Iris, grappling anguish and mucus, made noises.

"The idea of Larry and...you." Babs ground her teeth. "With your spangles-on-net dresses."

Word got out.

Matthew Ho, the doctor's son who lived next door to the de Souzas, waited for Iris after mass. She had known him forever. On the way home, he asked her to marry him. Hygiene and his Sunday suit notwithstanding, he went down on one knee on the pavement. A crowd materialized at once to offer advice and encouragement.

Iris, schooled in obedience, relayed the news to her father. "Damn Ching-Chong cheek," said Sebastian de Souza. He might have been enraged but chose to be amused instead. After a moment, Iris could see that amusement was what the situation called for. Father and daughter tittered together.

For weeks, a word was enough to set them off. *Chopsticks. Pigtail.*

Every four months, for three years, Matthew took Iris to lunch at the Golden Lotus and renewed his proposal. On these occasions he remained seated. It was not the kind of restaurant to tolerate a spectacle.

Then he married a distant cousin, a girl who had been in Nanking when the Japs invaded. It was rumored that unspeakable things had been done to her.

They did not seem to have caused any lasting damage, thought Iris, plucking the telltale hair from her scalp with vicious precision. Matthew Ho's wife had already presented him with three plump yellow sons. The baby was colicky. Iris would wake at night to his screams.

In a sea-stopped street, she passed Arthur Loxley. He peered in under the umbrella Iris carried for her complexion, and lifted his hat.

Change was flexing its claws, snarling the weave of Arthur's days. The maharani had announced that she was immigrating to Cincinnati. She was paying for the girls to retrain as shorthand typists. Arthur, feeling a brisk pattering across his stomach, had opened his eyes to find the prettiest one practicing her finger exercises while fellating him.

He would have been a pushover for Iris in any case. She was beautiful and set herself to be charming. His strength of will could be gauged from the quantities of papier-mâché knick-knacks and gaudy rugs he had amassed, the result of bazaar encounters with liquid-eyed Kashmiri merchants.

Arthur rented a sweltering cell in the house of a government clerk with nine children. It had a concrete verandah overlooking a strip of baked earth, where bold canna lilies, red and fierce yellow, grew in rusty tins. In that narrow place he passed sublime afternoons, dozing with a tumbler at hand and his landlord's mongrel bitch stretched panting beneath his Bombay fornicator. The younger children made a game of him, daring one another to drink the melted ice in his glass or deposit a spider on the hillock of his belly. Once, as he snored, the smallest girl placed a blue flower between his parted lips.

Iris, inspecting the setup, saw at once that it would not do. There was a swath of stink from the drains. The dog's teeth worked furiously at her ticks. The children, intuiting an enemy, gathered at a distance and dug in their noses.

Thus it was settled that Arthur would join the de Souza household. If he faltered at the prospect of his father-in-law's countenance over breakfast, he gave no outward sign of alarm. He was still flooded with gratitude that Iris had chosen to make him the gift of herself, a marvel that twenty years of marriage would not quite suffice to dim.

And the house, set on a hill, was wonderful. Like the de Souzas, it had declined over three centuries. First the grounds had shrunk, then the mansion itself had been divided and sold piecemeal and partitioned again. It had suffered concrete outgrowths and bricked-in colonnades. An elderly gentleman lived on a half landing; a balcony sheltered a family of seven. But the house wore its changes like medals, hung out strings of washing like flags. Flowering creepers fastened it to the earth. In the compound, goats and hens roamed among tall trees and lavish ferns. There was a bed of rangy, perfumed gardenias. The de Souzas' apartment on the ground floor retained a portico, pillars, ceilings that flaked but were plastered with garlands and painted with cherubim, windows that gave onto the puckered blue sea.

Arthur Loxley enjoyed this distinction: he was the sole individual to slip past his father-in-law's guard. The lessons of history notwithstanding, Sebastian de Souza had continued to believe in the supremacy of the English race. But illusions that the fall of Singapore had left intact could not long survive daily proximity to Arthur. Four days after Iris returned from her honeymoon, her father informed her of her mistake. The enumeration of his son-in-law's inadequacies occupied the following half an hour, and then the rest of Sebastian's days.

· · · · · ·

Yet the marriage was not unhappier than most.

Money was one problem.

Another was the lack of a child. Arthur made no reproach, but Iris, who had lied to him about her age, was frightened that barrenness would betray her. There was also the dread that Lawrence, fumbling *down there,* had passed on something unmentionable.

She consulted doctors, Western-trained and ayurvedic, two specialists, a soothsayer, a faith healer. A priest exorcised the house. Iris implored Saint Anthony to grant her father the blessing of grandchildren, and sent five rupees to a famous temple in the south.

Finally, when she had exhausted her stratagems, Iris discovered that she was expecting a baby. She was forty-one years old, but the pregnancy was uneventful, the delivery easy. They wrapped the infant in clean cloths and presented him to her. She hadn't known that the universe weighed five pounds, eleven ounces.

He was named Thomas Sebastian after his grandfathers. But Iris, preparing a bottle of Cow & Gate infant formula, observed his dark limbs and coarse hair, and beheld her mother the crow.

The danger of a throwback: one reason why respectable whites avoided Eurasians.

Prices went on rising. Arthur cut down his expenditure on drink to a fifth of his salary.

Iris had two barres of different heights installed in her large, rectangular hall and opened a dancing school for children. She felt the shame of it: a married woman obliged to work.

Her qualifications were four years of ballet at a school run by a Frenchwoman; much was made of this in Iris's prospectus. However, late in life Madame Pauline Duval had taken to appearing at mass draped only in a creamy lace tablecloth. The memory was still vivid in Mangalore. Iris was obliged to lower her fees. Her Academy of Dance attracted only a few dozen children, not all of them from desirable backgrounds. But it covered the cost of St. Stephen's Junior College, where Tommy was now an Upper Infant. Matthew Ho's wife, a bundle with her hair in a knot, turned up to enroll her twin daughters. Iris was pleased to observe that the doughy little tots were devoid of talent.

Sebastian de Souza died. A grim, protracted death ensuring maximum havoc for Iris and a succession of slovenly nurses.

Shortly before the end he had a bowel movement, fouling the air. Trying not to inhale, Iris approached with basin and sponge. Her father opened his sunken eyes and addressed her: "Dolt."

Later, turning it over in her mind, she thought he might have said, "Don't." It was in any case his last message to her.

Thirty years earlier, he had sold the apartment. A provision in the settlement granted him life tenancy, rent-free. Sebastian had not considered it necessary to impart these facts to his daughter. A lawyer's letter gave Iris thirty days to vacate the premises.

Abdul Mustafa Hussein, the new owner, received her in the tiny, lentil-smelling office attached to his dry goods store. "Kwality Remains When Price Is Forgotten," announced an ominous plaque above his head. But the man in the white cotton skullcap was not unkind, and when Iris began to cry he was sincerely moved. She was allowed to remain in her ancestral home at a rent that was only mildly scandalous.

The academy taught only the basics, flat shoe and barefoot dancing. But a parent withdrew her daughter, saying that Iris's marble floor was injurious to a dancer's feet. Iris protested, reasoned, argued, stormed; in vain.

There came a Saturday when the only children waiting on the verandah were the Ho twins, their pigtails secured with stiff red bows.

Old Mr. Lal retired, entrusting the export of cashews to his brother's son. Vijay Lal was twenty-nine and had spent two swinging years in Leeds. He had sideburns, and a secretary he called Mini. Vijay summoned all his workers over the age of thirty and explained what was wrong with India. "This is a very backward-thinking country. My uncle, for example, went on employing some people for the simple reason he had always done so. I am intending to change all that." Then he gave them a month's notice. "For the Age of Aquarius we are needing fresh blood." He rose from his chair and clicked his fingers. He might have been ordering up the massacre; instead his voice rose in song. He warbled, in a relentless whine, of times that were a'changing. When at last he had finished there was silence. Gradually it dawned on his audience that he expected applause.

Iris took it with remarkable aplomb. "Now we have to emigrate. What I've been telling you for years."

At first Arthur put up a resistance. But history was not on his side.

. . . . . .

Every year there were fewer and fewer of those whose hybrid faces branded them the leftovers of empire. The Pereira boy had gone; the Redden girls were going; the railway Gilberts, all eight of them, had scraped up the fares for Toronto.

Tom walked up to the lighthouse. The sea hurled itself at the land; went away, bared its teeth and renewed the attack. Passed for Canada. Passed for England. People he had known all his life had been scrutinized like cashews and declared fit for export. The past was sliding from under his feet. He glimpsed, for the first time, the flux inherent in human affairs.

The scene struck him as momentous. He felt he was witnessing it from a great height, fixing it in his mind like a memorable passage in a book: the figure in navy shorts on the headland, the turmoil below.

On Iris's settee, Matthew Ho turned a sisal brim in his fingers and declined Arthur's offer of whiskey and soda.

He was one of those who had prospered since Independence. But eight months earlier his mother had died, and now Dr. Ho had resigned his registrarship at the government hospital. His wife had a cousin in San Diego, and the Hos would be joining his household later that week. "There are the children to think of," Matthew said, his thin eyes directed at a vase of plastic roses on a teapoy. Altogether the fellow was a queer fish, as Arthur remarked afterward. "Gives the impression he might come out with something neither of you wants to hear."

Two bookend children had accompanied Matthew Ho, as

if he required material evidence for his case. Tom, instructed to "go and play" with his guests, led Opal and Pearl onto the verandah. There he scratched a mosquito bite, limp with envy. At the house of a wealthy school friend, he had seen a Coca-Cola bottle. Acquired at a diplomatic sale, the empty bottle was displayed on a cabinet along with other trophies. Tom had coveted it at once: teenage, curvaceous, modern; a glass America. He looked at the twins, whose half-moon upper lips showed no indent, and was compelled to say, "I'll probably get a transistor radio for Christmas."

Pearl and Opal inspected him in silence. Then their round little mouths twitched. Side by side on the verandah wall, they kicked their four patent-leather feet and laughed in his face.

"Not America."

"Not England," countered Arthur.

"Not England," agreed Iris. "Why should we suffer the European Winter?"

Arthur blinked.

"Audrey," she reminded him, with quiet triumph. "Australia."

Audrey, Arthur's youngest sister, was the one who had kept in touch. She was not a trivial correspondent, reserving her flimsy blue aerograms for weighty communications: the death of their father, a brother-in-law's appendectomy, the coronation, her marriage, the decline of England, the prospects that glittered elsewhere.

Iris, the least practical of women, possessed the foresight that is a by-product of fear. Against just such a day, she had found the postage for Christmas cards, birthday greetings, a studio photograph of the three of them taken against a cardboard Taj Mahal.

Passed for Australia.

. . . . . .

At the thought of a New World, Arthur felt great weariness. He was not sure he could be dusted off for it. But there was his son's face, etched with excitement. He had realized, in the first week of his marriage, that his wife was vain, capable of pettiness, and not in love with him. In all that concerned the boy, however, her faculty for selflessness outstripped his own. She would willingly plow herself into the dust for the sake of the future quivering in their son. Arthur thought of rain falling in a far country; one day, turning to grain.

Old Mr. Lal sent his ancient, gleaming Bentley to take them to the station. Friends and neighbors gathered on the steps. At the last moment, with faces already arranged for farewells and all the luggage squeezed in, Tom said he had to use the lavatory.

In the yawning rooms of childhood he raced hither and thither, touching a doorframe, a tile, thinking, The last time, the last time. Glancing through a window to fix a view forever — the last time, the last time — he saw a dog on the shadowed edge of the lawn: a tiny, heraldic beast, one forepaw raised; milky as marble. Then it was gone. Fear opened its wings under Tom's heart. Already a neighbor had acquired a dog he didn't recognize. It was a glimpse of the terrible future: a world he knew as well as his own face altering by degrees, never entirely alien but riddled with strangeness. One day he would pass through these scenes like a ghost, everywhere encountering proof of his irrelevance.

In 1972 in Australia there was work even for a man of fifty-three. Even for Arthur Loxley.

When Arthur left the pub that Thursday evening, his breast pocket contained what was left of his second week's wages from the bottling plant where he had been taken on for a month's trial.

Any number of things might have been on his mind as he approached the tram tracks. The need to find a flat, as they could not stay with Audrey forever. The discovery that Australia, or at least this southern corner of it, was not a warm place. The certainty that he would not keep his job, as the senior accountant didn't like Poms and had told him so.

In fact, Arthur was gazing at the sky and remembering a Sunday School picnic on a manored estate, where there were blue pools under trees. Then he wondered why violets look purple close up but blue at a distance. There came into his mind something barely remembered, and perhaps, after all, only dreamed: the discovery of blue petals on his tongue.

He heard a shout, and the wild tinging of a bell, but did not immediately understand their significance. When he saw the tram swaying above him, he hopped smartly back. There was time to register surprise and pleasure at his nimbleness; then the car hit him. He heard his knee crack as he went down.

AT FIRST Tom was not afraid. The dog was given to running off. In parks, beside creeks, over waste ground: tracking a scent, he vanished, emerged as a white band glimpsed among trees or on a plunging hillside, disappeared again. In time, half an hour or so, he would turn up, grinning.

But this was the bush: a site constructed from narratives of disaster. Tom thought of dogs forcing their way into wombat holes, where they stuck fast and starved. He thought of snakes. He thought of sheep, and guns.

There came the sound of barking.

Twenty yards away, a track led up to the ridge. Tom took it at a run, air tearing in his chest. The pale trunks of saplings reeled past.

Away to his right it went on: a high consistent barking designed to attract the pack's attention. So the dog barked when dancing around a tree where a cat or a possum clung among leaves. After a while, it would be borne in on him that he was alone in his venture, that the man would not assist in capturing the prey he had gone to the effort of flushing out. Like marriage, their relations had entailed the downward adjustment of expectations. A dog: Tom had pictured a faithful presence at his heel, an obedient head pressed to his knee. And the dog, thought Tom, arms hanging loose, breathing hard on a bush track, what had the dog hoped for from him? Something more than the recurrence of food in a dish, surely; surely some untrammeled dream of loping camaraderie.

Over the years, with patient repetition and bribes of raw flesh, he had taught the dog to fetch. But when he picked up the ball and threw it a second time, Tom would feel the dog's gaze on him. He tried to imagine how his actions might appear from the dog's point of view: the man had thrown the ball away, the dog had obligingly sought out this object the man desired and dropped it at his feet, and behold, the man hurled it away again. How long could this stupidity go on?

"Anthropomorphism," Karen would have said, his wife being the kind of person who mistrusted emotions that had not been

assigned a name. But what was apparent to Tom in all their dealings was the otherness of the dog: the expanse each had to cover
to arrive at a corridor of common ground.

Where the bushes fanned less densely, he pushed his way
through and found himself on an overgrown path. There was a
smell: leafy, aromatic.

The barking now sounded higher up the hill; somewhere to
his left, where a wall of gray-green undergrowth barred the way.
He pressed on ahead, hoping to loop around behind the dog.
His jacket grew damp from the branches that reached across his
face. Water found the place between his collar and his skin.

He was so intent on moving forward that at first he didn't notice
the silence. When he did, he stopped. Silence meant the dog had
given up hope that the pack would come to his assistance, and
with it, the chase. Silence meant he was making his way back.

Tom Loxley returned, under a thickening sky, to the place
where the wallaby had bounded across the track. Well after the
rain came he was still standing there, a slight man in large wet
sneakers, calling, calling.

By lunchtime the dog had been gone five hours and the rain over
the trees had fined to drizzle. Tom remembered Nelly's raincoat,
hanging from a hook behind the bedroom door; it would be too
short in the arms, but the hood was the thing. When he took it down,
he discovered a promotional calendar from a stock agent stuck to
the door. May 2001: no one had torn off a leaf in six months.

The forested crest of the hill was hemmed on the east by the track
that ran down from Nelly's house past paddocks and a farmhouse.
To the north was the trail Tom had followed that morning; another

led up the hill to the south. Both came out on the ridge road that curved around the top of the hill and turned down into the valley, where it met the muddy farm track. Tom set out along the perimeter of this bush trapezoid, calling and whistling and calling.

He told himself the dog was making the most of freedom, running where his nose led, through the crags and troughs of unimaginable scentscapes.

He reminded himself of the time when two children selling chocolate to raise money for their school left a gate open and the dog escaped into the street. Karen and Tom ran along pavements, checked parks, trespassed, knocked on doors, called animal shelters. Then the phone rang. A woman who lived half a mile away had returned from work to find the dog asleep on her step and her cat's bowl licked clean.

The dog was still hard-muscled, swift and strong. But he was twelve now, old for a dog his size. He spent less time darting after swallows and more snoozing in his basket, dream paws scrabbling. He would not willingly be out in this rain.

The ridge road was deserted. But it was the route taken by the logging trucks. The drivers, quota-ruled, were always in a hurry. The dog had no traffic sense. With the wind in his face, Tom tried not to think of these things.

He followed a path that led into the bush from the southern track. It took him to a clearing where a treadless tractor tire held the charred traces of a fire. There were crushed cans, cigarette butts, and balled-up tissues disintegrating in the scrub.

The past four days were already assuming the unreal glaze of an idyll: a time of rain broken up by windy sun; the soft, mad chatter of Tom's keyboard; the dog curled like a medallion before the fire.

. . . . . .

In the evening he walked down to the adjoining farm.

Turning off the ridge road on Thursday evening, he had pulled over to let a mud-freckled Land Cruiser pass. It slowed; the driver leaned across the passenger seat. Tom saw a man with sparse gray hair and eyes half as old as the rest of his face: Nelly's neighbor Jack Feeney.

There was a trailer to one side of Jack's drive, and a prevailing air of practical untidiness: old seedling trays loosely stacked, lengths of pipe covered with a plastic sheet, lax coils of wire netting. But the farmhouse clad in biscuit-brown bricks was a suburban box, neat with window awnings and potted plants, as incongruous in that setting as if aliens had placed it among the paddocks and left a flying saucer disguised as a satellite dish on the roof.

The man who came out of the door raised his voice over the racket of dogs who lived a dog's life on the end of a chain. "Help you?"

When the Australian desire to provide assistance meshed with the Australian dread of appearing unmanly, it produced the bluff menace that was Mick Corrigan's default setting:

"Yeah, I reckon this wallaby would've kicked your dog's brains out for sure, mate."

"Tell you what, he's dead meat if he goes after sheep."

"Saw a kangaroo hold this kelpie down and drown it in a dam one time."

"Can't blame a bloke that shoots a stray first and asks questions later."

Tom had seen those helpful blue eyes in schoolyards: "What about you fuck off back to the other black bastards?"

The Land Cruiser was in the carport, but Mick said his wife

had driven Jack to the medical center in town. "He'll be tucking into a counter tea by now while Nees finishes up work."

"Nothing serious, then?"

"Nah, checkup. He's got a crook heart. Tough as shit, but. Got to hand it to these old bastards," said Jack's son-in-law magnanimously.

He insisted on accompanying Tom to the gate, contriving to suggest, under the guise of courtesy, that he was seeing off an intruder. He walked on the balls of his feet, the fingertips of one hand jammed in his pocket. There was something heroic — at once absurd and touching — about his gait.

When there were bars between them, he looked at Tom. Who saw looped gold in a lobeless ear, a bracelet of coppery blue tattoos, a handsome face that had started to melt under a cap of dull yellow curls.

"Known Nelly long?"

Tom shrugged.

Mick leaned in. "Tell you what, mate, you want to watch how you go. Look what happened to the poor bloody husband, eh."

Tom walked back up the hill in the dirty light of a day that had gone on and on, despair dragging through him like a chain.

IN APRIL, a week or so after he first met Nelly Zhang, Tom was driving home from work when a storm broke. On Swan Street golden-eyed tramfish glided through tinsel rain. There were the oily dabs of streetlights, pedestrian doubles fleeing through shop windows.

The traffic trickled past a travel agency plastered with images plucked from dreams. "Sorry," said the bone-white script on the hoarding next door, suggesting that graffiti is only the grit deposited by the passing of a larger story.

A woman dashing between awnings crossed her bare arms over her chest. Tom put his hand on the horn.

Nelly said, "But you're going the other way." Water was running off her hair and her arms. It glistened on her cheekbones, which were broad as a cat's.

He turned up the hill, into the monumental sky.

She directed him through postindustrial streets, factories reinvented as offices, cafés, galleries, apartments. In a cul-de-sac behind the train station were four grimy brick stories, the remains of a painted advertisement still visible on a wall whose lower reaches were covered in tags. Tom's headlights revealed corrugated iron nailed over windows, bins and sodden cardboard in a concrete yard.

The building, a minor landmark in the area, was known as the Preserve, said Nelly, after the old ad for marmalade on the wall. "The Fat Orange. Who Needs the Big Apple?" She had lived there for thirteen years, she told him, illegally, because her lease was nonresidential.

"There used to be a printing works on the ground floor. They held out until Christmas. Now there's only us." Nelly indicated an estate agent's board: "Your own slice of history." She had small, creaturely hands. "Not for much longer."

Posner, he thought. *Us.* He noticed that she had a way of pausing between sentences that rendered her talk mechanical. It was faintly disconcerting; he found himself tensing for the grind of levers.

Nelly was saying, "No one actually makes things anymore. It's all lawyers in lofts around here."

The complaint of trains, and wind lifting like a voice. Carapaced in steel, Tom Loxley was lashed about by sentiments as large as weather.

Among other things, he was disturbed — aroused, intrigued, repelled — by her spoor of spice and sweat.

She was fumbling for keys. He switched on the overhead light, and saw, in her gaping bag, a little cardboard folder that fastened across the corners with elastic.

"Come up and have a drink," said Nelly.

A hundred years earlier the Preserve had been a textile mill. By the 1970s, it was housing several small industries. On the top floor, before Nelly's time, children's shoes had been manufactured. She showed him a box, retrieved from the rubbish on a landing, which contained wooden shoe molds. "Brendon's after them for an installation but I can't bear to give them up." She set them along the edge of the tall, scarred bench that served as a kitchen counter.

Brendon, Rory, Yelena: the artists who rented studios from Nelly. The Preserve was huge. An echoing central space included a kitchen corner: sink, ancient stove, microwave, ramshackle cupboards. There were two cavernous studios and two merely large ones, a cubicle in which Nelly slept, another she used for storage. Five lavatories side by side. Each artist had claimed one, with a spare for visitors. On the facing wall someone had stenciled "Cannery Row."

Tom sat in a vinyl armchair and drank whiskey from a glass

that had once held Vegemite. Rain rollicked against the grid of frosted panes that filled one wall. A game of Go was set out on a table. He noticed things on that stormy autumn evening that he would not notice again as familiarity blunted attention: an orange-glazed lamp base, grubby gray walls whose grazes showed blue. The heavy folds of a Pompeian red curtain that, partly drawn back, exposed a door set halfway along a passage. Tom looked twice before realizing that both curtain and door were painted on the wall.

The other thing that struck him was the makeshift air of the place. It was cheaply and carelessly furnished with disparate items. People had come and gone from here, leaving marks of their passing: a lampshade that was too small for its base, mismatched cups on a mug tree, assorted chairs.

Nelly was draping the plum-colored towel she had used to dry her hair around the wire shoulders of a dressmaker's dummy. It stood behind a long table on a dais by the window. A *Concise Oxford* with a peeling spine had fetched up under a couch. A plant pot displayed Barbie's and Ken's heads impaled on rulers marked off in inches.

One reason these things would stand out in Tom's memory was that the Preserve was brightly — in fact glaringly — lit that first evening. That was unusual. He would grow accustomed to seeing the room velvety with shadows, in which a lamp or a string of tulip-shaped lights acquired dramatic force.

Nelly Zhang under flat strip lighting with damp hair falling about her face was older than she had appeared at the gallery. Tom saw the loosening skin on her neck, the hips thickened by ill-fitting trousers.

A great draft of rain-smelling air entered with a girl in a slick yellow jacket. "Oh, oh," shrieked Yelena. She swooped on the row of little wooden feet. "Oh, Nelly, they look so sad. Like something left by a war."

She had waves of golden and bright brown hair, a wide red mouth. On her feet, below long, bare legs, she wore lacy orange ankle socks and peep-toed golden stilettos. From a bag she drew plastic containers that snapped open to fill the room with the scent of coriander and lemongrass and rice cooked with coconut.

Tom saw the legs, the face made for the camera. It was inevitable perhaps that such perfection would throw up a kind of smoke screen in his mind. Consequently, in those first few weeks, images of luminous flesh and a geranium-red mouth accompanied Tom Loxley's self-administered pleasure. He would believe, during this interval, that it was for Yelena he returned.

That initial misdirection led to others. So that months later, when he said, "Why didn't you tell me?" Nelly answered, "But I thought you knew."

"How could I have known?"

"Didn't Yelena tell you? You were always hanging around her." Nelly's tone was severe, and bubbles of joy effervesced in Tom.

Reproached in turn, Yelena stared. "You're Nelly's friend."

"Yes, but at the start . . . I'd only just met her."

Yelena shrugged. She was the kind of female who shrugs superbly. Men circled her like moons. The beam of her attention might alight now and then on their affairs, but only a fool expected sustained illumination.

What Tom misconstrued was mostly trivial. Like Brendon and Nelly's talk. "Did you know Dan Kopensky?" one might ask, and the other reply, "The completely undetectable hairpiece?" Then they would be off, their conversation splicing student houses in Darlinghurst, rip-off art dealers, Cyn Riley's film, dancing to the Sports, assorted bastards, that Canadian girl with the amazing tits, a waiter in a café in Glebe Point Road, someone called Freddie.

Tom concluded, not unreasonably, that these two were old friends. Until a chance remark revealed that they had met at a millennium party.

"Brendon's from Sydney," explained Osman. He kept his voice low, reaching under the rackety music. "Nelly and he knew the same crowd when she spent a year there so long ago. But" — his broad hands fell open — "they never connected."

He smiled at Tom. That slow smile was what people remembered of Brendon's lover, who had the kind of face that hasn't set itself a plan. "Look at Brendon dancing, so terrible," said Osman, who did not know, on that June evening in the Preserve, where they were holding a party to mark the winter solstice, that he would die on New Year's Day. His mind had reverted to an afternoon in Istanbul in 1993: heavy bees fumbling the lavender outside his window while he translated an Australian poem. *"To go by the way he went you must find beneath you / that last and faceless pool, and fall. And falling / find..."* He looked at Tom. "Find, find...what? Do you remember what comes next?" His right hip had begun to ache.

Tom would tell himself there was no design at work in the misunderstandings. They arose because Nelly and her friends had forgotten how recently he had arrived among them. It was a compliment, this taking for granted that spared him explanations. He acknowledged, too, his own part in the confusion, his preference for observation over asking questions. He wondered, not for the first time, whether the trait was symptomatic of arrogance or caution, the clever boy's reluctance to expose ignorance or the outsider's fear of what might follow if he did.

No one had set out to mislead him. The agent at the controls was concocted from inadvertence and poor timing. It was the selective vision of hindsight, he reasoned, that set a figure in the carpet. There could be no motive for deceiving him, and only a mind corroded by evil or disease deceives without purpose.

But not everything he failed to grasp was insignificant. And by accumulation, even minor errors take on density and cast shadows. Reality is an effect produced by the accrual of detail, a trickery whose operations Tom had traced in the pages of countless fictions. He was unable to shake off the impression that a similar process governed his relations with Nelly, staging elaborate scenarios that mimicked the solidity of truth. These, if probed, readily revealed their flimsiness; yet who could be sure that the vista thus arrived at was not equally contrived? The bottom of the box might always be false; so Tom Loxley feared.

There was the matter of Rory.

Nelly, clashing cutlery in the sink one afternoon, addressed the boy over her shoulder. "You've known for ages Gretchen's interested. She sets up a meeting to look at your folio. And you ring up the day before and cancel?"

"Yeah, whatever. How come you're suddenly so keen on Gretchen anyway? You've always said she had crap taste."

"You've got to put the effort in. With any dealer."

"Easy for you to say. Like when did you last have to —?"

But he interrupted himself to answer his phone: a sullen, square-set boy with a patch of black fur under his lip. "Sweet!" he said to his caller. And to Nelly, "Gotta go." Tom he ignored.

They heard the crash of his boots on the stair, the jump that took him to the half landing.

It was a scene that returned to nag at Tom. It reminded him of something he was unable to name. He had recognized Rory, of course: the dark boy who had laughed with Posner that first evening at the gallery. It was obvious Rory didn't remember him, but he rather thought Posner did. At the solstice party, the dealer's eyes had considered Tom as if he were something on a plate; something Posner might eat, or send back to the kitchen.

Yet Posner set himself to be attentive. The reedy voice, so at odds with the man's bulk, held forth about Tom's book. "James and the uncanny: it wouldn't have occurred to me. His novels seem so thoroughly materialist. All those people hankering after all those things." He filled Tom's glass from the bottle he was holding and inclined his head, flatteringly deferential.

Encouraging a man to display expertise is the shortest path to gaining his trust. It seemed a transparent tactic.

"And money! It's everywhere in James," went on Posner.

Tom thought, And what's more elusive, more ghostly, than money?

On the other side of the room, Nelly was laughing.

"Mind you, it's a long time since I've read him." Somehow it was clear Posner was lying. Tom thought, He's prepared for this conversation. Now he'll trot out some lit crit crap he thinks is profound.

"There's a sentence in one of the notebooks about going to the Comédie Française a great deal in 'seventy-two." Posner said, "I came across that, quite by chance, years ago. It had the effect of marooning James forever in the past. Eighteen seventy-two: unimaginable from the perspective of the nineteen seventies. But I've never forgotten it." He smiled: a wet, pink-lipped, humorless occasion. "As it happened, I was living in Paris at the time. And I did go, now and then, to the theater. I imagine a young man reading that in my diary one day." Posner looked up from his glass. "Quite a jolt, realizing that the life you remember so vividly exists for someone else as so much historical dust."

Tom thought, I've felt that too. Was, despite himself, moved. Yet the man made his flesh crawl.

Nelly had said, "We had a thing...oh, you know, ages ago. Before I was married."

"I thought he was gay."

Her hand made a rocking motion. "He's not too fussy, Carson."

The idea of her young. There was a faded Polaroid pinned to her lavatory door: high-necked blouse and tight skirt, pouty mouth, jet hair drawn into a topknot with strands falling around her face. She was twenty and looked thirteen. She looked desirable, bruised, corrupt, infinitely oriental. "Very *World of Suzie Wong.*" Posner's broad-knuckled fingers carried the knowledge of her flesh.

Tom knew that Rory had dropped out of university, that he lived in Posner's house. He imagined them together: the silver head grazing a dark line on the boy's flat stomach.

At the solstice party, he watched Posner's terrible eyes seek

Rory out; and the boy not noticing, stroking the hair under his lip, then crossing to the throng around Yelena.

Later, when things were breaking up, a group left to go clubbing, Rory swept up in the clamor.

Watch out, thought Tom, he's slipping your leash. He felt a small, mean joy: Posner, wakeful and alone.

It was to Yelena, early in their acquaintance, that Tom spoke of Nelly's painting. "I can't get it out of my mind."

The girl was spooning baked beans straight from the tin onto white bread. She had a predilection for vaguely repellent snacks: fruit-flavored yogurt eaten between bites of gherkin, crackers topped with peanut butter and chocolate sprinkles.

Her great dark eyes rested on Tom. "You say it like a criticism."

"It's just..." He began again. "I keep coming back to how beautiful it is."

Yelena spoke through a mouthful of beans. "So?"

Acutely aware of that angled face, he answered with deliberate scorn. "It's an amateurish response. It doesn't exactly advance understanding, does it?"

When she had finished her sandwich, Yelena set down her plate. She reached under the couch and retrieved the *Concise Oxford*. "Amateur: one who is fond." There was something semi-literate about the way she read aloud: sounding each word distinctly, as if testing it out. "It says here, from *amare*, love." She looked at Tom. "Love is amateurish. You wouldn't say it advances understanding?"

She abandoned him soon afterward. Then Nelly turned up and noticed the plate Yelena had left on the kitchen counter. She picked it up and came and perched beside Tom, on the broad arm of his chair. "Look."

The plate, smudged here and there with sauce, was rimmed in faded gilt. It showed a man and a woman conversing in a garden where a fountain played against a backdrop of pagodas and snowy peaks. Opposite this scene, a tree blossomed pinkly beside water, while overhead a plane flew through rags of blue.

Tom could see nothing remarkable about this object. If anything he was faintly disgusted by the combination of smeared surface and pretty patterning.

Nelly was saying, "Plates like this, they're usually old-world. They have these pictures of frilly ladies and hollyhocks and stuff. But this one's got a plane."

He looked again.

"It would've been the latest thing when it was designed," she went on. "A tribute to air travel, maybe."

But there was something about the plane, the oriental scenery: recognition flashed in Tom. "It's Shangri-La." He took the plate from her and turned it over, scattering crumbs. Together they read the inscription: *Lost Horizon.*

"Oh wow. I remember that movie from when I was a kid."

"The book the film's based on was the first literary paperback. Late thirties, something like that."

"How cool is that!" Delight stretched in Nelly's face. "So this plate would've been doubly modern."

She had come in from the street. Was stitched about with thready peak-hour fumes that fluttered in Tom's nostrils.

He rubbed his nose, and said, "That's not quite how I'd describe it." He was not sentimental about secondhand crockery, having expended energy in putting some distance between himself and that kind of thing.

"But that's what gets me." Nelly said, "Modern can never keep up with itself. Nothing dates quicker than now."

A few days passed, and Tom found his thoughts returning to the sauce-smeared plate. He couldn't understand the pull. Then, without warning, the plate slipped sideways in his mind, revealing an object he had once yearned for with the absolute, concentrated longing of small children and later quite forgotten.

Auntie Eulalia Doutre, who was not his aunt, had a long, low cupboard with angled legs and sliding doors in her hall. When Tom and his mother called on her, Auntie Eulalia opened one of the doors and handed the child a wooden object for his amusement. It was a pencil box with a range of snowy mountains and a pink flowering tree painted on its lid. Tom ran his fingers over it and the cover slid to one end. He found this wonderful, the box that opened sideways, doubling the cupboard door's smooth glide. He moved the lid back and forth, glancing now and then at the cupboard. In bed he would think about the wooden box lying in the wooden cupboard. He pushed his sheet away and drew it back over himself, and felt pleasure thrill in his marrow. The big door slid open and so did the little one. The child wished to keep that marvel safe forever.

The plum-blossom plate had this consequence too: it focused Tom's attention on Nelly.

WEDNESDAY

Tom slept in socks, tracksuit pants, a T-shirt, a flannel shirt, a sweatshirt. There was a blanket on the bed, and a quilt patterned with shambolic roses. He woke at first light, needles of cold in his limbs.

Falling asleep, he had told himself he would wake in the night to the scrape of the dog's paw against the door. The moment he opened his eyes, he knew this to have been absurd.

It was scarcely colder outside. Preferring not to face the earthy reek of the dunny, he urinated off the step into a clump of coarse-leafed vegetation. In the paddock beyond the gum trees, cattle showed as solid, blocky forms.

He filled a saucepan from the tank, heated it on the two-burner butane stove in the kitchen. The tin of ground coffee he had brought with him from the city was still a quarter full, but the milk had run out on Sunday. He tipped two spoons of sugar into his mug as compensation.

His jeans were damp, despite having hung in front of the fire all evening. His shirts were dirty. He needed wet-weather gear. He needed boots and clean, warm clothes. His scalp felt greasy, the backs of his knees itched. He hadn't had a shower since Thursday; getting dressed, he held his breath against his body's fragrance. There was no bathroom in the house; superficially spruced up, it remained primitive in its lack of amenities. It occurred to Tom that eighty years earlier, when the house was built, his odor would have been literally unremarkable. It was the transition to a modern way of life that rendered his mustiness conspicuous.

There was no more muesli, but he discovered a plastic container of oats in a cupboard. Long afterward, the taste was still in his mouth: distilled staleness.

He was stacking dishes in the washing-up bowl when he remembered the thunder of small steps he had heard the previous night. The image of a snarling, stunted child raging across the tin roof had jolted him from sleep. He had lain wakeful for minutes, listening to the possum, the dream still runny in his mind.

His mother was expecting him that evening. He would call her in a few hours and make some excuse. Without having to think about it, Tom knew he wouldn't tell her that the dog was missing. Iris greeted news of a sore throat or mislaid keys with screams of "My God. What are we to do?" In lives where the margin of safety is narrow, mishaps readily assume the dimension of calamities. Iris was fond of the dog; her son wished, genuinely, to spare her distress. But his protective reflex was partly self-directed. At the age of twelve, he had realized he could endure most sorrows except the spectacle of hers. Slight, dark-skinned, bad at sport, he was able to withstand the humiliations that awaited him in an Australian schoolyard by keeping them from his mother. He reasoned that she could offer no practical aid; and that this proof of her inadequacy would be more than either of them could bear. At the same time, he grew sullen, half aware that something fundamental, the obligation of parents to shield their young from harm, was lost to him.

In this way, the strands of evasiveness and protection and resentment entwined in his love for her were determined.

. . . . . .

The bleached bone of a dead eucalypt pointed skyward near the heart of the place where the dog had vanished. Another, stumpier, but still taller than the surrounding canopy, rose to Tom's right. He decided to begin by searching the area between the two. He would proceed systematically, with calm, and due recognition of his limits, a methodology that had seen him through examinations, four months of postdoctoral unemployment, rejection by the first two, more prestigious universities to which he had applied for work, the failure of his marriage: the crises he had known.

He planned to break off twigs to mark his way. He noted the position of the sun. In his pockets were handfuls of sultanas for the dog, who would be ravenous, not having eaten since Monday evening. These precautions struck Tom as sensible; therefore as presages of success.

His watch showed ten minutes to eight.

One difficulty was that the ground wasn't level. Trying to walk in a straight line, Tom found himself scrambling in and out of gullies. Tree ferns crowded in one. A steeper trench was knitted with fallen logs, the rotting wood treacherous underfoot. When he flung out a hand to save himself, his fingers encountered a growth as springy and slick as liver.

His sense of direction was good, but obliged to proceed in arcs he began to fear doubling back on his steps. He had been snapping off twigs and thin branches in passing, but the undergrowth had a way of pushing back to obscure these scars. Along with this elastic quality, it was tall — often as high as Tom — so that in every direction his eye met only the thrust of leaves.

The hillocky terrain was playing tricks with his marker trees. The shorter of the two had disappeared. The other was farther to his left than he would have liked, and looked different, less skeletal than it had first appeared. A foreshortening brought about, Tom reasoned, by the angle of his view.

Despite these difficulties, he drew closer to the tall eucalpyt. He had, after all, made progress.

Cheered, he ate a few sultanas. The dog would understand.

By the time Tom reached the tree, the light dropping through the leaves had dulled. He sniffed the air: humus, and the aromatic scent he noticed the day before; and behind these, the faint, distinctive odor of rain.

The scrub was thinner here, his progress easy. But Tom had the impression that something was not right. It came to him that someone he wouldn't want to see would be waiting beyond the trees. He stood still, ears straining.

Then, as he advanced, and the track faded into a clearing, he saw: the tree was wrong. It was the stumpy one, split at the top like a broken tooth; the jagged crown, smoothed by the direction of his approach, was plainly visible now. He looked over his shoulder and saw the tall tree far behind him, pointed in warning.

For two hours he had crashed about a modest wedge of scrub and trees, an area of perhaps three acres.

Rain began to fall.

Tom stepped over a log and felt his sneaker sink through the ooze of leaves covering a shallow depression. His ankle turned a little.

He patted one pocket, then another. A picture came into his mind of the kitchen table: radio, laptop, spare batteries, his papers and books, the mobile phone he had taken from his wet jeans the previous evening. It would almost certainly be out of range here. Nevertheless, he had been negligent.

Overnight, these had become his familiars: fear, rage at his carelessness.

Back at the house, he added hot water to pumpkin soup made from a packet he found in a cupboard. Its savor was chemical; trust Nelly to buy a generic brand. His feet were icy, there was a dull ache in his ankle. He swallowed a second cup.

AT FIRST Tom rationed his visits to the Preserve: several days had to elapse before he would let himself return. Very soon he saw that Yelena did not register his presence except in the abstract, as the homage her beauty extracted. Her friends would gather at the Preserve of an evening before going on to clubs or pubs. There were those among them whose faces hungered for her. Tom saw the girl's consciousness of her power. She was amiable with him, including him in the casual sweep of her attention but making it clear that he held no particular interest in her eyes. Although beautiful, Yelena was kind.

All the same, as autumn gave way to winter, Tom was a regular presence at the Preserve. The ease with which he had slipped into familiarity with Nelly surprised him. He was not given to swift intimacies of the mind, but it was almost as if he had known Nelly of old.

Her laugh was huge, disgraceful. It broke loose over small things. Yet when he was away from Nelly, Tom discovered that he was unable to picture her amused. Try as he might, he could call up only a frozen version of her face. One effect of this was that the mobility of her features delighted him afresh every time he saw her. Another was the brief, disconcerting sense of a known face overlaid with strangeness.

It was only when his loneliness lifted that Tom realized how acute it had been. The Preserve offered companionship and conversation. It offered Brendon, who designed Web sites by day and was usually to be found in the Preserve at night. His presence was signaled by music: fugues, cantatas, concertos turned up loud. He was secretive, allowing no one into his studio. At intervals he emerged to prepare tiny, lethal cups of coffee brewed in a blue enameled pan. Brendon brought handfuls of flowers into the Preserve, and mandarins and walnuts, and colored leaves. When his imagination stalled he would build these, along with the apples Nelly loved, into Arcimboldo-like fantasies, a cork serving for an eye, a paper napkin pleated into a ruffle.

He was a spidery man. Tom would watch, entranced, the deft movements of his long arms. He noticed that Brendon was compelled to touch beautiful things: the curve of a jug, the buttery leather of Yelena's new bag. Once, leaning over the girl, he lifted a strand of her hair: "Gold enough to eat."

Nelly lived on awful food, squares of soft white bread, instant noodles, tinned soup. (Brendon: "I had this bag of peas in the pod once. Nelly goes, 'What are they?' I say, 'Peas,' and she goes, 'Very funny, Brendon, I've eaten peas, they're *round*.'")

It was one of the things that endeared her to Tom. Early in life, he had encountered too many people who did not have enough to eat. It remained with him as the only thing that mattered about food: who had it and who did not. In a city where friendships grew brittle over the merits of rival olive oils or the correct way to prepare a confit of duck, Nelly's lack of interest in what she ate was bracing.

Yet in odd pockets of diet she was faddish, returning laden with Gravensteins and Royal Galas from the Saturday street market. Once a week she dosed herself, rather ostentatiously, with an infusion of senna pods and ginger. "Get plenty of fresh air and keep your bowels open. Ancient Chinese wisdom."

It grated on Tom. "You're, like, what? Third, fourth generation? Why do you pretend you're Chinese?"

"You think I should pretend I'm Australion? Well, the Australians won't let me, for one thing. Want to know how many weeks I can go without getting asked where I'm from?"

Nelly's mother was a Scot. Among her ancestors she counted a Pole and an Englishman. The cast of her adulterated features was only vaguely Asiatic. She exploited it to the hilt, exaggerating the slant of her eyes with kohl, powdering her face into an expressionless mask. Stilettos and a slit skirt, and she might have stepped from a Shanghai den. A sashed tunic over wide trousers impersonated a woman warrior. She wore her hair cut blunt across her forehead and drew attention to what she called her "thick Chinese calves."

She was not for the taxonomy-minded. Sometimes a rosary strung with mother-of-pearl served her as a necklace, while a red glass bindi glittered on her brow. Her palms might be intricately patterned with henna, or her chin painted with geometric tattoos. She was smoke and mirrors, a category error. Yelena, noting the attentiveness with which Tom was examining an old photograph of Nelly with dreadlocks, remarked, "She is not some kind of sign for you to study, you know."

There was wit in Nelly's self-fashioning. Sometimes she fastened her hair with chopsticks. Her fondness for a particularly unflattering set of garments had Tom baffled for weeks. Then suddenly he understood. Baggy trousers that ended above socked ankles, a red quilted parka, a man's felt hat jammed on her head: it was the anti-chinoiserie favored by the ageless Chinese females who can be observed presiding over bok choy and cabbages in vegetable markets.

Tom could see Nelly's choices as parody, as a defensive flaunting of caricature. There was playfulness in her imagery, and something sad. It was also kitsch. By that time he was half in love with Nelly Zhang. Anything that seemed to diminish her was painful to him.

An empty easel was a miniature gallows at one end of her studio. Tom's gaze took in a large-screen Mac on a workstation, portfolios leaning against a wall, a pear made from solid green glass. Nelly's painting overalls hung from a hook by the window. There were tall rolls of canvas under a table and remnants on top of a cupboard. Music he didn't recognize was playing on a paint-splattered boom box. Nelly hummed along for a few discordant bars. She was incapable of holding a tune.

Long benches displayed tubes of paint, bottles of medium and thinner, jars of brushes. Tom wandered around the room, noticing things, touching them. Nelly showed him the spectacles of different magnification that she wore for detailed work. There were shelves stacked with folders and file boxes. Oddments in a milk crate: rags, a hammer, a pair of pliers, empty jars. A sheet of glass that served Nelly as a palette: "It's easy to scrape clean."

A notebook lay open by the computer. *The collision between photography and painting,* read Tom. *Their circular conversation.* And below that: *There are now more photographs in the world than bricks.*

These jottings were the remains of ideas, said Nelly. She was only just starting to feel her way toward her next show. "I need fallow time. Dreaming time." Then she said, "Scary time. When you doubt you'll ever be able to do it again."

Tom told her that Renoir, reproached for doing everything but settle down to paint, had answered that a roaring fire requires the gathering of a great deal of wood. He saw that this pleased Nelly, although she didn't remark on it.

With the evidence of making all about him, he remembered something he had heard her say to Yelena about an artist's muscles retaining the memory of the gestures required to lay paint on canvas. "It can become automatic. Like you don't notice your wrist turning a certain way, producing this effortless brushwork. That's when you start repeating yourself. Competency: it's the enemy of art."

A page torn raggedly from a magazine was tacked to the far wall. Tom moved closer: Goya's ambiguous dog, poised between extinction and deliverance, gazing over the rim of the world.

"That's a painting I can hardly bear to look at," he said.

Nelly was standing near him, close enough for him to smell her scalp. She was not entirely appetizing: her hands were often grubby, her red parka was grimed about the pockets. All Tom's Indian fastidiousness rose against her musk, even as he was stirred.

When he sought to represent her to himself, there came into his mind the image of a great city: anomalous, layered, not exempt from reproach; magnificent.

. . . . . .

The realization of what she meant to him came about like this. One morning, he was conducting a seminar in a room where a row of interior windows opened onto a corridor. The lights were on against the darkness of the day, and Tom caught sight of himself in a window as he listened to a student read her paper. The glass was deceptive, a distortion in the pane or a trick of the light endowing his reflection with a vague double. In both incarnations the middle fingers of his left hand rested lightly on his upper lip. It was one of Nelly's poses. He recognized her in him at once.

What was more, he was familiar with the symptom. The mimicry of those he wished to impress was a reflex with him. Certain distinctive gestures or turns of phrase, the pronunciation he gave to some words, a habit of leaving his cuffs unbuttoned, a dislike of salads that combined lettuce and tomato, an idiosyncratic way of looping his capital Ks: these and other traits that identified him were old borrowings. Imitation is the trace of a compulsion to consume another; it proceeds by assimilation and regurgitation. For a split second the windowpane held enemies, gurus, lovers, a neurotic procession winding back to Tom's childhood. Nelly now had her place in that diaphanous parade.

Tom glimpsed, at unwelcome moments, something clenched within him: a hard pellet of suspicion. In this he knew himself his mother's son. Like Iris, he calculated and judged, fingered the world to assess its worth. His father, by contrast, had been on good terms with life, greeting it with interest and pleasure. In the ease with which Nelly laughed, Tom caught an echo of Arthur Loxley's readiness to be charmed by the great extempore adventure of existence.

Nelly was endlessly forbearing, tolerant of the dull, the deluded, the earnest, the video artist who steered all conversations to his gallbladder meridian. Vulnerability provokes one of two responses: the impulse to protect or the desire to crush. Tom could see — it was plain as sunlight — the sweetness that ran in her depths.

Yet he was driven also to remark the ambiguities eddying her surface. One of them concerned money. Tom learned — from Yelena, from Brendon, from others he met at the Preserve — that Nelly sold steadily. Museums across the country sought her out for projects and collected her work. The flood of talent and ambition that characterized the group was not without a resentful undertow. Now and then, in the detailing of Nelly's good fortune, Tom detected a sidelong envy: she was someone her peers kept tabs on.

Running counter to this narrative of success was Nelly's perennial consciousness of money. She was thrifty in ways uncommon in her cosseted generation, a single bag yielding two or even three cups of tea, meager leftovers scraped together and refrigerated. Once, when Yelena was preparing a meal for them at her house, Nelly helped by chopping zucchini. Tom saw her slice off a stem, then trim the scanty flesh from around it that anyone else would have discarded.

Nelly taught painting at a visual arts college one day a week. It was reliable, coveted, ill-paid work. She frequented thrift shops, coaxed Yelena into cutting her hair, stored money away in envelopes marked "Gas," "Rent," "Electricity," rode her bike to save on fares.

Tom watched her going about the Preserve hitting switches, grumbling that her tenants were wasteful with lights and heating. This regard for the conservation of resources might have been deemed admirable. But something in his gaze caught her attention.

"Haven't you heard? We Chinese invented cheap." It was as stagy as a pirouette. But Tom feared stumbling on an essential, submerged narrowness beneath the pose.

He glimpsed calculation in her friendship with Posner, who served Nelly in ways well beyond the commercial. She had a key to the dealer's house, a five-minute walk up the hill; a room was set aside there for her use. Posner would lend her his car, take her out for meals and films, buy her books. The digital camera she now used for preparatory images was a recent present from him. When she needed root canal work on a molar, it was Posner who paid.

At times, Nelly seemed to want only to appease the dealer. Posner would be delivering himself of an opinion, and Nelly would murmur, "Exactly. That's like, just so exactly right"; her dutiful, daughterly manner at these moments approaching cari-cature. On other occasions she was offhand with Posner, barely acknowledging his presence; and then it was he who was defer-ential, who cajoled while his eyes remained watchful. It was as if each possessed something the other wanted and feared would be withheld. Knowledge lapped between them, and need, and tenderness. They might have been conspirators or siblings. They had that air of mutual reliance tinged with resentment that tells of consanguinity or crime.

Yelena's work was included in a group show in Fitzroy. After-ward, in a bar, a curator said, "The thing is, Nelly's slow. Too long between shows." His fleshy, egg-shaped skull was adorned here and there with feathery stubs. He had the soft, greedy air of a baby bird: beak wide, waiting.

Tom bought a round, and the curator edged closer. "You wouldn't happen to know if what they say about the paintings is true?"

"What do they say?"

"Ah, well." A claw flipped, dismissing private hope. There remained the pleasure of imparting gossip. "There's a whisper that Nelly doesn't actually get rid of her paintings after they're photographed. That they're stashed away, accruing value." The voice was malicious and admiring. "She'll make a killing one day."

Once, after Tom had gone with her to a gallery in a suburb of tall houses and broad-leafed European trees, Nelly said she had some shopping to do and showed him the list inked on her palm: milk, cheese, bread. He drove to the nearest supermarket, where he picked up a few things he needed himself.

At the checkout, Nelly arrived with a carton of milk and a sliced loaf.

"Is that it?" he asked.

She had her purse out and he saw that it held only a five-dollar bill and a few coins. Not enough for cheese at the prices charged by the small, expensive store.

TOM WALKED UP to the top of the farm track, where he knew his phone would have coverage. The air over the paddocks was a substance between liquid and paper. It held, on the horizon, the trace of a mountain: a watercolor blotted while wet into almost blankness.

There was a message from his aunt, left that morning, asking him to ring her urgently.

No message from his mother.

He imagined her dead, of course. He had failed to call her the previous day, and now she had died. Plains and cities and snow-headed peaks filed before his eyes, vast India passing with her. The ground of history gave way. Tom Loxley swung in sickening freedom.

He pressed the numbers that would bring about a changed world.

In the farmhouse at the bottom of the track, Jack added an artificial sweetener to his mug. The shading of hair on the sides of his hands gave them the look of a drawing of themselves.

Tom said, "I left the gate ajar. And some food in a bowl."

"Foxes'll have that."

"I'll be back tomorrow night. Friday morning at the latest."

On the wall behind Jack was a frayed piece of tribal cloth in a wooden frame, a beautiful scrap in buff and dull ochres. Baskets woven from grass hung beside it. Yellow and red kangaroo paws crowded a greenish metal beaker on a table. The sleek couch, gray with a thin stripe of lemon, was a replica of the one Tom owned.

He sipped the tea that Denise Corrigan had insisted on making and felt her gaze on him. She was an unremarkable woman, with her father's remarkable eyes. Tom saw that she was enjoying the effect of the room, its calculated undoing of assumptions created by brown brick veneer. He looked away, to the window framing fields with a filmy backdrop of mountain.

Jack said, "Rain'll ease up later. I'll go up and have a gander. Take one of the dogs."

When Tom rose to leave, he was confronted by another anomaly. A set of hanging shelves by the door paraded kittens, boots, thatched cottages, mermaids: each miniature and doubled, a display of china salt and pepper shakers.

"Mum used to collect them."

Denise's voice, utterly even, defied him to betray disdain. He was familiar with that tone.

On the step, he asked, "Is your father OK? I mean, to go looking...?"

"Yeah, he's good. The pacemaker's made a difference." Denise added, "I'll go with him."

"I didn't mean to trouble —"

"No trouble. Wednesday's my afternoon off." She nodded at him, smiled. In flat shoes, she was taller than Tom by inches.

She said, "You must be worried about your mum."

"It's nothing serious. But I have to get back." He clicked open Denise's umbrella. "She's eighty-two. Arthritis in both knees. When she gets up from a chair, there's this tearing noise..."

Denise nodded again. She told him she was a physiotherapist at the local health center. She pulled up the hood of her raincoat. "It's cruel, arthritis."

He lowered the window and thanked her again.

"No worries. Drive safely."

Tom had started up the engine when she leaned forward. "They turn up, you know. Dogs. I'll ask people at work to keep an eye out."

Children draw rain as a finite thing, a band of broken strokes descending through fine weather. The rain curtain: Tom, driving at a crawl along the breakneck road curling down from the hills, could remember searching for its watery beads all through a monsoon, but the rain never showed itself until it had him surrounded.

Hours later, the rain had eased and the city was a thrust of tombstones at the horizon. Soon the freeway would catch up with fast food, shopping malls, showrooms, car yards with flying shrouds of plastic bunting. But for the moment there were pale, flat paddocks that went on and on. This was landscape that could only just remember color, as time fades bright experience. There remained the faintest recollection of something called green.

Coming up behind a truck, Tom saw sheep pressed against slats: eyes, dirty fillets of shoulder and breast.

Jack Feeney kept a few beef cattle, large polled gray beasts, in Nelly's paddock. For the rest he ran sheep.

Light stretching in the sky pulled silver through charcoal, transforming clouds into a softly expensive pelt.

Tom pulled out and overtook the truck as soon as he could.

At home, the first thing he did was step into the shower. With water streaming over his turning body, his mind occupied itself with shit.

"I knew something was wrong. It was almost nine thirty and I hadn't seen her and you know we have a cup of tea at nine. When I knocked, she was still in her nightie. And there was a smell..." Here his aunt's voice had faltered. "She'd done you-know-what on the floor. And trodden it into the carpet."

"But why? How...?"

"She says she didn't realize she'd done it. 'It must have slipped out.' That's all I can get out of her. I'll never be rid of the stains."

The last thing Tom had done in the country, in accordance

with the instructions taped to a wall in Nelly's kitchen, had been to lift out the toilet pail and bury its contents.

As a boy, sharing a lavatory with his mother, it had been impossible to avoid the stench of her feces. It was not until he left home and shared living spaces with other people that he realized their shit smelled different — from one another's, from his — even though they all ate the same food. But his mother rose unaltered from that elemental reek when he buried his waste in a hole by Nelly's fence.

Did that mean the odor of shit was genetically determined, in part at least? Toweling himself dry, he thought there must be a book about it, one of those fashionable volumes offering packets of whimsical facts, histories of fish, biographies of numerals. *An Archaeology of Excrement.* It's got to have occurred to the French, thought Tom.

A low, black iron gate swung open into his aunt's garden, where a red man had been strung up in a tree; outlined in fairy bulbs, he held a sign that blinked "Season's Greetings." November still had a few days to run, but Audrey was always early with her decorations. She prepared for Christmas as for a catastrophe, warning, "It'll be here before you know it," weeks ahead of the feast, observing its advance with the grim satisfaction of an Old Testament prophet notified that the first wave of locusts had been sighted.

Tom went down the path that led to Iris's door, which had once been the side entrance to his aunt's house. The slippers aligned on her doormat were deep pink with golden chevrons across the toe. He crouched; the fabric was still damp.

He thought about the moment when his mother must have realized what had happened. Iris, whose knees made it impossible to stoop, to pick up a coin or a pill, to scrape her own filth from the carpet.

"She'd been sitting there for an hour." Audrey, on the telephone. "You'd think she could have told me sooner, instead of just sitting there with it all around her."

Tom thought of his mother trying to come to terms with the disaster, preparing the words in which she would have to confess what she had done, the moment when the shameful evidence of age and incapacity would be made public, when it would be clear that she had lost control of her body and couldn't hide the consequences.

He made tea-bag tea for Iris, instant coffee for himself, carried the mugs into the living room. His nostrils identified chemical lavender.

"The biscuits," said Iris. "Where are the Tim Tams?"

In adolescence, Tom had devoured packet after packet of chocolate biscuits, unable to desist. He no longer liked the taste. But his mother went on buying them, and he could not deny her the pleasure she derived from being able to offer him this small indulgence.

He sat on the wooden-armed sofa bed, on which he had slept for six years, and ate a biscuit.

On the wall was the starburst clock that Iris had bought on lay-by with her first wages. Every time Tom saw it he remembered the passions it had ignited. He had sat at the card table in the corner, a book about the First Fleet open before him, while Audrey remarked that in her opinion, it was nothing short of robbery to squander money on ornaments while living on charity. For did Iris imagine that the pittance she paid would rent her two rooms and the use of a Whirlpool anywhere else in this day and age?

"The amount was agreed," Iris cried. "The rent was set by you. When my husband was alive and you were ashamed to try this highway rookery."

A week later, Bill presented Audrey with a starburst clock for their wedding anniversary. He was a heavy, peaceable man who sold surfaces; on the subject of laminates, he approached eloquence. The clock was larger, more elaborate, than Iris's, about which nothing further was heard.

Australian history for Tom would henceforth be inseparable from economics, high dudgeon, and the sense of entrenched moral positions.

His mother sat in the straight-backed chair she preferred, her walker within reach. Tom's earliest memory of Iris placed her in an armchair beside a wireless, with her legs in a bag made of flowered cretonne. It fastened below her knees with a drawstring, protecting her calves from mosquitoes.

The bag disappeared when Tom was very young, and for the rest of his childhood a table fan and Shelltox kept the living room mosquito-free. But he could still see the large red blooms on the creamy cretonne, the ivied trellis against which they climbed.

Iris was eating a biscuit with the audible, laborious mastication of those who no longer have molars.

"Ma, is everything all right?"

His mother sucked melted chocolate from her front teeth. "Knees are bad today. This weather."

"Audrey told me what happened in the morning."

"I knew she would ring you and carry on. There was no need at all."

"But, Ma, if you can't manage —"

"I can manage," cried Iris. "You all want to get rid of me. You all want to put me in a home."

"Ma, be reasonable."

"It's hard to bear when you're rejected by your own child."

Tom jumped up. He walked to the kitchen door and back; a short distance. His gaze fell on an arrangement of dried thistles he had always detested. The room, unchanged in thirty years, returned him to the helpless rage of adolescence, the sensation of being trapped in poverty and irrational argument and ugliness.

"How can you say that? I see you regularly. I do everything I can. How can you say you've been rejected?"

"No need to get worked up," said Iris.

Tom had decided to say nothing about what had happened the previous day, telling himself that the dog would be found and that there was no need to cause his mother unnecessary grief. Yet now he resented her not inquiring after the animal.

With her talent for irritating her son, Iris asked, "So how was your holiday?"

"It wasn't a *holiday*." He was shouting again. "I was *working* —"

Long-past Sunday afternoons: "I'm not *reading,* I'm *studying.* Why can't they wash their own car?" And so Tom Loxley still leaped to defend the life he had chosen against the imputation of idleness, the reflex as immutable as arithmetic.

He made himself breathe in slowly, feeling his ribs move sideways. He breathed out again. He said, "Let's go for a walk."

A three-inch step led down from the living room into the passage. Iris approached the brink, then stopped. "I'm falling," she cried, and clutched the handles of her walker still tighter. "Tommy, I'm falling."

"No, you're not."

"Hold me, darling, hold me."

"Ma, you're fine."

"Easy for you to say, child."

"Be sensible, Ma. I'm right here. You're not going to fall."

The front wheels clunked into the abyss. "I'm falling, I'm falling."

They shuffled up and down the passage, between the entrance to the annex and the door that led to Audrey's part of the house. Rain kept up its steady gunning on the tin roof. On the other side of the wall, there was the shapeless noise of TV.

Tom was thinking of an almirah made of Indian calamander that his mother had once owned. Now and then Iris had unlocked its single drawer, lifted it out, and placed it before her son. The child was allowed to look but not to touch. Naturally, he disobeyed. He turned his grandfather's ivory teething ring in his hands. He examined a thermometer and a tiny pink teacup painted with fiery dragons. An empty, redolent bottle with an engraved label and the enigmatic legend Je Reviens. Three glass buttons shaped like tiny clusters of purple grapes. A satin-bowed chocolate box with a basket of fluffy kittens on the lid. A jet and diamanté earring. A cardboard coaster stamped with a golden flower. A leather case in which a satin-lined trench held a silver Biro; when the case was opened, a puff of cool, metallic air was released into the world.

At random moments, the child Tom would shut his eyes and call up these items one by one. It was his version of Kim's Game. The almirah was doubly implicated in remembering: there was the memory game, and there were the stories attached to each object, the past glimmering into life as Tom pondered the provenance of a foreign coin or a small brass key.

In Australia, Iris had a wardrobe, utilitarian as equipment. History sank beneath the imperatives of the present, its kingdom conquered by objects with no aura, by bulky blankets and woolen garments that spoke only of household management and the weather. Who transports coasters and old chocolate boxes over oceans? Practical considerations had ensured that Iris was no longer the custodian of memory. But there was worse: within her new setting, she appeared archaic. It was as if a malevolent substitution was at work, so that she had begun to assume the aspect of a relic herself.

Iris moaned, "I'm tired. I want to sit down."

"Five minutes more."

"My knees are paining."

"Just up and down twice more. Exercise is good for you."

"Oh, I'm tired. I want to sit down."

Side by side, they carried on.

When he kissed her good-bye, he said, "Ma, if it happens again, call me."

She peered up at him. Fear moved in her eyes, a rat scuttling through shadows. "I was good up to eighty." Her hand tightened on his arm.

"Tell Dr. Coutras about it when you see him, OK?"

"He'll say it's cancer and want to open me up."

"No, he won't."

Iris's perm, the thin hair in airy loops, stood out from her skull like petals, like a child's crayoned sun. "All right, I'll tell him," she said.

The docility, the large, nodding head: Tom thought of beasts, waiting to be killed or fed.

While he was still on her doorstep, Audrey said, "I draw the line at nursing." There were many such lines, existence taking on for his aunt the aspect of a dense cross-hatching.

"It must have been awful. So humiliating."

"Yes, well." Audrey patted the back of her hair, hitched up her cardigan at the shoulders. "I've got the professional training, of course. And when I think what I went through with poor Bill."

"I meant humiliating for Ma." Tom knew he was being foolish, as well as unfeeling. His aunt, too, had had a bad day, and he could not do without her. Yet it seemed important, at the outset of the discussion he knew would follow, to establish Iris as a distinct being before talk took away her particularity, positioning her as the object of sentences.

He said, "What a terrible shock for you. You've been tremendous."

"Yes, *well*." But, her heroism acknowledged, Audrey favored the version of herself that was selfless and uncomplaining. "It's second nature to me, rendering assistance. Remember when Shona did my personality on the Internet?" She drew her nephew into the house, ignoring his murmured protest. She had been waiting for this conversation all day.

A glass-fronted cabinet held a harlequin, a corsair, a ballerina, a drummer boy, a Bo Peep with a crook wreathed in flowers and a lilac dress bunched up over a sprigged underskirt. Once a week

Audrey murmured of love to small porcelain people while hold-ing them facedown in soapy water.

Tom turned the flowered mug in his hands. He couldn't bring himself to drink another cup of bad coffee. A plump tabby left her cushion by the heater and crossed the room to rub her ears against the visitor's legs. She sprang up, a warm purring weight.

Tom thought of how wolfish creatures are tolerant of cold but dislike damp. He tried willing himself to believe that the dog had made his way to the ridge road and was lying safe, dry, sated, in a trucker's kitchen. At this minute a woman might be reaching for the phone, while a child read off the number on a tag.

The picture was overlaid by another: night and bedraggled fur, a thin wind blowing.

Audrey was given to summary: the review of offenses that confirms authority and justifies punishment. Cushioned in crisp chintz, she outlined what she called "the situation." Iris would not venture into the passage alone. "What if the heater bursts into flame when I'm out? She'll be burned to a crisp." Audrey had lately begun providing her sister-in-law with dinner as well as lunch, Iris now being capable of no more than tea and toast. "And even then, I don't like to think of her with electricals." Audrey knew for a fact that Iris no longer risked the shower, making do with washbasin and facecloth. "You have to ask yourself about hygiene." It went without saying that Audrey was happy to do what she could; nev-ertheless, she said it. "But I can't be bound hand and foot."

She had a genius, this woman upholstered in rosy flesh, for conjuring bodily abuse. "She's got her nose out of joint." "I was running my head into a brick wall." Images that recurred, scenes from a censored film, on the bland screen of her talk.

"I told her, I made it clear: if this goes on, you'll have to go into a home." She looked at Tom with small blue eyes, the sapphire chips he had first seen in his father's face. "No one can say I haven't made it clear."

"No."

"Did you see my Berber? Ruined."

"If you could arrange steam cleaning, I'll pay, of course."

But that was too simple an outcome.

"Well, if you think I didn't do a good enough job on that carpet."

"Of course not. I could hardly see the stains. Steam cleaning would get rid of them completely, that's all."

"I work my fingers to the bone for your mother."

Driving home, his mind glazed with fatigue, Tom thought he should have offered his aunt more money. But for Audrey, money was a subject veiled in elaborate rituals; best approached, like a god, by cautious increment, facedown in the dust.

There was her resentment that Tom should be in a position to offer money. On the other hand, if money was not offered, there was resentment at being taken for granted. And then there was the question of how much, settled by indirection and insinuation and inspired guesswork, a process strung between accepting the figure named by Audrey and exceeding it by too wide a margin, either error occasioning tightened lips, silences charged with grievance, oblique accusations, and small, roundabout acts of revenge.

The rain had stopped. At a traffic light, Tom lowered his window; a cold breath arrived on his cheek.

Audrey and he both knew he would rather write checks than confront the devastation time had worked on his mother, as a man will make donations to charity the better to turn his face from the misery of the world.

This shared awareness diminished him in all his dealings with his aunt. It was Audrey, after all, who prepared meals and washed clothes, who drove Iris to the doctor and the hairdresser, who arranged for nonslip soles to be attached to shoes, who shopped for chocolate biscuits.

On Punt Road hill, Tom saw the city laid out before him like a parable. The sky was clear but blank, its lights obscured by electric galaxies. The hubris of it always thrilled him, that jeweled fist raised nightward in defiance. Age brings increased delight in the natural world, or so tradition holds. But Tom was all for artifice, for the resplendent, doomed contrivances of his ingenious kind.

Toward morning he snapped awake, his mind on the loose. He drained the glass of water beside his bed; burrowed back down into warmth.

The dog's muzzle was scattered with liverish spots, darker than the rest of his fox-red markings.

Animals do not suffer as we do. They do not live in time, they are not nostalgic for the past, they do not imagine a better future, and so they lack awareness of mortality. They might fear death when it is imminent, but they do not dread it as we do.

So Tom Loxley reasoned and tried to believe.

He thought of the stray dogs of India: question-mark tails raised over the lives they witness and endure.

He thought of the clearing he had seen on the hill, the tire holding charred wood, the soggy remains of activity, and was visited by brief, lucid images of things that can be done to animals.

THURSDAY

Tom checked the weather for the hills on the Internet: heavy rain with intermittent hail and a gale warning.

Straightening up, he was conscious of stiffness in the small of his back. As a student, he had worked part-time as a storeman, had set himself to heft cartons with the casual aplomb of the muscled boys beside him. Now he spent too many hours reading, or in front of a computer: the scholar's hunched existence.

Palms on the desk, he stretched, relishing the voluptuous ache along his spine.

He wondered how his mother was faring that morning. Age, he thought. The undistinguished thing.

LESS THAN A MONTH EARLIER Osman had said, "I'm forty-seven. I won't die young." He had been allowed to go home at the beginning of November, the cancer in remission; although, as he told Tom, the respite would almost certainly be brief. A hospital bed filled the living room, where chairs had been pushed against walls and a new flat-screen TV set up on the sideboard.

"My welcome-home present," said the effigy on the bed. "We watch DVDs. I can't read anymore. And who can bear the news? This election they will win for leaving people to drown." He looked at Tom. "Tell me a poem."

"Yet might your glassy prison seem/A place where joy is known,/Where golden flash and silver gleam/Have meanings of their own."

When Osman closed his eyes, the curve of the ball was prominent under the lid. Cancer had made him thin-skinned. His face was in the process of being replaced by a skull, an ancestor stepping forward to claim him. Yet his ability to bring ease into a room remained.

Afterward, he said, "So many poems. How come you know so many old poems?"

It was a question he had asked before, but the medication had made him forgetful. So Tom told him again about evenings with anthologies, seeing a vein-blue binding in Arthur's hand. "My father taught me to read a poem aloud and repeat it line by line. You learn without noticing that way."

Tom could still hear entire poems in Arthur's voice, a good voice, clear and unaffected. Arthur Loxley had been an indiscriminate reader. He had pages of Keats and Browning and Hardy by heart; also much his son would learn to call third rate. In resentful moods, Tom saw his mind as an attic crammed with an incongruent jumble. Groping for treasure, he was just as likely to come up with a gimcrack oddment.

Nevertheless, what had stuck was delight in words arranged well.

On a chair wedged between bed and bookcase, he said,

"Even the Gatling jammed and the colonel dead is a lesson in rhetoric."

"You know, a thing that astonishes me. How quickly poetry has slipped from the culture. I mean what lives in memory. The remembering of poems: a collective inheritance, vanished." Osman shifted, trying to raise himself against his pillows. Tom sensed Brendon, squeezed in beside him, grow tense; watched love fight itself down to grant its beloved the dignity of struggle. "I have seen this happen in my lifetime," Osman went on. "In democracies, with no dictators to burn books. So many centuries of poems, and then—"

He looked at Tom. "There are people when I say this who think, How come this Turk lectures us about poetry?" His eyes were black olives, now and then still shiny.

On his way out, Tom came to a halt in front of a picture. "It's one of Nelly's."

"Yeah, it's from last year's show." Brendon said, "I've only just got 'round to having it framed."

The image had the depth and richness of painting. You had to look closer to see that it was a photograph. Then you realized it was both: a photograph of a painting.

"The way the paint's laid on, you can see it even in a photo. Nelly can get these really amazing effects with brushwork." Brendon's hand moved out to an abacus of railway tracks depicted at the blue hinge of evening. "It really gets to me, you know. I can't bear to think of her destroying work like this."

Tom ate breakfast while loading clothes into the machine. Then he scattered the contents of drawers, searching for a photograph.

Meanwhile, his mind busied itself with this production: he was making his way down the farm track with the dog snuffling ahead on his rope when a wallaby flashed out from the bush. The dog sprang forward. But Tom kept his grip on the rope, using both hands to wind it in. The dog twisted, barking furiously. They walked on.

He had begun sketching in this scenario within hours of losing the dog. Each replay introduced a detail: his shoulder wrenching as the dog lunged forward, his skidding half steps in the mud before he mastered the animal. An ancient corner of Tom's brain insisted that if he could bring sufficient intensity of imagination to this sequence, it would in fact be true.

At eight he began calling animal shelters. "Hang in there, mate," said a ranger. Tom put the phone down and found tears prickling his lids.

There was an odd spaciousness to the morning: a dreamlike drawing out of time. At some point he realized it came from not having to walk the dog.

The campus jacarandas were staining concrete pathways blue. Exams were over; deserted courtyards and empty corridors lent the university a shifty, malingering air.

Tom settled down in his office to read a late essay from his seminar on the modern novel. The topic was "It was Henry James's ambition to break with melodrama and romance and establish himself as the master of the new psychological novel. Discuss with reference to at least two works by James."

This had elicited the following response: "Henry James failed completely in his ambition to be a modern writer. For example he invented point of view but could not always rise above omniscience. His problems are demonstrated in his last work called *The Sense of the Past*. There are the implications of the title. Furthermore the novelist provides many juxtapositions of melodrama in the text, ie when Ralph, a modern character because he is American visits a family house in London (old world) that is haunted. A ghost is one of the most well known symbols of romantic discourse. Similarly the protagonist travels back in time and meets his ancestors who are dead. Time-travel is a modern device (for the time), however —"

But Vernon Pillai was rolling through the door. "Thomas, Thomas, how I have missed you. No one to scuttle with, claw in ragged claw."

Vernon was a small circle balanced on a large one, an anomalous black snowman. He wheeled hither and thither, turning his round head sideways to decipher a spine, picking up letters and perusing them with frank interest. He tapped a photocopied article lying on Tom's desk. "Have you read this?"

"Not yet. Have you?"

"Terrible. But short." Then Vernon pointed to a mug beside the computer. "That is a disgusting object."

It was the survivor of a set of four once presented by Iris to Karen. Tom had felt the shame of it when the wrapping paper came away: his gleaming, expensive girl with a lapful of super-market china. His agitation was accompanied by a fierce protective surge. If his wife were to betray, by word or sign, what she must think of the gift, he would have no choice but to leave her.

Karen's impeccable manners brought her safely through the peril, as manners are designed to do. But the mugs remained in a cupboard. Iris, visiting some months later, inquired after them, choosing a moment when she was alone with her son. Her little finger, with its salmon-painted nail, flew like a flag from the handle of a cobalt-rimmed cup. They had lunched off the same service, a wedding present from Karen's godparents.

Tom said, "The mugs are great. But I needed some at work, and Karen said I could have them. So now at last I can offer people a coffee in my office."

He saw Iris's satisfaction in picturing his clever friends sipping from her mugs. Whatever she gave his wife was in any case an indirect offering to her son.

And so her gift ended up in Tom's office. The mugs were patterned with white hearts on a red background, or the reverse. Three quickly broke or vanished. The last persisted, with the stubbornness of the unwanted. Time scoured the hearts closest to its rim, leaving a row of pinkish smears. Recently the mug had acquired a chip. Stained with coffee, it was indeed sordid. Tom was helpless before it.

Vernon inserted his plump buttocks into the most comfortable chair and scrutinized Tom. "Where have you been darkly loitering?"

"I took a couple of days off to work on —"

"That will do." Vernon held up a startlingly pink palm. "I have students to bore me. You were due back yesterday, I believe."

"My dog ran off into the bush. I went looking for him."

Vernon considered this briefly, testing it like a loose tooth. "I am very fond of animals," he announced. "I intend to eat many, many more before I die." He hoisted one foot, encased in a tiny, shiny shoe, onto the opposite knee. "Now let us give ourselves over to scurrilous reflections on our fellow inmates. Who is your preferred candidate for the lectureship? I am in favor of the Lacanian from Rotterdam who would like to live in Australia because of our beautiful horses."

"Oh, Christ."

"Thomas, you deep cretin." Vernon removed his spectacles and dangled them by an earpiece: always a sign he was enjoying himself. "You had forgotten that we're to produce a short list by Monday."

"Can I get out of it? Are there lots of applications?"

"No, you cannot. And yes, indeed. Including a distinguished professor who's published extensively on James."

"Run along and research something lovely, Vernon."

Tom finished marking the essay on James, dropped a faculty directive about Strategic Learning Outcomes into his recycling bin, wrote a scholarship reference for one of his postgraduates. Among the many messages in his in-box from strangers offering to extend his penis was an e-mail from a student protesting her exam results. "How am I supposed to get into Law if I get a 2B in Textual Studies?"

He ran off a copy of the flyer he had mocked up at home. The photograph reproduced well, picking up the dog's markings and the feathering along his legs. Tom ran off forty more, but even as he did, was conscious of plaintive notices passed with barely a glance as they peeled from lampposts. *Have you seen Angel?* That one, with its smudged image of a cat, had caught his eye just the previous week. He remembered also: *Missing blue heeler (mainly red).* At the time, he had smiled.

At a shelter for lost dogs, a woman said, "So let me get this straight. Your dog...disappears into the bush...right?...with twenty feet of rope...you've tied to his collar."

"Yes."

"You don't *deserve* an animal." She hung up.

ONE OF THE MADDENING THINGS about Nelly was that she didn't have a phone. She could give the impression of existing in a fold of time. Walking to the Preserve to see her that winter, Tom was transported to India, to that era in his life when talk meant looking into a human face. His dealings with Nelly often uncovered these souvenirs of the past, little lumps impeding the smooth flow of time.

It was not that she was anachronistic. Nelly was open to youth, novelty, the stir of their times. She was only two months younger than Tom, but in her company he was often conscious of having lived forty years in another century. She used words not yet codified in dictionaries. It was from her that he first heard of MP3 files, of memory sticks. There was also her casual familiarity with new kinds of music, the CDs Rory and Yelena burned for her, their three-way conversations about the bands playing the Corner Hotel.

Once he had seen Nelly absorbed in a game on someone's laptop, moving about on her seat in excitement, little splashes of colored screen light reflected now and then on her face. She was technological, thought Tom. And then, more potent than any sign, was his sense that, as an artist, she inhabited the modern age, the age of the image, while he was marooned in words.

At some point in the previous decade, consumption had turned gluttonous. There was more stuff around. More people were buying it. Democracy had become a giant factory outlet. It was as if endless wealth had been converted by a malicious spell into endless want. Sometimes, late on a weekend afternoon, Tom would head to a café on Bridge Road. People crowded the pavements, shopping gathering up all classes and kinds in its dreamy pull. Isolated, spotlighted, displayed in glass niches, everyday objects took on fetishistic power, a vase or a pair of shoes acquiring the aura once enjoyed by religious icons. Such things could mean whatever people needed. They were repositories of dreams. Over espresso and the papers, Tom observed the spending that made the getting bearable: a last high-kicking performance on the public stage before the curtain of work came down.

Early one Sunday he went hunting with Nelly at the flea market in Camberwell. There was a purposeful air to her, signaled by the black bag worked with yellow daisies carried over her arm. She avoided the professional dealers; lingered among the offerings of stallholders who had turned out their cupboards so they could go shopping again.

Strolling along packed aisles, Tom marveled at the ease with which articles changed status, transmuted by the alchemy of desire. The flea market was a resting place for the debris piling up behind the whirlwind of the new. Wishes were its currency. Their force might resurrect objects no longer animated by collective yearning. A turquoise and black dress with shoulder pads, Jim Reeves's *Greatest Hits* on vinyl, a brown-glazed biscuit jar sealed with a cork, a Smith Corona typewriter in a pale blue, rigid plastic case: Tom saw each of these leavings pounced on. Invested with fresh, private meaning, they passed once more into the treasure albums of someone's mind.

At a bookstall there were volumes Tom could scarcely bring himself to touch: liberated from libraries, they displayed their violet stamps and yellow stains like prisoners exhibiting proofs of torture. A pile of comics looked more inviting. He flicked through them, and saw Huckleberry Hound and Top Cat take flight, forgotten comrades spinning up from the pillows where he had lain with measles; as if memory were one of those little flip books that need only correct handling to bring their trapped images to life.

Nelly bought a pair of fingerless gloves, an openwork cardigan threaded with Lurex, a hand-tinted panoramic postcard of the lake at Mount Gambier. Tom bought her a hot jam doughnut and a pot of pink hyacinths.

She negotiated with stallholders: "Would you take four for it?" "Any chance you could make it two-fifty?" He looked away from these scenes, ashamed for her. He always paid whatever was asked, not wishing to appear *typically Asian*.

From a tray that held a clutter of brooches, single earrings, and broken chains, she drew a strand of greeny-blue plastic pearls. It lacked a clasp and cost fifty cents.

They had arrived, at her insistence, by seven. When they were leaving she said, "If we'd come early, we'd have got the real bargains."

Not long afterward, Yelena arrived at the Preserve wearing Nelly's necklace over pale cinnamon wool. Against that setting, it turned extraordinary: the pearls glowing, otherworldly.

Tom could hear his father: *They are better than stars or water,/Better than voices of winds that sing,/Better than any man's fair daughter,/Your green glass beads on a silver ring.*

The girl noticed Tom noticing; slipped her fingers under the necklace and held it up. "Isn't it gorgeous? My birthday present from Nelly."

Why not? Nelly had restrung the necklace, fitted it with a new catch. The gift was enriched with her labor. Tom was reminded again of childhood: of bazaar handkerchiefs embellished with lace or stitched monograms in the weeks leading up to Christmas, of birthday greetings fashioned from images cut from hoarded foreign cards and glued to colored cardboard with flour-and-water paste. Such things were more than links in a disaffected chain of production and consumption. They bore a human tang.

All the same, he thought, She spent fifty cents on Yelena.

It was Nelly's habit to roam the streets of their suburb after dinner, padded against the weather in her scarlet parka. On a June evening when a southerly carried the memory of icebergs, she had coaxed Tom out with her. It became their usual way of being together.

In invisible gardens on the hill, pale camellias were the ghosts of girls locked out after balls. There was the wintry fragrance of daphne, and once — but they could never find it again — a scented drift of violets escaping through pickets. Each dark street climbing west climaxed in a peep show of a radiant city.

On Victoria Street they bought rice-paper rolls from a man with exquisite hands. A soft-bellied god smiled over joss sticks and golden mandarins. The public housing towers showed scattered patterns of light: the concrete punch cards of a superseded technology.

A girl going past said, "Forgiveness is really important. I forgive myself all the time now." Tom and Nelly shunned the narrow pavements, sauntering down the middle of the street, as people will.

Window displays drew them with the theatricality of light-defined space. A stage in Swan Street was a favorite. For weeks it held nothing but a backdrop of translucent cloth, ivory striped with gold. It floated and shimmered, a stream, a veil. It was sacred and profane. It was almost not there. It was lively with the magic of money.

From this temple they would cross to a discount department store. Here sly comedies were enacted. Bald mannequins clad in cheap, belted raincoats thrust suggestive hips at passersby. A boy in pajamas straddled a man's thigh, offering him a power tool for Father's Day. Two women who appeared to be laden from a shopping spree at the store were discovered, on closer inspection, to be bag ladies in gaping sneakers and clothes held together with pins. Everything on display looked trumpery. That was the crack through which parody made its entrance, mocking the shoddiness of all such enchantments.

Between the river and the railway lines lay a semi-industrial zone where lights were few. Streets that began with auto repair shops and small foundries ended in yards packed tight with vegetables and vines. There were herbs planted in old paint tins, ashtrays on verandah tables, rusty bed frames, palings crooked as bad dentistry.

They passed an electricity substation and an overgrown quarry. Late cars zipped by on the freeway. Mists crept up from the river. Sometimes there were fireworks staggering about the sky.

When his wife left him, Tom moved to this inner suburb because it was one of the few he could afford on his own. In that hellish interval when the humiliation of Karen's choice was a blade endlessly drawn across his soul, he had a singular stroke of luck, buying his flat just weeks before the property boom doubled its value.

It was a neighborhood on the way up. The butcher had taken to stocking free-range eggs. The doctors no longer bulk-billed. Wooden plantation blinds were replacing cutwork nylon in windows. Tibetan prayer flags fluttered across verandahs; neighbors fell out over parking for their four-wheel drives. Pubs that had featured topless waitresses now offered trivia nights and wood-fired pizza. It was easier to buy a latte than a liter of milk. The roomy weatherboard places on the big corner lots were coming down; town houses were going up. There were fewer lemon trees and more roof gardens. Construction sites gave off the odor

of cement dust and prodigious money to be made. Vistas ended
in angled cranes, colossal needles knitting up the future.

The marvelous city built by gold and wool had once voided
its filth in these parts. The sweet-watered river of the early days
of settlement had been swiftly converted into a reeking flow. A
sludge of cheap housing appeared, row after row of wooden cottages: so many flimsy coffins in which to bury the ambition of
another century's poor. It was the kind of suburb where people
had lived in tiny buildings and worked in huge ones. Tanneries
set up beside the river; later, factories. They were symbols of a
great metropolis, signs that the colonial city was no longer raw
material but an up-to-the-minute artifact.

Now the echoing shells of these industrial mollusks promised
"prestigious river frontage," or what one copywriter called "an
envious lifestyle." The riverside path had taken on rural airs, with
poplars and gums and unruly willows. Men and women sweated
doggedly along its length or lunched on terraces overlooking the
water. Wealth was inserting itself into this newly fashionable terrain, as decoration accrues on a renovated façade.

In the course of their walks, Nelly and Tom noticed that some
shop fronts displayed a commemorative plaque. "William Merton, bootmaker, conducted business on this site in 1899." "Alice
Corbett ran a bakery here in 1920." The memorials were puz-
zling in their arbitrariness, offering no indication as to why
these places, dates, and citizens had been singled out. Tom discerned the willed creation of a sense of the past: a municipal
mythmaking. It produced the inscriptions in parks that signaled
a site pregnant with meaning for the people who had lived here
first: a tree where corroborees had been held or one whose bark

had served to fashion boats. Cloaked in virtuous intention, these signs functioned insidiously. They displaced history with heritage, plastering over trauma with a picturesque frieze. A spectator might have their detail by heart and no inkling of the chasm that separated bark canoes and William Merton, bootmaker.

The unofficial past flared more vividly, illuminated in match-lit glimpses. Tom and Nelly paused before roadside shrines dedicated to lives that had ended violently: makeshift memorials composed from soft toys and plastic flowers. There were dates, photographs, greeting cards on which the ink had blurred. Each shrine was a little gash in the illusion of continuity. Propped against walls or fastened to poles, what they proclaimed was the terrible fact of rupture.

Nelly talked of people in cities needing to find places that seemed to speak to them privately; places that detached themselves, *like spots of time,* from unmemorable surrounds.

They discovered that they were both drawn to a convent school that stood beside a traffic-choked intersection a few miles to the north. Stiff pine trees lined its high perimeter wall. Painted white, an arcaded verandah on the upper floor glimmered in the apertures between dark branches.

It was the trees, they agreed, that gave the place its aura: setting it off from the polluted streets, suggesting an enchanted domain. At the same time, the pines were ambiguous presences, their green-black wings suggesting menace as well as protection.

Tom said the scene reminded him of a woodcut in an old book of children's tales. It was like something remembered from a dream, said Nelly. "Something marvelous and strange you can almost see under the skin of reality."

. . . . . .

Tom described a tiny pair of opera glasses, imagined by Raymond Roussel, to be worn as a pendant. The writer had envisioned each lens, two millimeters in diameter, to contain a photograph on glass: Cairo bazaars on one and a bank of the Nile at Luxor on the other.

Nelly yearned for this virtual object; as Tom had known she would.

One day she produced a calico bag from her pocket, unfastened the drawstring at its neck, and tipped its contents into her hand. When she opened her fingers, her palm was full of eyes. They had belonged to her grandmother, who had inherited them from her great-grandfather, who as a small boy in London had been apprenticed to a manufacturer of dolls. It was the child's task to separate the black and brown eyes from the gray and blue ones, and then to sort each group again, in precise gradations of hue.

Nelly moved her fingers. Blue eyes shuddered in her palm. Kingfisher, cornflower, steel. Smoke crushed with violets. Tom looked at them, and they looked back. It was impossible not to avert his gaze.

They spoke of the past, discovering each other. Tom learned that Nelly was an only child. Her mother had died when she was fifteen, her father was *into serial marriage.* There had been a goldfish called Fluffy.

It was not much to go on. He knew that Nelly had once been married, but little beyond that bare fact. A stray remark of Posner's confirmed that the union had been short-lived. Tom longed to know more, of course. But he wouldn't question Posner; and Nelly had a trick, to which he did not immediately tumble, of deflecting questions about herself with inquiries of her own. She drew from him stories of childhood, women, sorrows, travel, his preferences in matters trivial and weighty. What's the first thing you remember? Would you rather live in the mountains or by the sea? What's something you regret not doing? Describe a perfect city. Tell me something you've never told anyone else.

It was the kind of talk that takes place in bed. Except that Nelly, despite the force of her attention, withheld all bodily intimacy. She never touched Tom. Her hand didn't accidentally brush his; an occurrence that, in any case, is never accidental, and requires collusion. It struck Tom that even her enthusiasm for their walks might be a device for avoiding closeness. There was the Wordsworth precedent: William and Dorothy out striding the dales for fear of what might take place between them in the confines of Dove Cottage.

One day he came to a decision as he was leaving the Preserve with her. On an unlit landing, he grasped her arm: "Nelly."

"No."

"Why not?"

The dark, confined space seemed to concentrate her odor. A succession of scenes, purely pornographic, was unreeling in Tom's mind.

She disengaged herself and continued down the stairs.

He swore that was the end of it. He lay on his bed compiling an inventory of the ways she repelled him; his cunning flesh working all the while at its own satisfaction.

Over the days that followed, what remained was his need for her. And beyond Nelly, for the world she had created. He missed the drift of people in and out of the Preserve, improvised meals and conversations, the jokiness. The sense of being caught up in a wide spate of imaginative work.

Small scenes haunted him. Nelly and Osman bent over the sink with dripping raspberry ice pops. Someone's kid in stripy leggings riding a Razor scooter up and down the passage. He left a café without ordering, because a shelf behind the counter held a pink plastic sugar canister with a gray lid, identical to one in the Preserve. Lifting a glass from a sink of soapy water, he noticed the rainbow membrane of detergent stretched across it. His first thought was, Nelly would like that. Then he remembered. Her footsteps retreated through him down a cold stair.

To the raw ache of solitude he applied his usual balm of work: marking essays, reading, typing words onto a screen late into the night. The dog would leave his basket to settle on a rug in the study, first turning around thrice, an apprentice sorcerer. Later he would go out into the yard. When he returned, his fur carried the mineral scent of earth into the room.

Tom went to the cinema; out to dinner with colleagues. Then, at the end of a blunt winter's day, in the act of transferring a packet of buckwheat noodles from a shelf to a supermarket cart, he froze. Pride, which had seemed insurmountable, lay in ruins: toppled, like that, and the view a sparkling clarity. What counted was that Nelly was not indifferent to him. He might learn from the discipline she imposed. An obstacle might be a gift, deferral conceived of as a slow striptease.

There was also the novelty of the situation. Tom was a product of his times: what he knew of preludes was swift and unambiguous. Among other things, his curiosity was pricked.

THERE WAS NO POINT going back to the country on Thursday night, Tom decided. He would sleep more soundly in his own bed, would rise early and drive up to the hills.

So he went looking for Nelly at the Preserve. But found only Rory, who told him that Nelly had not been well and was staying at Posner's. "One of her headaches."

It had happened before. Tom told himself again that what mattered was Nelly having somewhere to go, someone to look after her. Once again the formula failed to counter his jealousy.

He became aware that Rory was studying him; covertly, the narrow eyes rapid and darting. Tom could not remember having been alone with him before. Silence lay between them, as awkward as a beginning, heightened by the weather slapping at the panes.

Tom said, "Could you tell Nelly I need to hang on to her keys? I've got to go back to the bush for a few days."

The boy nodded.

"I'll be off, then."

Rory said, "You OK? You look a bit shabby." Having blurted it out, he glanced away.

Tom thought, I forget how young he is. What he had diagnosed as sullenness, he now saw as the caution of someone who was trying to find a way of being in the world.

He told Rory about the dog.

"That's awful." The boy tugged at the hair under his lip, fingered the zipper on his sweater. He was in the habit of touching himself, as if to make sure he was still there. "You should go up to Carson's," he said.

"But Nelly —"

"She's OK. Out of bed. I saw her at lunch." Rory pulled the zipper down a little way, then did it up again. Tom understood that the boy was looking for something to offer him.

Rory said, "You should tell her what's happened." His sympathies were engaged by Tom's predicament, but what had just entered his mind was the place mat his mother used to put under his bowl when he was very young: a sunny circle stamped with bright blue butterflies.

"Go up to Carson's," he repeated.

"Yeah, thanks. I will."

ON AN EVENING in late July, Tom had arrived at the Preserve to find Brendon angled over the stove. He resembled a hinged ruler, his long body forever obliged to fold itself into deficient spaces.

Nelly, on the couch with her feet tucked under her, was talking about Rory. "So now there's this band. I mean it's good he's going back to music, he used to be a really good violinist, and these guys are great, he'll get a lot out of playing with them. But that's the end of painting, although he says it isn't."

"No reason he can't do both," said Brendon.

Nelly's hair was fastened on top of her head, her eyes and mouth were painted. Her face, always pale, had been powdered rice-paper white. Her concubine look. Tom had known her long enough to understand it signaled defensiveness.

She said, "But he won't. Not seriously. He won't paint in a focused way because all his energy'll be directed at this band. He always gives a hundred and ten percent to whatever he's just taken up."

"Well, that's not a bad thing," said Brendon easily. He looked at Tom. "Coffee?"

"Yeah, it's not a bad thing if it lasts." Nelly twirled a vagrant strand of hair around her finger. "But there's this burst of enthusiasm and then —" She exhaled theatrically. "I don't know, sometimes I wish he wasn't coming into all that dough. It's like he doesn't have to make an effort, you know?"

Tom sipped Brendon's heart-stopping brew and was stabbed with impatience. Nelly, grimacing, her jaw tense, was almost plain. "Why do you let Rory get to you?" he asked. He remembered the earlier exchange he had witnessed between the two, and in that instant knew what it mimicked. "You act like you're his mother or something."

Afterward, he would remember their faces: aimed at him, oddly still.

Until: "I *am* his mother," said Nelly.

Nelly poured herself a glass of wine. Pushed up the sleeves of her sweater.

Brendon said, "I'll leave you guys to it," and carried his cup into his studio. Moments later, a cello began to flow.

Tom felt the familiar jolt: he had misunderstood. The thought dropped open, and what lay underneath was the suspicion that he had been misled.

But he knew Nelly had been married. And then, with hindsight sharpening his vision, he could see the resemblance between mother and son: attenuated, but discernible all the same in the shallow-set eyes, the rather heavy molding of the chin.

It was the kind of oversight to which Tom was prone. He lived in a country where he had no continuity with the dead; and, being childless, no connection to the future. Most lives describe a line that runs behind and before. His drew the airless, perfect circle of autobiography. What he missed, in the world, was affiliation.

He felt immensely foolish.

Nelly was talking. He retained facts. Her husband *taking off* — a phrase Tom would remember — when Rory was four. The turmoil; life going awry. "It was like the plates shook and fell off the wall." Her in-laws trying to get custody of the child.

She continued to speak of these things as if Tom should have had prior knowledge of them.

"I used to spend more time at Carson's place when Rory was still a kid." Nelly looked into her empty glass. "He's been really good to us, Carson."

It sounded stilted. Tom looked at her averted face and thought, You know I don't like him. He said, "I should have connected the dots."

Nelly gestured: *Oh well.* "Rory's not 'round here much when you are. I guess you never heard his surname."

Tom said slowly, "Atwood. Rory Atwood. I've heard him on the phone."

He saw that Nelly was, among other things, fearful.

She made a noise: half laugh, half groan. "Oh, crikey. You really don't know, do you?"

It was Tom who felt afraid, then, of what he was about to learn.

"I used to be Nelly Atwood." The voice was gentle. "Nelly's Nasties. Remember?"

POSNER'S HOUSE, on a corner lot, was high and broad, built of grim bluestone hand-chiseled by men in chains. A wrought-iron fence around the garden brought impaling to mind. Formal beds restrained by low box hedges contained the kind of roses whose icy perfection was impervious to common rain.

Tom had steeled himself for Posner, but a stocky brown man answered the door. He wore blue overalls with a logo on the pocket. Tom asked for Nelly, gave his name. There was the sound of vacuuming from a room off the hall.

"Ah, Nelly." The cleaner smiled, stepped aside, pointed to the stairs.

An overalled woman looked up as Tom passed an open door, but went on with her work.

The arched window on the half landing looked out onto a deep back garden: bowery, treed, a stone birdbath on shaggy grass. Just then, as so often at the end of a rainy afternoon, the sun shone. The garden showed shadows and splotched light. Flowers were everywhere, fat spillages of cream and pink, belled blue spikes, frothy lemon. Leaves and grasses moved, the scene shaking in light.

"Hi." Nelly had her arms on the banister. Light was dangling in her black hair.

They stood awkwardly, not having, in all these months, evolved a satisfactory way of greeting each other.

Tom indicated the window at his back. "So glorious."

Nelly was wrapped in a shawl he hadn't seen before, swarthy red stamped with tiny cream and golden flowers. She said, "Going from the front to the back of this place is like one of those movies where the librarian takes off her glasses and starts to unbutton her blouse."

"That's exactly right. That garden's wanton."

"We could sit out there." Nelly peered at the landing window. "No, everything'll be wet. Let's just look at it from my room."

He said, "How are you? Rory told me you were here, that you've been ill."

"The usual. A headache. Such a drag. I'm heaps better, thanks," said Nelly. "I should've gone to college today. But there's all this." A gesture. "I'm getting soft."

All this was a long room, light-filled. The bed was high and wide, a disarray of square and oblong pillows, dull silk contrasting with smooth cotton. Tom took in a lacquered cabinet with intricate locks, a glowing rug, books with opulent jackets on shelves and tables. Things Posner could give her.

He conceived of it as a transaction between Nelly and the dealer: unvoiced and understood, with the gleaming presence of Rory at its core. His early sense of Posner's relations with the boy had since wavered from certainty. Rory's manner toward the former seemed unencumbered, wholly free of the lover's charged style. Nevertheless, time and again, Tom had seen Posner's gaze find and follow the boy. Need settled on Rory, and sucked.

A book, partly obscured by another, lay on Nelly's bed: *Vanished Splendors,* and the fragment of a name, Balthasar Klos —. It was a name Tom recognized and didn't recognize, a name on the edge of memory.

Nelly had crossed the room and was pushing up the sash. Beads of water edged sill and window.

"And your book?" she asked. "Did you get it finished? Was the house OK?"

Tom sat in a low embroidered chair by the window and began to talk.

"I'm coming with you," said Nelly.

She had placed the decanter and a glass beside him and prepared tea for herself, saying she was off the hard stuff. Now she sat with fingers laced about a translucent gray bowl. "I'll help you look for him. We'll cover more ground than if you're by yourself."

But Tom had observed the indigo stains below her eyes, the tight, whitish lips.

"Do you think you're up to it?"

"Sure." But her eyes traveled to the table by the bed, and he saw the pills there on a wicker tray.

"Why don't you see how you are over the next couple of days? It's pretty bleak up there with all this rain."

He expected her to protest and, when she didn't, understood that he had been right not to take up her offer.

"I'll be back by Sunday," he said. "I've got to see my mother. And there's a meeting I can't get out of Monday morning. If he doesn't turn up tomorrow, we could go back together next week."

She was refilling her bowl, her head bent over the task. There was something unfamiliar about her presence; then Tom realized it was the clean smell of her hair. It had been washed in something herbal, faintly medicinal. Rosemary, he thought.

Later he carried his glass and Nelly's tea things into a recess off the landing that had been fitted up with a sink and cupboards. When he came back into the room, an object caught his eye. It was the small folder with elastic fastenings he had first glimpsed in Nelly's bag all those months ago. Its blue and red marbled cardboard was furred, as if much handled.

She was still sitting by the window. The weather had turned, and the room was cold. Tom lowered the sash. Two lorikeets, feathered purple and crimson and green, flew up from the mus- cled mauve arms of a eucalypt: a Fauve canvas come to life.

Nelly said, "You mustn't be hard on yourself." She leaned for- ward. "You were doing the right thing, keeping him on a long lead."

Tom allowed himself to place the back of his hand, very lightly, against her cheek.

He could find his own way out, he insisted, and left her settled in her chair. But he was still on the stairs when he heard her call and turned to see her come out onto the upper landing. "Your book. Did you get it done?"

"Yes."

"Hey!" Nelly crowed with pleasure. "That's great."

Gazing down on him, hung with heavy ruby folds, she had the air of a tiny idol, one who might save him or do him great harm.

Downstairs, lamps had been switched on against the gathering evening. The glare of parquet was everywhere. A spotlighted alcove sheltered a pre-Columbian figure carved from stone. For a split second Tom saw the miniature double of the squat brown man who had let him into the house.

Paintings filled the walls. But Tom would not allow himself to linger before Posner's trophies.

Nevertheless, as he came to the open door of the room where the woman had been vacuuming, he halted. Gleaming wood and muted jewel tones repeated the message of wealth tempered by taste that the house had been designed to communicate. But what held Tom's attention was the landscape on the far wall.

He had forgotten how small it was. With light steps he crossed the room until he stood in front of it; and felt again the force of something that could not be contained in rational dimensions.

A reedy voice at his back murmured, *"How with this rage shall beauty hold a plea, / Whose action is no stronger than a flower?"*

The pale pillar of Posner was rising from the black scoop of a chair. For a large man, he moved as if oiled.

A dribble of dismay made its way down Tom's spine. That he should be in this place, twitching in Posner's snare. That he should have been discovered coveting what Posner possessed. That Posner, a gross, material creature, should have Shakespeare at his disposal.

"Not at all," said Posner, although Tom had not apologized. He spread his hands. "It exerts such a pull. I feel it myself."

He came up close to Tom. Who was conscious, unexpectedly, of Posner's appeal, of the calm that would follow submission to that pearl-glazed mass. He could offer up the gift of himself, and Posner would keep him safe in his pocket. He would take him out now and then and polish him on his sleeve.

"I mean, just look at it." Posner's hand rested on Tom's shoulder, urging him gently around. "I think...I *think* what makes it extraordinary is the way it risks sentimentality. How it doesn't shy away from sheer gorgeousness. The way she's laid on that paint. And this." His finger hovered above a rectangle of gold and burnt orange. "The whole thing's such a huge risk. And she confronts it and makes use of it. Subordinates it to a larger design, like this scrap of Chinese paper. It's an exorcism, in a way. It looks something dangerous in the face and accepts it. Controls it. And you think, How absolutely fucking marvelous."

His fingers tightened a little on Tom's shoulder. "Would you like to touch it?" His mouth approached Tom's ear. "Touch it, if you like," breathed Posner.

After dinner, Tom assembled clothes, food, the equipment he had bought that afternoon. He checked his list again, aware that he was not entirely sober. He had begun drinking as soon as he had gotten home and had kept it up more or less all evening.

It was his habit to try for private truthfulness. He paused in his preparations to acknowledge that what disturbed him most — more than his sense that Posner had anticipated the entire episode, more than his flustered, schoolboyish retreat — was the flicker of acquiescence Posner had drawn from him.

A CHAMPAGNE-BRIGHT AFTERNOON in winter, the blank interval that July during which Tom had sworn off Nelly.

In a paddock by the river, where a post measured floods in imperial feet, he unclipped the dog's lead. A giant metal man stood sentry over the place, one of a series of pylons striding beside the freeway. But there were also eucalypts and acacias deep in waving grasses or leaning over the water. To leave the bike path for the leafy corridor that dipped into the paddock was like returning to a scene almost forgotten.

The dog vanished over a bank, reappeared eventually with damp paws. He never went out of his depth but stood in the sluggish current even in the coldest weather, attentive to ducks. Sometimes a dog on the far side of the river made him bark.

Time passed. Shadows stretched over the beaten tin surface of the water. The sun was easing itself earthward with the caution of an old, exhausted animal. In the yawning sky, which was still full of light, a dark path opened and lengthened. It was the city's daily visitation from horror. The bats streamed up from the botanic gardens, following the river's chill road to the orchards waiting in the east.

Tom walked back into the baroque ruins of a sunset, rose and gold curds whipped up in a Roman dream. It was a city that put on wonderful skies. He thought of a cloudscape in one of Nelly's pictures: oyster-gray puffs blown over a yellow bed. *Up above,*

what wind-walks! what lovely behaviour / Of silk-sack clouds!
Then he remembered believing, as a very young child, that the
sun and the clouds followed wherever he walked.

A voice from a hedged garden hissed, "You've had every opportunity." But when Tom turned his head, there was no one there.

Without having intended to, he found he had deviated from
his course and was in the vicinity of the Preserve. He began to
fantasize about turning a corner and coming face-to-face with
Nelly. This flight of imagination was so persuasive that the smell
of her entered his nostrils. He saw her hand, emerging from its
padded red sleeve, in the dog's fur, and noticed what had escaped
his attention until then: a tiny cork-colored blemish between her
thumb and index finger.

He came to a halt at the junction of two streets, beyond which
the bulk of the Preserve detached itself against the darkening
sky. The upper stories could be plainly seen above the surrounding buildings. Nelly's studio, which lay on the far side, was invisible, but the wall of panes in the central room was a sheet of
gold, and Rory's windows were lined with light.

The dog clicked to and fro on the corner; he wished to return
to his dinner. With the onset of evening, it was very cold. Tom
slipped his free hand into his pocket.

At that moment something pale moved in the shadows above
the Preserve. In Tom's chest a muscle jolted. With that first
shock, he took an instinctive step backward. Then, straining to
decode the vision before him, he stood stone-still and peered.
Posner was walking on the roof of the Preserve.

It was where Nelly and the others went to smoke. What business Posner, a nonsmoker, had there on an icy evening was not
apparent. Then it occurred to Tom that he might not be alone.

Nelly might be strolling there, hidden by the parapet, drawing poisonous spice into her lungs, while the dealer regaled her with a witty dissection of the motives of the figure shrinking on the pavement below.

Posner came to a halt, the whey circle of his face directed at Tom. Who told himself that in his dark fleece, at that distance, he was invisible to the watcher on the roof. He mastered an impulse to look away, made himself return that blind gaze. For a frozen passage Posner and he remained motionless, stricken with each other.

But there was the dog, a patch of light shifting at Tom's feet. He placed his hand on the furry spine and pressed. The dog sat.

This obedience so surprised Tom that he glanced down. When he looked up again, Posner had vanished.

The chill of the street, seeping up through his boots, had entered Tom's marrow. He shivered and heard soft growling. The dog's hackles had risen. There must be a cat somewhere close at hand, crouched in the darkness that had spread like leaves.

TOM WENT IN AND OUT of rooms in his flat. In the laundry, a blanket-lined basket still held the dog's smell.

He found himself flicking through his address book. The dog had belonged to his wife. Tom had picked him out with her from the animals with their noses pressed to the mesh at the shelter, but he was Karen's birthday present, technically hers.

The presumption of it struck Tom now: that one should speak of ownership in relation to nerved flesh.

He sat on his bed and punched in a series of numbers.

On the other side of the globe, his wife said, "Karen Clifford." She had retained the crisply professional manner she had honed as a solicitor, crisp professionalism being a quality by which she set great store.

In those same clear tones, designed to purge conversation of the pungent and ambiguous — to make speech over as communication — she had informed Tom that she was leaving him for a human rights lawyer who had just been appointed to the Hague. "Hugh's doing absolutely vital work for asylum seekers," she had announced, with her little characteristic gesture of tucking her hair behind her ears.

Hugh's manifest superiority thus established, it was plain that she expected her husband to raise no objection.

With time, as he picked over the rubble of his marriage, Tom Loxley realized that its end repeated its beginning, each having its origin in the erotic coupling of virtue and transgression. Karen was the product of the usual liberal, middle-class upbringing that tolerated Asian immigration while not expecting to encounter it at the altar. The prospect of union with Tom had satisfied both her need to rebel and her social conscience, the same erotic fusion she sought, years later, in adultery sanctified by the pro bono advocacy of Hugh Hopkirk.

Yet Tom knew he was not blameless in what had failed between them. With hindsight it was obvious enough: a fact as large and plain as a wardrobe.

A few months after he met Karen, she got pregnant. They had been unlucky: a condom had burst. Neither wavered over their course of action, their dialogue regretful but charged with practicalities. Afterward, they were sad together; also relieved. They had been sensible. There was the feeling of having averted something that had the capacity to engulf them. They held hands on the beach at Queenscliff, and what Tom noticed was the unimpeded horizon.

They spoke of the business of children now and then in the years that followed, prompted by the arrival of other people's babies; or, as their generation aged, by protracted, harrowing encounters between depleted flesh and biotechnology. Meanwhile, Karen would roll her eyes, telling him of this or that colleague who had chosen "the mummy track."

She worked fifty, sixty hours a week, often spending a day and a night and another day at the office. When she was made a partner, they celebrated with five days at a resort in Tahiti. In the airport bar, waiting for their flight home to be called, she looked up from her second vodka tonic. "Look: this whole children thing. I just don't want to go there, OK?"

Her pale eyes, always very clear, were luminous in her tanned face. Tom was visited by a brief, brutal need to take her to a private place and ram himself into her. A blurred voice overhead announced destinations, delays.

He said, conscious of awkwardness, "Of course it's OK."

"Sure?"

"Positive. It's exactly the same for me."

"That's good."

Time passed. Tom witnessed the lives of men and women he had known for years bent into new configurations by the impact of children. He understood, with the brain not the heart, as one understands a syllogism, that paternity might represent an enlargement of experience; to him it seemed dilution. Babies arrived and individual histories thinned, became difficult to distinguish from the great biological tasks. The small parcel of clotted tissue he had helped bring into being rarely crossed his mind, and never as a lost possibility in his marriage.

It didn't occur to him to doubt that these things held true for his wife as well.

Yet a year after she left him she had a child, and then another. A boy and a girl, the right number in the right order. It was all very Karen: perfectionism in everything she undertook. Malicious friends reported on impeccable toddlers, sleep-schooled and potty-trained within months of arriving on earth. There was a rumor that the three-year-old had begun violin lessons.

It was gossip Tom relished and propagated. At the same time, recognizing that Hugh Hopkirk had addressed what he himself had neglected to notice in Karen: an aptitude for love infinitely larger than any caricature concocted from her flaws.

It was to that sense of something private and true in the woman who had been his wife that Tom spoke now, across the silence of oceans, telling her what had happened.

She said, "Oh, God. Oh, it's too horrible."

When leaving Tom, she had wept for the dog. Who could not be conveniently transported to the Hague.

Tom talked of the cold in the hills, the unseasonable spring. Then he spoke of the dog's strength, his freedom from the diseases of old age. Ending weakly with, "I still stick to that diet you came up with for him. Always."

It became clear, to him at least, that he was trying to prove he had not fallen short of her standards.

"I'm going back first thing tomorrow. I'll keep looking. I haven't given up hope."

He massaged his neck, his temples.

Into the silence Karen said, "He must have hanged himself." Her voice, which had wavered earlier, was now firm. "The rope would have got caught up around a tree or something, and he'd have gone over the edge of a gully and broken his neck."

When Tom didn't reply, she said, "It would have been quick. He wouldn't have suffered."

She sounded quite calm, even contented, having found consolation in picturing an animal she had loved dying at the end of a rope.

THE MICROFISH darted through Iris's mind, flashes of emerald and garnet and iridescent opal. She never thought of the little fish without feeling comforted, even though they had taken away her job as a filing clerk in the department store, where she had been happy, in her pale blue uniform, for four years, splurging once a week on a hot lunch in the cafeteria, choosing chocolates from the revolving assortment in Confectionery to take home on a Friday. Even now, so many years later, as she sat on the toilet slow with sleep, the warm, sharp scent of dollar bills rising from her pay packet remained distinct to her.

Then Mr. Parker called everyone together and said the microfish were taking over. Some of the girls began to cry. Mr. Parker was a knife-faced man with an infinite capacity for kindness. His pinpoint eyes moistened readily; when the girls chipped in for a layered sponge on his birthday, for instance. His mustache quivered as he spoke of redundancies throughout Clerical. "Length of service doesn't come into it. My own future's on the line."

Tommy had said that the microfish weren't fish at all. "Christ, Ma, I can't believe you thought they'd trained fish to take over the filing. That's really dumb." He was sixteen, a scornful age. Iris had long forgotten, having in the first place not understood, his impatient explanations. But she could remember the long filing room, with its green-shaded lights and the row of potted plants that Mr. Parker tended under the high window. It looked to her not unlike an aquarium. And whatever her clever son had to say, Iris had heard from Mr. Parker's own lips that his future was on the line. Henceforth she would always picture him perched on a filing cabinet, long legs dangling as he hauled in one tiny fish after another, filling the green-tinged room with their brilliance.

Iris grasped her walker and began the process of hauling herself off the toilet. Pain was a drawn-out shriek in her knees as they straightened.

Every Sunday she had lunch at Tommy's, where the toilet seat was lower than her own. Audrey dismissed this as nonsense. "There's a standard measure for everything." Iris's knees knew better.

Upright at last, she looked down at her hands: two plucked birds welded to her walker. Her rings were buried in flesh. But the cabochon ruby Arthur had bought for a knockdown price from a fellow who once managed a mine in Burma glowed on her finger.

Her father had taken one look: "Glass."

Lowering herself onto her bed, Iris sighed. She wriggled her buttocks into position. Swiveled from the waist — slowly, like a tank on maneuvers — and brought her right leg up, then the left. She reached for the jar beside her bed and began rubbing an herbal cream into the swollen hinges on which verticality depended.

Her bathroom cabinet contained a mess of half-used tubes and bottles. Each had marked a station on a path that shimmered before Iris, promising to lead her from pain.

Sometimes Iris would listen to late-night talk shows when she returned to her bed; sometimes she reached under her pillow for her rosary. Tonight she lay with her eyes closed and listened to the wind, which was breathing among leaves with the sound of the sea. She thought of miracles, of waking to find her knees strong and supple; of hunger satisfied with loaves and little fishes.

The rain started up its brisk conversation. Standing under a banyan tree, a child looked into an amber mask in the fork of the trunk. A monsoon was crashing in the compound and, "Come on," shouted Matthew Ho over the din. "Climb up the rain."

Iris sucked the end of a ringlet; balanced on her right foot, her left. Then she tucked her drenched skirt into her knickers, hoisted herself skyward, and began swarming up the ladder of rain.

FRIDAY

Tiny feet fled when Tom entered Nelly's house. In the kitchen, there was a Morse code of mouse shit on the sill, the sink, the table.

He unpacked the car, then sat on the back step with coffee from his thermos. It was shortly after eight; he had risen at four. His mind brimmed with metal and oncoming lights, with images slippery as speed. He concentrated on the stream of his breathing, trying to absorb the saturated calm of the place. Cattle raised their heavy heads to look at him, then lowered them once more to their table. Magpies drove their beaks into the damp earth.

The dish of oats he had left by the steps, partly covered with a piece of Masonite, was soggy but undisturbed.

He noticed that his ritual magic had taken a variant turn. His latest revisioning of the scene with the wallaby began by Nelly's water tank, where, instead of fastening a length of orange polypropylene baling twine to the dog's collar, he merely clipped on his lead. The wallaby crossed in front of them. The dog bounded into the bush. He reappeared shortly afterward, shamefaced but unrepentant. His lead, too short to tangle with the undergrowth, was dragging through the mud.

The replay was relentless. Tom was learning that disaster is repetitive: animated yet inert. Offering neither the release of change nor the serenity of detachment, it was merely always there; always terrible.

· · · · · ·

His purchases the previous day had included builders' tape and a pocketknife. Short lengths of bright yellow plastic now flagged his passage through the bush.

There were fugitive smells: humus, rotting wood, the pungent green tang he had already remarked.

Tom would call the dog, then listen, straining to hear a whimper, a rustle. But if he was silent and still for too long, he had the impression that something was listening to him. Very quickly, the feeling grew oppressive. It was necessary to keep moving, keep shouting.

Then he saw it: close to the ground, a patch of white. He tore and pushed his way through recalcitrant vegetation, came to a standstill at a sack that had once contained superphosphate.

The rain held off all morning, then fell in sheets.

The road from the hills coiled tightly down through forest to the highway. For four or five clenched minutes Tom was tailgated by a truck until the road widened sufficiently for him to pull over. The monster ground its way past, horn blasting. The air shook. Tom crouched in his car, the rain and his heart drumming, and saw the cargo of dead trees rock as the truck took the bend. To his left, the abyss inches from his wheels held the towering calm of mountain ash.

The logging traffic had pocked the road with potholes. A second truck with its consignment of giant pencils passed Tom farther down the hill. Water swooshed over his windshield. Friday afternoon: drivers racing to meet their quotas at the sawmill.

. . . . . .

The road broadened and improved when it reached the coastal plain. Paddocks came into view, a windbreak of dark pines. The noteless staves of fences, hymning possession. When a driveway appeared, Tom pulled over; dashed out, and dropped a flyer into a mailbox. The sodden fields had the pulled-down look of a bitch who has whelped too often.

Here and there, stringy eucalypts had been allowed to live. They ran counter to Tom's idea of a tree, which was wide as centuries and differently green. These had failed an audition. They loitered, dusty tree ghosts, bungled sketches signed "God" or whatever.

He thought of his progress that morning, the hillocks and gullies he had traversed. There was something humbling about uneven, wooded ground. He realized, peering past his laborious wipers, that it came from the absence of vistas. Here, he was a surveyor of horizons: mastery was in his gaze. There, in the hills, vision came up against the palpable folds and pockets of the earth, was obliged to follow the lay of the land.

Forward motion: it was the engine of settler nations, where there was no past and a limitless future, and pioneers were depicted gazing out across distant expanses. The man in the car remembered, *The pleasure of believing what we see / Is boundless, as we wish our souls to be.*

He was a citizen of a country that had entered the modern age with a practical demonstration of the superiority of gunpowder over stone. To be impractical on these shores — tender, visionary — was to question the core of that enterprise. Yet the place itself was hardwired for marvels. What was a platypus

if not the product of a cosmic abracadabra? So much that was
native to Australia seemed to be the invention of a child or a
genius. Minds receptive to its example had grown sumptuous
with dreaming.

It was true that local characters and scenes slotted effortlessly
into a global script. Muscled teenagers in big shorts crowded
the nation's shopping malls. On neat estates where every house
replicated its neighbor, young women pushed strollers containing babies of such plush perfection that it was difficult to believe
they would grow up to eat at McDonald's and pay to have their
flesh tanned orange. There was comfort to be derived from this
sense that the nation was keeping up with the great elsewhere.
What claim does a new world have on our imagination if it falls
out of date?

But a stand of eucalypts in a park or the graffiti on an overpass might call up a vision of what malls and rotary mowers
had displaced. Australia was LA, it was London, and then it was
not. Here there was the sense that everything modern might be
provisional: that teenagers, news crews, French fries, might vanish overnight like a soap opera with poor ratings. The country
shimmered with this unsettling magic, which raised and erased
it in a single motion.

The past was not always past enough here. It was like living
in a house acquired for its clean angles and gleaming appliances;
and discovering a bricked-up door at which, faint but insistent,
the sound of knocking could be heard.

NELLY ASKED to borrow a copy of *The Turn of the Screw,* and Tom lent her an edition that included a selection of critical commentaries. When she returned it, she said, "Do you think we create mysteries because we crave explanations?"

She could unsettle him in the way of certain students: seeming to miss an idea, yet leaving the after-impression of striking to its core.

When she asked about his book on James, Tom talked about the novelist's desire to be modern. "He wanted to distance himself from the literary past, from old forms like gothic. But that stuff wafts around his work like a smell he's too exquisite to mention."

There was James's fascination with the supernatural. "He tried to contain it by writing ghost stories. Sidelining it, trying to keep it out of the major work, out of the novels. But even in *The Portrait of a Lady,* which everyone agrees is a realist masterpiece, the heroine sees her cousin's ghost at a crucial moment."

Over time the monumental *Portrait* itself turned spectral, said Tom. Its presence showed and faded and shimmered again in *The Wings of the Dove,* a novel written when James had grown old, and haunted, like its predecessor, by his memories of his cousin Minny Temple. She had died young, leaving James with the uneasy thought that he had not loved her well enough.

This conversation was taking place in the Preserve. While he was speaking, Tom was conscious of many things, of the sound produced by Nelly's teeth biting into an apple, for instance, and of the unexpected mildness of the evening. Someone had placed a double row of candles all down the long table on the dais, the only illumination in the cavernous room. Tom's eyes kept returning to that bright, unstable path. But what he was seeing had no material form. Over the years, as he worked on his book, he had begun to picture James's oeuvre as a massive, stooped figure, its progress along the passage of time impeded by a dragging shadow. Tom understood that the name of this darkness was history, that it represented unwelcome aspects of the past that blundered into James's fiction.

Nelly said, "But isn't that the way it works? I mean, doesn't setting out to reject the past guarantee you'll never be free of it? It's like being modern means walking with a built-in limp."

Her almost magical divination of the halting colossus Tom had pictured so astonished him that he couldn't reply. The lurching figure advanced in his mind again, a grotesque portrait stepping clear of its frame. The vision was central to his argument, and it frightened him. He feared being unable to convey its force in reasoned prose; and of this fear he said nothing to Nelly.

I USED TO BE Nelly Atwood. It had sent Tom to his university library early the next morning. There he learned that sixteen years earlier, in 1985, the disappearance of a man called Felix

Atwood had made headlines across Australia. A graduate student in the States at the time, Tom had missed the story. Now he began piecing it together from archived newspapers, leaning over the shining glass of a microfilm reader.

Atwood, aged thirty-three, a trader in bonds at an investment bank that had financed the Napoleonic Wars, vanished while spending Easter with his wife and young son at their holiday house in the bush. His wife was reported to have been unconcerned when she woke on Saturday morning and found her husband missing and no car in the drive. Atwood, an early riser, liked to go bushwalking on his own. The property was surrounded by forest. It seemed likely that he had left the car at a trail head and set off into the bush. Equally, he might have driven down to the coast. He was a keen swimmer, and half an hour away was a beach he favored.

Mrs. Atwood, who suffered from headaches, had woken to familiar symptoms that day. With an effort she dressed; stumbled with her child to a neighbor's farm, where she left him. It was not an unusual arrangement; the four-year-old had a pet lamb there and was spoiled by the farmer's teenage daughters.

Atwood's wife said she returned to bed. Around noon she woke to find herself still alone in the house and started to wonder if something had gone wrong. The Atwoods were expecting a visitor from the city later that day, and surely only a mishap could have kept her husband from being there to greet him.

Still the woman did nothing. She was quoted as saying she was *not thinking clearly*. The Atwoods' friend arrived and, learning what had happened, went immediately to the farm, where he made the call to the police.

The machinery of process clicked on. In the days that followed,

the police interviewed the missing man's relatives and friends
and began sorting through the reports still coming in from people
who claimed to have seen him. Atwood's BMW was found almost
at once, parked in ti-tree scrub by the beach where he liked to
swim. His clothes lay folded on the passenger seat. Forensic testing yielded numerous traces, none of them of use in determin-
ing what had happened to him.

Then a statement issued by Atwood's employer revealed
that he was under investigation for irregular dealing. While his
managers had supposed him to be exploiting low-risk arbitrage
opportunities, Felix Atwood had in fact been gambling spectacular sums in directional bets. These unauthorized activities
produced substantial profits at first, consolidating Atwood's
reputation as a trading star. What greed, complacency, and lax
internal controls failed to discover was the secret account he
had opened. Here he hid the monumental losses that his high-
risk strategies produced, while posting fabricated profits in the
account where his performance was evaluated.

Atwood was clever and lucky — just not enough. The bank's
auditors presented their findings within a week of his disappearance, causing a fresh wave of speculation. For as the auditors
closed in, Atwood could scarcely have failed to notice the stench
blowing his way. It was an old story: a man faced with public
ruin walking away from his life. Perhaps literally, for suicide was
quickly assumed to be the solution, Atwood wading into the sea
as his wife and child slept, preferring death to disgrace.

It was discovered that the Atwoods' house in the city was
double-mortgaged. There were personal loans and credit card
debts and irregularities in income tax; the tax office was about
to launch an inquiry of its own. Ready-made phrases appeared

on the sheet of light under Tom's eyes: *luxury lifestyle, cocaine habit, assets seized.*

Tom studied the photographs. Felix Atwood: curly hair, an angular, inviting muzzle. He was pictured on a beach with long breakers at his back and a surfboard under his arm; bow-tied, with curls slicked down, outside a concert hall. He looked straight into the camera and smiled. He had good, or at least expensive, teeth. Somehow it was clear he did not make the mistake of underestimating his effect.

The Atwoods' friend from the city was identified, predictably, as Posner: dark hair emphasizing his pallor, but the rest astonishingly unchanged, as if that large, smooth face had repelled even time. Posner was in fact everywhere: escorting Mrs. Atwood to a car, at a fundraising dinner with her husband, grave-eyed outside police headquarters on Russell Street.

But it was Nelly who held Tom's attention. In the early photographs she was anonymous in sunglasses. But as events gathered speed and density, a different set of images prevailed. She appeared in an ugly ruffled dress with jewels at her throat: a photograph taken at the same opening night at which her husband had been snapped, with this crucial difference, that she gazed stonily at the lens. To Tom's eye she looked — oddly — older than she did now, her cropped hair and frumpish frilled bodice making her seem dated, compounding the rigidity of her stare.

Elsewhere she was pictured in such a way as to bring out the prominence of her jaw. Then a new photograph showed her with her arm raised and mouth wide, screaming at the camera. She might have been trying to hide her face, but the gesture, coupled with that glimpse of her tongue and teeth, suggested a harridan's attack.

In this way, from multiple images, a single portrait was being composed: of a hard-faced, alien female, operating from unfathomable motives, capable of losing control.

Nelly was never photographed with Rory. He was always pictured alone, and looked, as children do in such circumstances, fearful and exposed.

There would have been other pictures, gleaming and persuasive. But what television had made of Nelly was left to Tom's imagination.

His university archived most of its newspaper holdings on positive film. However, a two-week period was stored on negatives. Their velvety darkness coincided with the least flattering images of Nelly. Bat-black with silver-foil lips, she hung inverted in the machine's overhead mirror.

Tom avoided microfilm whenever possible, was thankful for the digital imaging that had replaced it. There was the fiddle of loading the film onto the spools and threading it correctly. Librarians breathed at his shoulder with ostentatious forbearance as his hands thickened into paws. The film jammed or slipped from its reel.

Blurred columns of newsprint rolled toward him, the past advancing with speedy, futuristic menace as he tried to locate what he needed. The jumpy, black-on-white batik of fast-forwarding hurt his eyes and brought on intimations of nausea. As time passed, his arm began to ache from rewinding each spool. His body had accommodated itself to the demands of his laptop and was protesting the readjustment. He rotated his head and heard a vertebral click.

He awarded himself a break; drank coffee issued in sour gouts from a dispenser while thinking of the way bodies changed with technology. Handwriting, assuming the speed of a body, was marked by its dynamic. Technology reversed the process, leaving its impress on corporeal arrangements. The history of machines was written in the alignment of muscles.

A scene from the previous year came back to him. One evening, as he was putting out his rubbish, he had noticed a woman wave at a car pulling away from the curb. Then she rotated her forefinger rapidly: she was asking the driver to call her. And Tom had realized that this gesture, once commonplace, had almost disappeared. He couldn't remember the last time he had seen it. The rotary-dial telephone, until recently an everyday object, was glimpsed now only as a ghost inhabiting a gesture; itself an ephemeral sign, transient as progress.

Public interest in Felix Atwood had started to wane, when a man walked into a police station in a country town and told a story. Jimmy Morgan was known locally as *a character;* a photograph showed a narrow brow above a drinker's unfastened face. He lived alone in a shack deep in the bush some miles from the spot where Atwood's car had been found. It was the kind of refuge Australia was still good at offering.

Very early on the day Atwood had vanished, Jimmy Morgan was walking along the beach. To what purpose was not evident, purposelessness being the end to which Morgan aspired, an aim harder to achieve than it appears. But he told the men who interviewed him that the date was fixed in his mind, for it marked the completion of his fifty-fourth year on earth.

It was still some minutes to sunrise, but the night had begun to dissolve. In the lengthening clefts of light, Morgan saw a woman climbing the track that bent through scattered ti-tree to the road. She didn't look over her shoulder. In any case, Morgan had the knack of not drawing attention to himself.

Eventually he followed her over the dunes. The empty road curved away out of sight to the left and right along the coast. Morgan might have heard a car. It was hard to tell. The wind was up and there was the sound of the sea.

It was a narrative of missed opportunities, thought Tom. If Morgan had approached the winding track from a different direction, he would have seen Atwood's BMW and whoever was or wasn't in it. If he hadn't hesitated before following the woman, he would have seen where she had gone. Crucially, if he had told his story sooner, the police would have stood a chance of finding her. But almost three weeks went by before Morgan heard a conversation in a pub and realized the significance of what he had seen; weeks in which drink went on washing relentlessly over his mind, and while the near past and the far faded equally into the dim unhappiness of so many things that might have been.

Yet Morgan would tell his story many times in the weeks to come, and over all those retellings his description of the woman never wavered. After the first sighting, the ti-tree had screened her; but then Morgan had seen her again, just before she disappeared, near the top of the track. One pale hand tugged at the dress stretched above her knees so that she might climb more freely. Morgan thought she was carrying a bag in her other hand, a small suitcase, perhaps.

There was another thing, a strange thing. It was the reason Jimmy Morgan had hung back on the track that night, the reason that had sent him, against instinct and experience, to lay his tale before pebble-eyed detectives. But it wasn't easy for Morgan to pin down what had occasioned his unease. Even sober, all he could say was that there was something peculiar about the figure on the track. It was an impression: distinct and elusive. Images slid about in Morgan's brain.

He told the same story to the journalist who was waiting for him when the cops were through. Some hours later, with two inches of Southern Comfort left in the bottle, Morgan confessed he had been *shit scared*. "I thought she was going to turn 'round." He passed his hand over his jaw and said, "I didn't want to see her face."

ONE OF THE PLEASURES that knowing Nelly had brought Tom was the rediscovery of images. Looking at paintings with her, he gave way to an old delight. The anxiety he brought to analysis was less urgent in her presence, subsumed in sensuous attentiveness to stagings of mass and color and line.

Nelly brought a practitioner's gaze to looking. She might talk of the problem of representing form in two dimensions, the use of perspective and shading versus the modulation of lines. She might say, "Warm colors advance, cool ones recede. That's what they teach you at art school. But what makes this bit work is she's used blue here, where the highlight is, where you'd expect yellow. It's a thing Cézanne used to do."

Or "This guy's so good. He's such a great colorist, and their work can look, you know, sort of vague. Just big, loose outbursts. But there's really solid structure here. It's so disciplined."

As Tom listened, what he had known as abstractions of period and style acquired immediacy. There was the mess and endeavor of the studio in Nelly's conversation.

He had a gobbling eye. Nelly was teaching him to look slowly.

She took him to an exhibition of precinematic illusions. They looked at dioramas and Javanese shadow puppets, and the *ombres chinoises* theaters that captivated eighteenth-century France. In the illusory depths of peep shows they saw a Venetian carnival, and baboons at play in a jungle glade. A snowscape dissolved from day to night before their eyes. They witnessed phantasms.

Then they found themselves in front of a display of parchment lithographs colored with translucent dyes and strategically perforated. As they watched, the overhead lighting dimmed while at the same time light shone behind the pictures. At once the little scenes came to life. A string of fairy lights appeared in a pleasure garden. The moon glimmered above a forest. Candelabra and footlights made luminous the gilded interior of a playhouse. Best of all was a huddle of houses at dusk by a wintry lake, for a lamp glowed in the window of one of the cottages, and the sight of that tiny golden rectangle in the night was incomparably moving and magical.

The gallery lights came up, and were lowered once more. Again the images shone out. Fireworks burst over an illuminated palace; lanterns glowed beside water and were answered by a scatter of stars. Tom and Nelly stared and stared. They were twenty-first-century people, accustomed to digital imaging and computer simulation and all manner of modern enchantments. They stood before the antique miracle of light, transfixed with wonder.

Searching for a corkscrew at the Preserve, Tom opened a drawer and found it full of silky folds. He shook out scarf after scarf, musty souvenirs printed with banksias and trams, marsupials and modernist skylines. Nelly said she had picked them up in thrift shops, collected them over the years.

She had boxes of postcards and photographs, and a collapsing Edwardian scrapbook with seraphim and posies of forget-me-nots peeling from its pages. A large blue envelope, rescued from a dumpster, contained three X rays of a scoliotic spine. There was also a plastic sleeve stuffed with stamps; a relic, Nelly said, from student days when she had made jewelry with a friend. She fished out one of their efforts: a Czechoslovakian hound, a tiny stamp-picture encased in clear resin and hung from a silken cord.

Nelly owned tin trays painted with advertisements for beer, as well as a little grubby brick of swap cards. She had a bowl of souvenir ballpoints bought for her by traveling friends. Within a window set in each barrel, an image glided up and down: the guard changing at Buckingham Palace, the chorus line cancanning at the Moulin Rouge.

Many of these objects were damaged: the scarves stained, the tin surfaces scratched. Watching Tom draw his finger along the creases sectioning a photo, Nelly said, "It's stuff people were throwing away. I got it for nothing, mostly."

That was no doubt true. At the same time, he sensed a deadpan teasing: her cut-price instinct dangled in his face. And beyond the self-guying, something deeper and more characteristic still: an impulse to salvage what had been marked for oblivion. An It girl peddling Foster's; the tottering, cotton-reel stack of a stranger's vertebrae; an archangel with upcast eyes and a faint reek of glue: nothing was too trivial to snatch from the flow of time.

A shelf in Nelly's studio held a modest array of view-ware: ashtrays, coasters, small dishes that might hold trinkets or sweets. Made of clear glass, each had a hand-tinted photograph embedded in its base: the war memorial at Ballarat, Frankston beach in summer, Hanging Rock, and so on.

These kitsch little objects fascinated Tom. He found an excuse to handle them. It was partly that their unnatural hues and thick glass glaze turned the commonplace images dreamily surreal. They were also faintly sinister. Their creepiness was intrinsic to the sway they exercised, these miniature honoring of national icons and fresh air and the healthy bodies of white nuclear families. And then, the view-ware drew on the magic of all collections. Redeemed from mere utility, its coasters and dishes were multiple yet individual. They were as serial as money and partook of its abstraction.

They exceeded the world of things. They erased labor, seeming to have been magicked into existence. Tom found himself fighting down an impulse to steal one.

IN THE TOWNSHIP in the country, he left flyers at the supermarket, as well as at the news agency–cum–post office, the town hall, the hardware store. The only bank he could find had been made over into a phone shop, but the owner of the Thai take-away, having studied a flyer, took ten for the Perspex menu holder on his counter.

The receptionist at the health center said, "Is that the dog Denise was talking about?" She took a pile of flyers for the waiting room and tacked one onto a bulletin board, beside a poster depicting an engorged blue-red heart with severed blood vessels. "He'll turn up when he's ready, love. My granddad used to tell this story how he got lost in the bush one night when he was first married? So he tied his hanky 'round his dog's neck and just followed it home."

The bakery had tables by the window. A woman with ropy brown hair caught at the nape of her neck was forking a cavity in a small emerald breast topped with a pink sugar nipple.

Denise Corrigan said, "Steer clear of the coffee. But these are a whole lot better than they look."

Tom bought a cup of tea and a cinnamon scroll at the counter. When he returned to Denise, she had picked up a flyer. "Lovely dog."

He nodded, looking past her at rain falling in an empty street. He did not wish to be undone by kindness.

"Dad and I had a look around, evening before last. Walked the tracks and that. Dad went back again yesterday."

"Thank you."

"I wish we'd found him." She set down her fork. "How's your mum?"

"Fine. Thanks." He gestured. "I don't know how much longer for."

"Does she live on her own?"

He explained briefly. "My aunt's been very good. But she's getting on herself now. It's all a bit much for her."

"Do you have brothers or sisters?" When he shook his head: "It's hard being the only one."

"Are you?"

"I've got a sister. In New Zealand. It's funny: I always wanted to get away. Jen was the one who loved the farm, life on the land and that. But she ended up marrying a Kiwi and now she's bringing up three kids on a quarter-acre block in Napier."

She told Tom she had worked in Papua New Guinea and Darwin after finishing her training. "But then Mum died…" She paused. "Dad was doing OK. But I don't know, there was something so not OK about the way he was OK. He rang me one time and asked how you make what he called 'proper mash.' This was like two, three years after Mum died, and all that time he'd been boiling potatoes and just smashing them with a spoon." She looked at Tom. "I couldn't bear the thought of him alone at that table where there used to be the four of us, eating his smashed potatoes and trying to figure out what was wrong. So I came back. And then I got married, and Dad's really glad of Mick's help, though he'd never admit it."

She picked up her cup, peered into it, set it down again. "How does your mum feel about going into a nursing home?"

"How do you think?"

She flushed a little. "They're not all bad. I've seen people who were struggling at home really improve when they went into care. Just getting balanced meals is a huge boost. You don't know how many old people live on, like, tea and bread and jam." Then she stopped. Said, after a few moments, in a different tone, "Yeah, you're right. They're places for when you've given up hope."

Tom thought that few people would have abandoned a line of defense with her ready grace. And that under different circumstances, he might have welcomed her into his bed.

He realized that this last notion had come to him because Nelly had been in his mind all day. The radio alarm had shaken him from a dream permeated with images of her, which had dissolved on the instant but left the filmy residue of her presence.

Some flicker of his thoughts communicated itself to Denise. Who said, "So what's the latest on Nelly? Still living with that guy Carson?"

There was something avid in her speckled eyes. Tom had not yet learned to anticipate the hunger Nelly provoked, her contaminated glamour.

From a van parked up the street, a voice cried, "Got this huge fuckin' tray of fuckin' T-bones for seven bucks."

Tom watched two children jump down a flight of steps, each carrying a cotton bag angular with the shapes of books. Denise had provided directions to the logging company's office on a road that looped around the back of the town. But he remained at the curb, behind the wheel of his car, reluctant to leave such comfort as was on offer, the domesticity of iced cakes and library books.

He was thinking of his mother; of the dog; of Osman, in whom death was advancing cell by cell. He felt malevolence gathering force and drawing closer. The children crossed the street, hooded figures from a tale. Life would set them impossible tasks; straw and spinning wheels waited. Tom crossed his fingers and wished them luck: lives reckoned on the blank pages of history. And thought of a night in September when Nelly and he had sat

contented in a pub, until people began to gather in front of the
TV mounted on the wall at the other end of the bar.

It was their faces that had drawn him: uplifted and calm as
churchgoers.

When they parted, Nelly said, "Everything changes when
Americans fall from the sky."

As a child, Tom was accustomed to thinking of himself as rich.
The Loxleys, no strangers to invisible darning and the last crucial pass of the knife that scrapes the excess butter from a slice
of bread, were nevertheless not poor; not as one is poor in India,
roofless, filthy, starved, diseased. There was a Protestant hymn
Arthur sang when he was drunk, compounding offenses. *The
rich man in his castle, / The poor man at his gate*. Beneath his
ancestors' vaulted ceilings, with cracked marble underfoot, it
was plain to Tom where he stood.

In Australia everything was reversed. The Loxleys were poor.
Tom learned this early, his cousin Shona losing no time in pointing out what he lacked: his own room, a tank top, Twister, a
beanbag chair, a poster of the Partridge Family. Yet within a few
short weeks the boy had amassed possessions undreamed of in
austere India, dozens of cheap, amusing objects, iron-on smileys,
plastic figurines, a rainbow of felt-tip pens. A three-minute walk
took him to a cornucopia known as a milk bar that disgorged
Life Savers, bubble gum, Coke, ice creams, chocolate bars, potato
chips in astonishing flavors. Among the novelties on offer in the
land of plenty was food designed to give pleasure to children.

Nothing in Tom's experience had prepared him for the beck-
oning display of so much that was both unnecessary and irresistible. Long before he encountered theories of capitalism and

commodity production, he had grasped that *things* — desiring and acquiring and discarding them — were the lifeblood of his new world.

Against that cascade of pretty baubles stood India: the name itself shorthand for privation.

Tom Loxley counted himself lucky to have escaped into abundance. It was a plenitude he measured in possessions at first; but he soon sensed that it exceeded the material. At school he met children from countries whose names he barely recognized. He looked up Chile in the encyclopedia; Hungary, Yugoslavia, Taiwan. An impression came to him of standing in a great public square hemmed by severe buildings, where all kinds of people came for work or amusement. It was a place of wonder and dread. The boy was jostled; sometimes he lost his bearings. But he glimpsed the promise of enlargement in that huge, variegated flow.

The real city was a gray and brown place sectioned by a grid of chilling winds. From time to time, when he should have been at school, Tom wandered its ruled streets: King, William, Queen, Elizabeth. Within a familiar history he was finding his place in a new geography. Sometimes he thought, No one in the whole world knows where I am.

It was his father's journey in reverse, a flight into modernity.

And still Tom would never be able to shake off the notion that the West was a childish place, where life was based on elaborate play. Reality was the old, serious world he had known when he was young, where there were not enough toys to deflect attention from the gravity of existence and extinction.

When Tom's father died, his mother decided — "took it into her head," in Audrey's phrase — that the calamity had to be communicated at once to a decrepit uncle in Madras. Tom was placed in charge of the telephone call, a procedure that, in those days, assumed the dimensions of a diplomatic mission, with its attendant panoply of intermediaries, uncertain outcomes, and fabulous expenditure.

The operator said, "Go ahead, Australia," and went off the line. Tom pressed the receiver against his ear in readiness for the old man's papery tones. But the ink-black instrument transmitted only a steady, inhuman whisper that flared now and then into a ragged crackle.

The fault was remedied; a death passed over oceans. But what lodged in the boy's private mythology was what he had been permitted to hear: the underground mutter of large, disagreeable truths that could be ignored but not evaded.

Twenty-nine Septembers later, he would join a crowd enthralled by images in time to see the second plane drill into the tower. Nelly came up to stand beside him, but Tom barely noticed her. He was remembering a flawed connection; the patient rage of history in his ear.

THE LOGGING COMPANY furnished its lobby in nylon and vinyl. A pink girl with mauve eyelids bent her head over Tom's flyer, biting her lip. The word *Joy* had been engraved in plastic and pinned to her breast.

On the wood-veneer counter a glass held water and the kind of flowers plucked over fences: daisies, fat fuchsias, coral and scarlet geraniums, blooms of passage. Tom noted this modest expression of the human and natural against synthetic odds.

"If you leave me a stack, I'll make sure they get to the drivers." Her face was a clear oval under her center parting. It gave her a stately air, but Tom guessed she was not yet twenty. She had the expectant gaze of those who still believe there must be more to life than other people have settled for.

She consulted the sheet of paper again. "Jasper's Hill. There's some funny stuff goes on 'round there."

Tom waited.

"My brother's a ranger? He's got all these stories. Like people have these dope plantations hidden away up there? And there was this bloke from New South Wales, drove his car into the bush and shot himself. The loggers found what was left twenty years later." Her voice was matter-of-fact, and Tom saw that this child had taken the measure of her world and neither esteemed nor trivialized it.

When he was at the door, she said, "I hope your dog turns up safe. I really do."

He had bought two refill cartridges for Nelly's butane stove. Stirring a take-away green curry on it that evening, Tom was absurdly cheered; the dread he had felt earlier in the day dispersed by the sense that he had taken action in distributing the flyers.

He ate straight from the pan, savoring flavor and aromatic steam, musing on smell as the sensory sign of transition. Odor marked the passage from the pure to the putrid, from the raw to the cooked, from inside to outside the body.

Tom's own scent was patrilineal. Its varnished wood with a bass note of cumin was one of the traces Arthur Loxley had left in the world. Even now, so many years after Arthur had died, Tom sometimes buried his face in the clothes he took off at the end of a day. By his odor, he knew himself his father's son.

When he woke, in the downy warmth of his sleeping bag, the room was hushed. He directed his flashlight at his watch: a few minutes past midnight.

He was certain something had woken him. The previous week, the dog had slept at the foot of the bed. Now, alone at night, Tom was conscious of the unpeopled woods and pastures about him. It was a country in which the old ideal of rural solitude had been bought with violence, and some hint of this lingered in the most tranquil setting, converting calm itself into an indictment.

He went outside and saw that the night was fine, the sky glittering with fierce southern constellations. When he came in he was careful to bolt the door.

SATURDAY

Tom would select a point on a track, mark it with tape, and walk into the bush. It was like trying to pass through a living wall. Ferns and vines swayed up from the murk of gullies. Fine scratches covered the backs of his hands.

There were rustlings and tickings, the inhuman sounds of the bush. The great blue forests of Australia were walked by strangers and ghosts. People like the Feeneys did not much go in for entering them on foot. It was an unvoiced taboo: the ancient human respect for wooded places, strengthened by memories of a time when the only people who trod these paths were blacks or fugitive convicts.

Flies settled on Tom's lids. The bush was full of light. In a northern forest, vegetable density would have brought gloom. Here light dropped straight down past vertical leaves. There was the disconcerting impression of being both trapped and exposed.

Mountain ash, clear-cut and rejected, rotted in the hollows where it had been herded by machines. Five or six years earlier the hill had been replanted with blue gums, chosen for the rapidity of their growth. Their puny forms were still struggling for supremacy over the undergrowth, an outbreak of mean skirmishes arising from a great defeat.

Felix Atwood had bought the house on the hill from Jack three years before he disappeared. It stood on land that had been selected late, the topography and weather deterring all but dirt-poor optimists, which is to say the Irish. Built in 1920 by a man called McDermot, the old farmhouse was testimony to the hardscrabble of his life.

Half a century later, his grandson gave up. Machinery and stock were sold, the house and its vertical acres to Jack Feeney. The McDermots moved to a town where a power station was hiring.

Framed photographs in Nelly's kitchen taken at the time her husband bought the house showed rotting boards, a sagging chimney. Even in a picture from the 1950s, when the McDermots were still living there, the house had a desolate look. A flat garment pinned to a rope in the background was suggestive of flaying.

Looking at these images, Tom understood the attraction of a brown suburban box with its own generator.

Jack grazed beef cattle in Nelly's paddock, clearing it of blackberries and ragwort in return and keeping an eye on the property. Nelly would go up to the house for a week or so at a stretch, and in the milder seasons friends were persuaded to rent it for brief periods. But in that comfortless place, the hard winters were harder. And bad summers threatened fire: a red beast rampaging over the forested hills.

The Feeneys had stored sheepskins in the house. When the rooms were first repainted, the sharp animal smell disappeared, said Nelly. Then it returned to stay.

ON HIS THIRD OR FOURTH VISIT to the library's archives, Tom learned that the police had re-interviewed Mrs. Atwood in light of Jimmy Morgan's evidence. The photograph that showed her shouting at the camera coincided with this development. It was at this stage of the story, too, that conscientious citizens began writing to the papers urging Nelly's arrest: *You've only got to look at her to know it was all her idea.* Nelly Atwood failed the first universal test of womanliness, which is to appear meek. She failed the first Australian test of virtue, which is to appear ordinary. Intangibles such as these, operating with a subterranean force unavailable to mere evidence, bound her to the figure Morgan had seen among the ti-tree.

Sources inevitably described as *close to the couple* claimed that the Atwoods' marriage had been unhappy. There had been arguments about money. *She was always on at him, wanting more.* Tom read reports of extravagance on a Roman scale. Mrs. Atwood was a brand junkie. She wore tights woven in Lille from cashmere and silk. A weekly florist's bill ran to hundreds of dollars. Confirmation came in the form of a photograph: the florist himself, righteous above an armful of triangular blooms.

And so, with the practiced ease of a sleight of hand, disapproval passed from the man to his wife. Atwood photographed well. He went surfing. His victims were bankers. He was halfway to being a hero in Australian eyes.

Nelly Atwood was also Nelly Zhang. She was A and Z, twin poles, the extremities of a line that might loop into a snare. She was double: a rich man's wife and an artist, native yet foreign. Duplicity was inscribed in her face.

But Morgan insisted he had seen a tall woman. "Same as me, about," and he was five feet nine. Nelly Atwood came in at barely five one. High heels might account for missing inches but seemed unlikely on a sandy track; in any case, the story kept running into Morgan. He was shown TV footage of Atwood's wife. The woman on the path had been "different," he insisted.

His objections were easily disregarded, of course. Morgan reeked of imbalance. One chop short of the barbecue. And then distance, darkness, the passage of time: these might deceive a far steadier witness.

But — and this was crucial — if Morgan was to be discredited over small things, he could scarcely be relied on for large ones. The woman on the dunes might have been elfin. Equally, she might never have existed. Elusive female forms were known to appear to men who lived alone in the bush. Folktales were told about them. The woman on the beach might have been nothing more than a splutter of memory, the brightest element in a story related by lamplight in the unimaginable kingdom where Jimmy Morgan had been young.

The police commissioner himself appealed to her to come forward. But the woman from the sand dunes never materialized. She had appeared in flashes among the scrub, then vanished. Like the hitchhikers who were her kin, she remained legendary, the latest variant of an old tradition.

There was a limit to what journalism could concoct from repetition and guesswork. There was a limit to what could be done with Morgan. The bush lent him a tattered heroism. Shabbiness, alcoholism, and eccentricity might pass as the decadent residues of a mythic past. But there was a fatal laxity to the man. He should have been shrewd and sparing of words. In fact he ran on endlessly, a garrulous drunk.

There was a hunger to equate the woman he had seen with Nelly. All those years later, Tom felt it quiver under the surface of tabloid prose. It would have been so neat. Perfect solutions make perfect stories. This one foundered on a paradox: the solution required Morgan, but Morgan undid the solution.

An interview with Carson Posner appeared in a Saturday supplement. The photographer had posed him against an early Howard Arkley abstract, and there was much obsequious filler about the dealer's reputation as a talent-spotter, his unwavering, unfashionable devotion to painting, and so on. But the real subject of the feature was never in doubt.

Posner said he had been devastated to learn what Felix Atwood had done. The evidence against the broker was overwhelming. Nevertheless, Posner felt sure his friend was not devoid of conscience. Atwood would not have required the certainty of punishment to suffer for what he had done. When they were both boys, he had spoken of drowning, that it was the way he would like to go. And so he, Posner, believed that his old friend had chosen to end his days in the southern waters he loved.

His interviewer raised the subject of a note. Wasn't the absence of one a serious flaw in the suicide theory? Posner's disdain was superb. "Art exists because there are realities that exceed words."

If it was plain that Posner's portrait of Atwood had been airbrushed into smoothness, there was admiration, in the days that followed, for the loyalty that had produced it. Mateship: the Australian male's birthright. Even stockbrokers were worthy of it.

Above all, Posner's opining added weight to the idea that Atwood had taken his own life. Perhaps not having really made a decision, merely going on swimming; the continent receding, and with it, the braided pull of life itself.

The most satisfying conclusions are bodily: a corpse or a coupling, death or its miniature. Tide patterns had already been
verified, currents monitored. Felix Atwood's body was never
recovered. Still, the story might have ended as the larger one is
said to have begun: in the huge, slow roll of the sea. But there
was the feeling that had built up against Atwood's wife. In time
it would find the outlet it required.

IN AUGUST, Esther Kade asked if Tom would like to meet for lunch:
a small, proprietary pat to check that he was still in place.

She arrived with amber and Mexican silver bound about her
wrists and said at once, "So, Tom, what's all this about Nelly
Zhang?" It being Esther's habit when faced with a closed door to
turn the handle and walk in.

Tom, chary of the scorn of Esther Kade at amateur trespass-
ing on her art historical terrain, repeated the hazy half-truth he
had devised in his e-mail to her: that he was considering writing
about literary and artistic controversies. "Nothing academic, of
course. You know how the vice-chancellor's always saying we
mustn't shut ourselves off from the marketplace. So I'm thinking
along the lines of feature articles. Eventually, maybe a book. The
kind you see in real bookshops."

Esther rolled her bright brown eyes, dismissing their vice-
chancellor's idiocies along with Tom's rigmarole. She had the
face of a friendly monkey and was much feared on committees.

In the course of their affair, she had said, "I'm like one of those cities about which people say, Oh, it's great for a day or two."

Now she produced a manila envelope from her bag. "Not exactly my field. But I asked around the department."

Tom took out a thin sheaf of photocopies: reviews, catalogues, the bibliography of a book called *Contemporary Australian Art,* in which entries had been highlighted with fluorescent pen.

Esther said, "A starting point."

When he thanked her, she replied, "I saw the famous show, actually. The one that caused all the fuss."

"I've read what the papers said. But I was getting my doctorate in the States at the time." A tiny irrelevant shard of history was rising to the surface in Tom's mind, the memory of walking with a visiting Australian friend down an avenue of lime-green leaves in Baltimore. The tourist had fashioned silver tips for his shirt collar from foil in a parody of the current fashion.

A waiter dropped cutlery on the table. He made cabalistic passes with a pepper grinder and commanded them to "Enjoy!"

Tom said, "Tell me about those paintings."

"How well do you know your Ernst?"

"*Two Children Are Threatened by a Nightingale.* It was one of Nelly's sources, obviously."

Esther said dryly, "How very clever you are." Then, as she scrutinized him over mushroom soup, her tone changed. "You know, I couldn't stop thinking about them for ages. You could see where that Nelly's Nasties tag came from. There were these Day-Glo colors and a sense of pure evil. *The bright day is done, / And we are for the dark.* Isn't that how it goes? Only the darkness was already there, inseparable from the bright day. But only implied. In one sense, it was all in your mind," said Esther. "That was the worst thing, in a way. It made you part of it."

When they said good-bye, she kissed Tom on both cheeks, with a little pause in between to convert affection into irony. "Good luck with Nelly Zhang." Another beat. "I'm so pleased you're pursuing a nonacademic line there."

NELLY, the least intimidating of creatures, could summon great aloofness at will. Her marriage, the events surrounding Atwood's disappearance: these remained virgin stretches in the map of their friendship. Once, when speaking of Karen, lightly sketching the ways he had failed with her, Tom mentioned Atwood. Nelly went on with whatever she was doing. The subject dropped between them like a stone.

Sometimes Tom suspected that she understood the fascination of taboo. That her silence was a way of ensuring his ongoing interest. Or they might be talking about anything at all — politics, TV, the perennial weather — and slowly there would grow in him the certainty that the real subject of the conversation was Felix Atwood. The very fullness of their dialogue was shaped by his absence. A string of banal observations seemed to contain him, in every sense. Tom's consciousness of the man would swell until it seemed that Atwood's name must burst from his tongue. Once or twice, at these moments, he thought Nelly was looking at him with something like dismay. He would make an effort, would force himself to say something entirely trivial. The danger was skirted. Once more, there would be nothing but ease between them.

Now and then a fragment of information came Tom's way, maddening in its incompleteness and particularity. When proposing that he rent her house, Nelly warned him of its inconveniences: hurricane lamps, tank water, a stone fireplace for warmth. Then she said, "Felix didn't want somewhere gentrified. It was before everyone went postmodern. People were still big on authenticity."

"It can't have been easy, weekends in a place like that when Rory was a baby." Tom was thinking, The selfish prick, no running water for his wife and kid so he could feel authentic.

Across the road from the bar in which they sat, a window displayed bra and panty sets in shell pink, vanilla, mint green. Tiny satin bows signaled the gift-wrapping of female flesh. A few doors away, a chandelier-hung lighting shop that specialized in "Never to Be Repeated Bargains" went on closing down.

Nelly remained silent for so long, staring into her glass, that Tom's mind drifted to a DVD he had rented. Then she said, "I didn't go up there so much. It was really Felix's place. His retreat where the city couldn't get in."

Tom waited.

She lit a cigarette. "But it's beautiful. You'll see, if you go. I think about living there one day."

His heart dipped. That she might speak so lightly of a future in which he had no part.

He always pictured her framed by the city, he said. Seeing, in his mind, her red parka blocky and vivid against a blur of traffic or suspended in a plate-glass door.

She exhaled clove-scented smoke in his face. "The Chinese is a creature of alleys."

But afterward, in the street, she spoke of watching shooting stars over the paddocks. Of the daffodils a woman long dead had planted around the house, golden and cream and orange-centered, hundreds of flowers quaking in cold August. She said she nurtured a dream of planting trees all over the property. "All the different trees that belong there, blackwoods, gums, acacias. I'd like to see it start to turn back into bush."

People were coming out of restaurants; a woman lifted her hair over the collar of her jacket. There was the scrape of metal on concrete as waiters began packing up the sidewalk seating. A voice said, "Remind me again who you are?" Nelly and Tom made their way through a stream of stills, a beef-pink face mounted on a pearl choker, two girls in studded denim turning away from each other on a corner, a taxi flashing its lights at a man with his arm raised.

"A perfect city is one you can walk out of," said Nelly.

Tom pictured the pair of them on a road striped by tree shadows: towers at their back, a mountain in the space between their bodies.

Nelly often sought his advice on what to read. She would quiz Tom about literary history, borrow his course readers. She studied his bookshelves like museum cases, hands behind her back. She squatted to peer at shelves where neglected volumes gathered, and fished out treasures: Kafka's diaries, an anthology of Victorian poems, *The Man Who Loved Children*.

"I only read about five books when I was growing up." But one day a chance remark revealed that having come across *Crime and Punishment* at the age of seventeen, Nelly had read her way through the nineteenth-century Russians. What she found there had stayed with her as a series of images. She might speak of a man striking a woman at a window with his riding crop as if describing a page in an illuminated missal. In Nelly's distillation of a famous story, there was a woman dressed in gray and an inkstand gray with dust; one day the woman's lover looked in the mirror and saw, from the color of his hair, that he had grown old.

Tom would have spoken of the formal qualities of Chekhov's tale, its understated, almost offhand treatment of love and its evasive resolution. All this Nelly omitted or missed in favor of detail and implication. But years later, when Tom himself was old, he would discover that what remained, when the sifting was done, was a dress, an inkstand, a man whose hair was the color of ashes.

What he missed in images, said Tom, was the passage of time. "Stories are about time. But looking's a present-tense activity. We live in an age where everything's got to be *now,* because consumerism's based on change. Images seem complicit with that somehow."

Then he said, "Sometimes I think I'll never really get what's going on in a painting."

He had never admitted this before. It required an effort.

"Is it so different from what you do?" Nelly said, "Reading a book, looking at a painting—they're both things that might change you."

Tom noticed that where he spoke of knowledge, Nelly talked of transformation. It confirmed his sense that pictures exceed analysis. Art was ghostly in a way, he thought, something magical that he recognized rather than understood.

He said as much to Nelly. Who argued, "But you can see a painting, touch it. Fiction's the spooky thing. The thing that's not there."

She stirred in her ugly vinyl armchair as she spoke. The movement caused her shirt to ride up; there was the glimmer of a bare hip. It was an intensely erotic apparition. Tom looked away. He thought there was nothing more present, more material, than her flesh; and nothing he found more disturbing.

When he told Nelly that he was thinking of writing about her work, she looked doubtful. "Yeah, right, that's good, I guess."

Next thing there was Posner, lying in wait for Tom at the Preserve. "Dear boy, this is tremendously exciting. The serious attention Nelly's attracted so far has been rather outweighed by sensationalist dross. The hour is ripe, *ripe,* for a scholar." He brought out his version of a smile, cautiously, like a man exercising an alligator. "Oh, I know you're not an art historian. But as I've been saying to Nelly, one must think over and through mere categories. The specialist is a contemptible modern creation. I consider the fact that you come to us from literature a veritable *atout.* Art and text: an illustrious association." A shirtfront loomed vast as a snowfield. "If I could help," said Posner, "I would be honored. Resources, contacts, suggestions....We could start with dinner."

Tom murmured that the project was in its infancy.

Nelly said, "You're scaring him off, Carson."

"But it's quite the other way around. I'm entirely awed." Then he was pressing something into Tom's hand, the bloodless fingers surprisingly warm. "My card. Whenever you're ready," crooned Posner.

"Tell me a story," Nelly would say.

It was oddly disquieting. The childishness of it: *Tell me a story*. It rang through their encounters like a refrain. Tom was unable to resist it, of course. Soon he was going to meet Nelly stocked with stories like charms.

He told her about April Fonceca, who sang in the last row of the choir and was a living example. When April was a little girl, she had lit a candle and placed her dolls around it. Afterward, she said she was only playing birthday parties. Afterward, who could tell exactly how it happened? But there was a golden flame and there was a celluloid doll, and then the doll was the flame. And there was April, reaching to save her pretty doll, and the flame reaching for April. April wore high necks and long sleeves, but there was nothing to be done about her face, and that was what came of playing with matches. Whenever Tom looked at her, he saw the girl and her doll flowering into light, a big candle and a small one. He didn't want to look at April, said Tom, and he couldn't take his eyes off her.

He told Nelly about a widowed Englishwoman his parents had known. She kept a little dog called Chess: tight white body, black ears. "The Civil Service terrier," said Arthur. One day Chess was bitten by a snake and died. Soon afterward, the elderly Indian couple who lived next door to the widow acquired a dun-coated mongrel and promptly named him Chess. This greatly amused Sebastian de Souza: "The fools! A brown mutt called Chess!" Passing their compound, he would call out, "Here, Magpie! Here, Domino!" Or, "I say, Prasad, how's Zebra today?"

He was a grown man, said Tom, before it occurred to him that the Prasads might have intended the name as a form of homage, a mark of respect, even affection. The old people had been gentle and ineffectual. Tom could recall a steady procession of beggars to their door.

He spoke to Nelly of marvels. Of arriving in Australia and finding clean water piped into every kitchen, every drinking fountain. He had drunk glass after glass of it: an everyday miracle on tap.

On a moonless night, Tom ventured a gothic little tale. It was a true story, said Tom, and he had heard it from his father. It was Arthur's earliest memory, and this was how it went:

What Arthur remembered was a red thing. It jumped up and fell back. Sometimes it vanished, but tiny red eyes still watched him. It had a name and that was fire.

Arthur had scarlet fever, which was red fever, and his head hurt. His arms and chest were on fire. In his mother's ivory-handled mirror he saw that his cheeks had turned red. But his tongue was white, coated with sugar or snow.

Snow dropped past the window. Arthur's throat burned. The next time he saw himself in the mirror his tongue was a strawberry. The red thing was growing inside him. It spread in his bed, and his sheets were on fire. The only cool thing in the world was his mother's white hand. She smoothed his hair. She filled a red rubber bag with ice and placed it on his forehead. She read him a story about Snow White and Rose Red.

His older sister sent him a picture on folded white paper. She had drawn a wreath of sharp green leaves and berries like beads of blood. "It's Christmas," said Arthur's mother. She draped a snowy pillowcase over the foot of his bed and left him in the dark. The red thing leaped about.

In the night it turned into a man. It was a red man, and Arthur knew him and he didn't know him, and he was coming closer.

Tell me a story. It led Tom to reflect on the book he was writing. Near the end of his long life, Henry James had written a story with a happy ending, having until then, in exemplary modern fashion, avoided the redemptive case. "The Jolly Corner" told of Spencer Brydon, who returned to New York after a long absence abroad. He was welcomed by Alice Staverton, an old friend who had loved him steadfastly over the years.

Not long after his return, Brydon began to suspect that a family property he had inherited was haunted. He took to prowling the house after dark and, after a harrowing pursuit one night, came face to face with the apparition. As Brydon had intuited, it was none other than his alter ego, the rich businessman he might have become if he hadn't left New York. The terrible figure advanced on and overpowered the hero, who, when he finally came to his senses, found Alice cradling his head in her lap. She had come to the house because she sensed Brydon was in danger. She spoke gently to the bewildered man of the need to accept the path his life had taken, and they embraced as the story ended.

Tom had devoted several pages of his book to this text. He had concentrated on horror, on the awful qualities that pervaded the story. He had traced the presence of doubles in James's fiction, had analyzed the mythic, cultural, and psychoanalytic import of the doppelganger; and remained unsatisfied with his efforts. The tale continued to elude him, as the ghost eluded Brydon. It was a complex, masterly work, far removed from simple childhood tales. But Tom suddenly saw that the fairy story, a humble, enduring form, might provide him with a fresh thread to follow in unraveling its significance. For Brydon, like the protagonist in a fairy tale, had bravely stared down peril, securing selfhood and winning union with a beloved other.

It was an insight Tom pursued with happy results. In this way, Nelly entered a chapter of his book: an enabling, untragic muse.

SATURDAY AFTERNOON PASSED in hopefulness and despair and bouts of icy rain. Images of the dog continued to present themselves to Tom. He remembered him sitting up very straight at the top of the hill above Nelly's house only a week earlier: calmly attentive to his wide surroundings, rich in world.

With wind stirring the trees into a formless boiling, Tom made his way back up the track toward the house. Felix Atwood's attachment to authenticity notwithstanding, his architect had clad the old farmhouse in galvanized iron. Seen at a certain angle, its corrugations shadowed violet, the house could, in fact, pass for the shed it impersonated. It was iconic, in its way, at once more and less than it appeared, a persuasive fiction.

Nelly had told Tom that Atwood had acquired the house in her name. After negotiations with the tax office, her solicitors succeeded in saving it. Whereupon Nelly put the property on the market. But no one wanted it. Its lack of modern comfort had no charm in rural eyes, and it was too far from the city for a convenient weekender. And it was in any case dismaying. "The estate agent said people would say, But it looks like a shed. They'd drive off without having left the car."

A house imitating a shed was an unprecedented object. Nelly said, "It takes time to see something new."

One of the old outbuildings on the property had been left to rot in peace: roof rusting, boards weathered to soft black and silver. Beside the shiny iron house it had the cringing look of an animal that fears attention.

The gatepost, gray with age, was patched with yellow lichen. Tom was lifting the wire fastening over it when he heard his name. He turned to see Denise Corrigan in her blue rain jacket.

"I thought you might need a hand."

He explained that he had to drive back to the city. "I see my mother on Sunday. You know how it is."

"Well, you get along. I'll head up to the ridge anyway."

She was wearing pale, faintly shiny lipstick, an unflattering choice. She saw him noticing it and looked away.

Her awkwardness, and the adolescent color of her mouth, prompted Tom to say, "You used to look after Rory, didn't you? You and your sister."

"Not Jen. She preferred tractors to kids back then. Probably still does."

"So you were the one who used to babysit Rory?"

"He was a gorgeous kid. I felt sorry for him, really. His dad liked to take off, go walking, head down the beach, whatever. And Nelly could get caught up with her painting and that."

"It was good of you to help out."

"Rory wasn't any trouble. And they were cool people to have

around. They'd have friends up from the city, sometimes a whole crowd. It was all pretty exciting for a teenager stuck out here."

Her lips were slightly parted; he glimpsed her tongue. In a delirious moment, considered to what uses it might be put.

She was saying, "I cooked for them sometimes. Felix used to say my steaks were the best he'd ever eaten."

Something about the way she said it. He could hear Nelly: *I didn't go up there so much. It was Felix's retreat.*

Denise and Atwood. Tom saw the man's hand in the ropes of her hair, a plate of bloody flesh on a table between them.

On an impulse he asked, "What do you think happened? With Atwood, I mean."

"I know one thing for sure. That setup on the beach, the car and that? It was so tacky. There's no way Felix would've gone like that."

Darkness, a deserted beach, clothes folded in a car: Tom could see that they might add up to a clichéd quotation from tragedy. But he disagreed with Denise's deduction. Why should banality be incompatible with seriousness of intent? It was like art that flaunted its lack of artistry; it was Warhol's Brillo box all over again. Atwood might have laid out the signs of his death in wry acknowledgment of their triteness, the sea winking hugely at his back. Kitsch might be no more than it appears, or a different thing altogether. The enigma was one of signification.

Tom moved involuntarily, a kind of half shrug.

It annoyed Denise. She said, "That was Nelly who Jimmy Morgan saw on the beach that day."

"Sure."

"Oh, you can think what you like. But I recognized that dress straightaway from how Jimmy described it. I'd made it for Nelly.

A surprise for her birthday. Felix got me the fabric, this lovely silky French stuff. Cost a packet." Denise said, "It wasn't the greatest fit. He got the wrong size pattern or something. But Nelly still looked gorgeous in it."

There was the distant sound of machinery in the paddocks. Nearer at hand, the pepper tree was flinging itself sideways with throaty noises.

Tom said, "Did you share this with anyone? Like the cops?"

A cool, dappled stare: "Why do you think Nelly and I aren't friends anymore?"

"What that amounts to is, the cops followed it up and got nowhere."

"Nelly'd have had some story ready."

"Morgan swore he saw a tall woman, remember?"

"Half the time Jimmy hadn't a clue what he was seeing. I know what he was like: he used to give us a hand with shearing before he went totally off the rails. But he was spot on about that dress. Like that Nelly'd hitched it up so she could climb the dunes better. It was that Chinese style with a slit skirt."

Denise Corrigan had a recurring dream of bleeding from the mouth in public, and the memory, passing through her mind at that moment, drew her tongue across her gums. It left tiny bubbles of spit between her upper teeth, which were translucent and sloped inward a little.

"OK, so maybe Nelly helped Atwood get away." Tom said, "You can't really blame her, can you? When it was a choice between prison or cocktails poolside someplace they don't do extradition."

Trying to lighten the conversation, he realized Denise was close to crying.

"I was the one who was home that morning. When she brought Rory down saying she wasn't feeling too good. She didn't look ill to me, she looked scared."

The wind was amusing itself with Denise's hair, heaving it about. She pushed pieces of it away fiercely, and said, "She wouldn't have helped Felix. Don't you know about those terrible paintings she did? Anyone could see she hated him."

FIVE MONTHS after Felix Atwood disappeared, an exhibition by Nelly Zhang had opened at Posner's gallery. It included a suite of paintings called *The Day of the Nightingale*.

Among the crowd at the opening was a journalist who had covered the Atwood story. The next day, his newspaper ran a front-page article under the headline "Nelly's Nasties." The phrase gained its own tripping momentum and circulated throughout the city. Nelly was arraigned in single-sentence paragraphs. The charges included cashing in on her husband's notoriety, trendy feminism, washing her dirty linen in public, ruthless ambition, sick navel-gazing.

The newspaper reproduced the photograph of Felix Atwood with his surfboard, beside the image of his wife's distorted face.

A rock star who collected art was quoted as saying he was struggling with aesthetic and ethical objections to Nelly's work. And a grand old painter described her as a she-artist whose frames displayed great promise.

The gallery's windows attracted eggs and a brick. The show sold briskly but closed three days later, the contentious sequence withdrawn from sale, destroyed by the artist, belatedly appalled by her own images, so it was reported.

In the art world, there was widespread dismay at these events. Artists and critics defended Nelly's right to display the controversial work. A virtuous rapping of philistine knuckles was heard.

Yet it was plain to Tom, reading through the material Esther had given him, that even among professionals the *Nightingale* paintings had caused unease. The same sort of thing kept turning up in reviews: *barely suppressed violence, eerie stagings.* Elusiveness was also mentioned, this last an affront, since reviewers who would have sacrificed their lives, or at least their columns, defending art's right to scandalize were stirred to outrage by its refusal to simplify. An eminent critic summed up the problem: *Zhang (re)presents the systemic violence of authoritarian modes in images as ambiguous as they are oppressive. Nowhere in these paintings is the phallocentric will-to-power explicitly critiqued. The refusal to engage in direct visual discourse is ultimately elitist and unsatisfying.*

PACKING UP at Nelly's house, Tom discovered a box of food he had set on a kitchen chair and forgotten: soup, chili sauce, olive oil, tins of tomatoes and mangoes. Grains of rice trickled from a packet, and he realized that the plastic had been nibbled away at one corner.

He remembered the stale oats; he would throw them away and use the container for rice. He eased up the lid and found a dead mouse inside.

He stood with his back against the sink, his jaw tight. He saw his hand, scooping oats into a stainless-steel dish. He saw himself carrying the dog's bowl outside and placing it on the grass by the steps.

In those minutes, the mouse had emerged, run up the table leg, and climbed into the oats. Tom had replaced the lid; and in time, the mouse had died.

The time it had taken was what Tom didn't wish to think about.

He drank some water, first holding the enamel mug against each of his temples in turn.

When he had finished his chores, he went outside and dug a hole at the foot of a gum tree. He tipped mouse and oats into the depression and covered them with earth.

Light was starting to drain from the sky. But as Tom was turning away, something glimmered white in the grass. He stooped and found that he was looking at a little heap of old dog turds.

That was when tears began slipping down his cheeks. He sat on his heels and wrapped his arms about his legs and rocked. He rubbed his face on his knees, leaving a glitter of mucus on his jeans, and went on crying.

On Saturday nights there was only TV on TV. Tired from the long drive home, Tom lay on his bed. A picture had come to him, as he inserted the key in his front door, of the dog bounding up the hall to greet him. This mental image had such power, the pale animal rearing from the gloom of the passage in such speckled detail, that it was like encountering a revenant. Tom had entered his flat convinced that the dog was dead.

Now he lay with whiskey at hand and his thoughts drifting, as they did in this mood, to a room with a polished concrete floor. Some years earlier, on a stopover in India, he had been persuaded by his mother to call on a relative, a third cousin who lived in Pondicherry. Eileen had married a man ten years older, a Tamil with cracked purple lips. He accepted Tom's bottle of duty-free single malt with both hands and placed it on a glass-fronted cabinet between a vase of nylon hibiscus and a plastic Madonna containing holy water from Lourdes.

Children's faces bloomed at different heights in a doorway hung with a flowered curtain. Tom smiled at a stumpy tot with plaited hair, who burst into tears. "Take no notice," said Eileen. "That one is needing two tight slaps."

A girl entered the room bearing a tray of tumblers in which a bilious green drink was fizzing. It dawned on Tom that his cousins were teetotalers.

Cedric held an obscure clerical post at a Catholic charity. Before her marriage, Eileen had worked as a stenographer. They had applied to immigrate to the States, Canada, and Australia and had been rejected on every occasion. There remained New Zealand, and what could be salvaged of hope.

Eileen summoned her eldest son: "Show Tommy Uncle your school report." On a settee covered in hard red rexine, Tom read of proficiency in chemistry and mathematics. A boy with fanned lashes stood beside him, breathing through his mouth. "He is pestering us all the time for a computer."

The scent of India, excrement and spices, billowed through the house. On a radio somewhere close at hand, a crooner was singing "Whispering Hope." A ziggurat of green oranges glided past, inches from the barred window. The walls of the room were washed blue, of the shade the Virgin wore in heaven.

Eileen brought out a heavy album with brass studs along the spine. From its matte black pages, de Souzas gazed out unsmiling, each new generation less plausibly European.

On his return to Australia, Tom struggled to find a rhetoric suited to the episode. When Karen had traveled with him through India on their honeymoon, she had made up her mind to be charmed by everything she saw. It was an admirable resolution and she kept it, heat, swindles, belligerent monkeys, spectacular diarrhea, and headlines reporting communal murder notwithstanding, her tenacity boosted by air-conditioned hotels and sandals of German manufacture.

Karen informed Tom that India was spiritual. From the great shrines at Madurai and Kanyakumari, she returned marigold-hung and exalted. At dinner parties in Australia she would speak of the extraordinary atmosphere of India's sacred precincts. Tom desisted from comparisons with Lourdes, where the identical spectacle of ardent belief and flagrant commercialism had worked on his wife's Protestant sensibilities as fingernails on a blackboard. The glaze of exoticism transformed *superstitious nonsense* into *luminous grace.*

Karen's good faith was manifest. Yet her insistence on the spirituality of India struck Tom as self-serving. It wafted her effortlessly over the misery of degraded lives, for the poorest Indian possessed such spiritual riches, after all. And then, there was the global nation: the India of the IT boom, the pushcart vendor of okra with his cell phone clamped to his ear, the foreign-returned graduates climbing the executive ladder at McKinsey or Merrill Lynch, the street children enthralled by Bart Simpson in a store window, the call-center workers parroting the idioms of Sydney or Seattle. The energetic, perilous glamour of technology and capital: spiritual India, existing outside history, was disallowed that, too.

Faced with Karen's curiosity about his cousins, Tom thought of Cedric's eyes traveling in opposite directions behind heavy-rimmed spectacles, of the way Eileen's hand flew to cover the deficiencies in her smile. In India bodies were historic, tissue and bone still testifying to chance and time.

In the former French quarter of Pondicherry, Tamil gendarmes in scarlet peaked caps strolled the calm boulevards; bougainvillea stained colonial stucco turmeric, saffron, chili. At sunrise, managerial Indians jogged the length of the seafront, where the waves were restrained by a decaying wall. The wines of Burgundy were served in the dining room at Tom's hotel. The maître d', who bore an unnerving resemblance to Baroness Thatcher, had once been a waiter at the Tour d'Argent. At mealtimes he was to be found surveying his domain with a cramped countenance. The table napkins, although freshly starched and mitered, were always limp from the heat. It is not the absence of an ideal that produces despair, but its approximation.

Eileen lived in a street of stalls and small, open-fronted shops on the wrong side of Pondi's canal, the Indian side, the *ville noire,* encrusted with time and filth. A crow picked at something in the gutter by her door. Tom feared that it was a kitten.

In Australia, sitting with his wife at a table made of Tasmanian oak, the racket and reek of the bazaar returned keenly to him. Eileen's azure room was oppressive with calculation and yearning. Children were its familiars. It held fleeting, unique lives. Tom could not find a way to convert these things into narrative. The dailiness of India was too much with him.

Yet his wife required an anecdote. He spoke of the bureaucratic pettifogging that dogged his cousins, of immigration officials who didn't have a clue, thus engaging Karen's sympathy and deflecting her attention. She was given to causes, her imagination too broadly netted for the merely individual.

Tom had taken his camera with him when he visited Eileen. He came home one evening with packets of newly processed film to find Karen drinking wine with a colleague. The two women sifted through his photos of Pondicherry, exclaiming over flame-colored blossoms arched above a pair of rickshaws, and a brass-belled cow grazing in front of a bicycle-repair shop painted sugar-almond pink. They loved India, they agreed.

Eileen and Cedric sat side by side, posed on red rexine. Tom recalled what he had noticed when taking the picture: that being photographed was not a casual affair for his cousins. The flash found them smiling and attentive. Their image would circulate where they could not. It was not something to be yielded lightly.

Karen's friend said, "That's funny." Her square-cut nail tapped a tiny picture on the blue wall above the dark heads: a minute Sacred Heart. "It doesn't seem right, does it?"

"What doesn't?"

"Well, the whole Christian thing. It's not like it belongs in India."

The memory of this woman's living room, in which a long-lobed Buddha reclined on a mantelpiece and frankincense smoldered beneath a portrait of the Dalai Lama, floated through Tom's mind. He let it pass. Evidence of the subcontinent's age-old traffic with the West rarely found favor with Westerners. To be eclectic was a Western privilege, as was the authentication of cultural artifacts. The real India was the flutter of a sari, a perfumed dish, a skull-chained goddess. Difference, readily identified, was easily corralled. Likeness was more subtly unnerving.

Tom Loxley, drinking whiskey on his bed, wished to lead a modern life. By which he meant a life that was free to be trivial, that had filtered out the dull sediment of tradition and inherited responsibilities, a life shiny as invention, that floated and gleamed.

In that respect he was an exemplary Australian.

His cousin's blue walls contained a life Tom might have led. He saw himself waiting on a red settee to be rescued; with no real expectation that rescue would come.

Recently, there were more and more South Asian faces in Australia. Each time he saw one, Tom felt a small surge of satisfaction. At the same time, he would think, But there are so many more waiting.

Whenever he thought of the waiting going on around the globe, Tom was afraid. He feared that the ground of his life would give way, that he would fall into a room where, powerless as a figurine, he would have nothing to do but wait. Transformed into a human commodity, he would find himself competing with thousands of identical products, all waiting to be chosen. It was an irrational, potent dread. It had visited Tom, assuming one shape, now another, for years. It whispered of the life led by millions, a phantom life characterized by stasis and the dull absence of hope, an unmodern life, where the best that could be expected of the future was that it be no worse than the past.

Of late, its mutter had grown louder. Tom knew that this crescendo was bound up with his mother. As Iris's body failed, he felt her claim on him grow forceful. He felt the proximity of history. The present makes use of what has gone before, feeding on and transforming it, and rejecting what remains. But Tom could remember the aromatic streets of his childhood, where feces, animal and human, lingered on display. The past waited too: odorous, unhygienic, surplus, refusing to be disposed of with decent haste.

Eileen and Cedric still lived on the black side of the canal, New Zealand having deemed superfluous such talents as they possessed.

But recently their son had won a scholarship to a midwestern college. Tom pictured him in a laboratory, calibrating instruments; on a sidewalk, astonished by snow.

Realism argued that the scholar would in time buy a Lexus and alter his idiom, would transfer money telegraphically, and put off lifting a phone to hear of a sister's disappointments, a parent's decline.

Yet it was apparent to Tom that people, like nations, grew stunted on a diet of realism alone. To soar, it was necessary to imagine the transcendent case.

. . . . . .

Arthur Loxley, pinkly moist in the tropics, spoke often of the cold. He described childhood winters: his eerie morning face in the basin's ice mirror; a flaw that opened under his skates on a frozen pond and raced, a flame along a lit fuse, toward the shore.

It was talk that horrified his wife. As a bride, Iris's great-grandmother had visited Lisbon in January. The sky was blue enamel, mosaic pavements sparkled in the sun. On her ninety-sixth birthday, Henrietta de Souza was still reliving the deception she had experienced upon drawing off a glove and holding out her hand to a slanted ray. "The sun was cold!" the old lady declared in cracked, imperious tones and thumped her stick on a tile painted with a spouting whale. "The sun was cold!"

That unnatural reversal worked powerfully on Iris's imagination. The European Winter: she pictured it as a beast. It lay open-mawed across the jeweled cavern of London, daring her to pass. In Lawrence Fitch's embrace, envisaging her English future as wavelets traveled from her thighs to her throat, she saw herself the plaything of icy paws; and shuddered, so that the captain, finding her name circulating with the port and himself the object of regimental envy, felt justified in referring to her as a ravishing little trollop.

When the earth cracked open in pre-monsoonal heat, Arthur evoked the geometric precision of snowflakes. Fanning himself with a newspaper, he spoke of wind-whipped sleet and the brown slush on Coventry pavements. He described the sensation of grasping iron chains in a frozen playground and how to fashion a man from snow.

He held his son entranced with tales of icy queens, and wolves howling through black, leafless woods. There was a story about a ship manned by wraiths that might be glimpsed in Arctic latitudes, hoarfrost diamonds in its rigging. A bookseller's warren yielded a musty yellow volume written by a Dane, and a five-year-old who had never known cold shed warm tears at the plight of a small girl freezing with her tray of matches.

Tom tilted a glass of whiskey, the better to observe the melting of icebergs.

In time he had encountered theories of cultural identity and discovered that his childhood had been deficient in reading that reflected the world around him. The argument had its force and was, like all orthodoxies, blind in one eye. It viewed Arthur's stories as nostalgic exercises in the colonial project of ignoring what was indigenous and vital in favor of alien constructions.

Tom saw the thing as more intricate and himself as happy to have experienced, when young, the empire of imagination. Stories with Indian backdrops offered the pleasure of recognition. Those that brought outlandish elements into play posed India as one reality among many.

It was precisely the disjunction between Arthur's anecdotes and the scenes unfolding before his eyes that had fascinated Tom as a boy. He was stirred by a tale of alpine snows as a northern child might quicken to palm-fringed lagoons: each thrilling to wonders that existed beyond the rim of perception.

The most blatantly trumped-up tale captured Arthur's sympathy, so that swindlers of every stripe sought him out with stories of widowed mothers or fail-safe investments. A lean, ageless individual who went by the name of Perry once laid siege to him for a month with whiskey and sagas of the Brazilian interior, at the end of which time Arthur agreed to relieve him of three uncut diamonds he claimed to have wrested at knifepoint from a dishonest *garimpeiro*. The contract had been sealed with a fresh bottle when Perry's angry blue eyes filled with tears. "You have driven me to honesty," he announced, and blew his nose violently. He reached for the soft leather pouch containing the pebbles and flung it over his shoulder into a bed of shocking-pink anthuriums.

The incident made its way back to Iris, who placed herself in her husband's path with her hands on her hips. "I told you about that Perry," she began, her voice ominously even. "As soon as I set eyes on him, large as life and twice as ugly, didn't I tell you, 'Here is a humbug'?"

It was true. Even Tom, then aged eight, had been struck by the unreliability of Perry: flagrant in every facet of the man, from his winking tiepin to his golden-cornered smile. "Perry's Pebbles": it became family shorthand for the preposterous; for a tale too good to be true.

Arthur had been dead a decade when an exchange occurred that cast the episode forever in a different light. Seeking to amuse a girl he was involved with, Tom had set about skewering a bombastic acquaintance.

Lizzie said abruptly, "For Christ's sake." She broke off whatever task engaged her and turned to face him. "There are alternatives to seeing through people."

"Why don't you run them past me." (Startled, but not out of irony.)

The girl opened and closed one hand. It was a gesture already familiar to Tom, signifying exasperation. She said, "Try seeing into them. That'd be a start."

Lizzie proved transient. But the rebuke lodged in Tom. He thought of Perry, with his glinting, ready smile. Arthur had seen honesty in the man, and his son realized, with a little stab of surprise, that it was Arthur, after all, who had been right.

If, on numerous other occasions, his father had been duped, he was surely not the party cheapened in the process. There are illusions that are glorious. If the shabby surface extended to the depths, it was still infinitely grander to project the other case.

SUNDAY

In the weeks that followed his lunch with Esther Kade, Tom read everything he could find about Nelly's work. What began as curiosity ended as need. His book on James lacked only its conclusion, yet he neglected it, led on from catalogue to periodical to Web site. Obsessive as a gundog, he tracked the glimmer of her, not caring if it led him astray.

It was easy enough to find reproductions of Nelly's more recent work, easy to reconstitute the stages of her career. But Tom soon realized that no visual record of the *Nightingale* suite existed. He had a copy of the exhibition catalogue, but it reproduced none of the controversial works; as if wily Posner had anticipated the furor.

More than one critic lamented the loss of the paintings, reporting that Nelly had destroyed them as soon as the show closed. But surely, Tom thought, surely they couldn't be gone altogether? He thought enviously of Esther, whose memory held their trace.

Five years after the *Nightingale* debacle, an exhibition of new work by Nelly Zhang opened at Posner's gallery. It marked a turning point in her career.

The new show consisted of photographs of original paintings. The catalogue essay was signed by a critic called Frederick Vickery, whose crumpled jowls and rectangular, black-rimmed glasses had since enjoyed mild notoriety on a late-night television arts program. *Zhang confronts us with work that follows Barthes in presenting realism as secondary mimesis,* wrote Vickery. *That is, not as a copy from nature but as the copy of a copy.*

The essay went on to explain that once photographed by a professional photographer, the paintings were destroyed. It struck Tom as a reenactment of the fate of the *Nightingale* suite, part protest, part catharsis, the deliberate repetition that controls trauma but refuses appeasement. Or so he reasoned, while flinching at Nelly's destruction of her paintings, at the calculated violence of the act.

He had heard Nelly and the other artists talk about Vickery. While there was a coolness between him and Posner now, the critic had once been integral to the dealer's set. His essay had Posner's spin all over it, decided Tom, noting its concluding sentence: *Here is an artistic practice that denies the market's lust for the original, offering an endless multiplicity of likenesses instead.*

Tom examined images of freeways, multistory parking garages, supermarkets, fast-food outlets. Nelly painted the strange, assertive beauty of constructions essential to the functioning of large cities. She painted hospitals, those nonplaces where modern lives begin and end. She had a fondness for changing light and liminal hours, for the theatricality of sunset and the frightening blue of certain dusks.

What was curious was the change she worked on her subjects. Inanimate things glistened and appeared to move in her pictures. The ugly musculature of an overpass or a high-rise estate turned dreamily vaporous under her hand. Hung about with the huge blackness of night, concrete and steel grew ecto-plasmic. Tom clicked on a link in an online art journal and was confronted with a shining tendon that might once have been a road.

These were images that had the quality of apparitions. Others struck Tom as forensic. A deserted railway platform suggested surveillance footage; a desolate mall might have been filched from the bulletin board in an incident room. He found himself looking at a city envisioned as the scene of a crime.

He made notes on technique, composition, the use of color and space. It was a methodology that had served him well as a student, the close scrutiny and faithful recording of what was before him producing gleams of insight, bright fissures opening in his mind. Noting the featureless architecture and nondescript vistas Nelly favored, he believed he saw why she was drawn to these anonymous elements. She lived in a city deficient in visual icons, a place without a bridge or harbor or distinctive skyline. It lacked an image. From that lack, Nelly had fashioned a style.

Tom analyzed and speculated. He had been trained to per-form these operations. He sat in his study before shining win-dows and filled them with words. It required connective tissue, conclusions; since one thing leads to another in narrative. He was aware of a degree of wrenching entailed. But a story need not be true to be useful. He was happier in those weeks than he had been in years.

A photograph called *Secured by Modern* showed tramlines, a half-demolished office block, the Victoria Street neon sign that advertised Skipping Girl Vinegar.

The metal sign modeled to resemble a skipping child was one of several forms in Nelly's work that recalled the human. There were effigies in a shop window, a plastic-sheathed jacket on a dry cleaner's rack, shadows thrown by invisible bodies, two silhouettes entwined on a dance studio's sign. But there were no people in Nelly's scenes. They suggested dramas from which the actors had fled.

As his intimacy with her work grew, Tom noticed the evidence of decay Nelly included in her streetscapes. Rubbish overflowing a bin, weeds pushing through concrete, broken or missing tiles. The cracked, outdated faces of seventies and eighties buildings. These signs told of a city that was neither ancient nor exactly new, but mutable. Inscribed within them was the memory of the maggoty cheeses and rotten fruit once painted into still lifes as warnings against excess and reminders of the transience of earthly splendor.

The conflation of work and author is an error into which novices fall; so Tom Loxley believed and sought to impress on recidivist students. It had the inadequacy of all law. How could his obsession with Nelly's work be distinguished from his desire for her? He was governed by a hunger for possession, images serving to paper over a bodily absence.

It was a substitution he literalized. In one of the regular sessions he devoted to Nelly, he lay in a darkened room, gazing by the unsteady light of a tea candle at a photocopied page. When he had finished, the edifice of her imaginings was tagged with his luminous urgency.

Iris's eyebrows, long vanished, reappeared every day as two greasy, coquettish arcs. The bronze puffs over her skull showed white at the roots. The events of Wednesday had caused her to miss her appointment at the hairdresser and she would not pay the extortionate prices of Thursday and Friday.

At the sight of Tom, her mouth unscrolled like a scarlet ribbon.

She was delivered to his door on Sunday morning by Audrey. A horn sounded, and Tom went into the street with an umbrella to extract his mother from the car. As soon as he reached for her, "I'm falling," cried Iris. "I'm falling."

Braced between the car door and her son's arm, she staggered upright at last. Many of her parts still worked, but she had been obliged to renounce high heels. With her feet crammed into pink ballet shoes suitable for a six-year-old, she knew herself to have grown old.

Expertly assessing the room for recent acquisitions, Audrey declined a cup of tea. She was running late; Iris had misplaced her eyebrow pencil that morning.

Audrey patted the back of her head: "I can't imagine why you use one in the first place. People should age naturally, if you ask me."

She stood before them, the product of skilled professionals — hairdresser, manicurist, orthodontist, podiatrist — and delivered herself of this view.

······

Iris Loxley, née de Souza, had triumphed over pain, rain-slick pavements, and the treachery of bucket seats to accomplish the repositioning of her flesh from her living room to her son's. The successful completion of any journey represented a victory. A girl who moved like water was present in her thoughts from time to time, but in the detached way of an actress familiar from a long-running serial.

Her double-handled bag of imitation leather on her lap, Iris sat motionless as an idol. A picture was sliding about in her memory of a gray stone half sunk in tough-bladed grass. Matthew Ho from next door squatted on his heels in front of it, reading aloud. His stubby finger, moving over the writing cut into the stone, was green-rimmed from scraping moss. Iris could see the ivory silk ribbon threaded about the hem and pockets of her blue batiste dress. She could hear Matthew saying, "Snowflake." Then he said, "A Merry Companion." She could remember a date, 1819. One hundred years before she had been born.

By the time Iris was seven, that part of the de Souza compound had disappeared under concrete. Matthew said the stone had marked the place where a small dog was buried. He said that the laborers working on the new extension had dug up its remains. He had seen them, he said. "Three bones. And an eyeball." He put his face close to Iris's: "Now its ghost will haunt you forever," he hissed.

Audrey, disliking waste, never disposed of a grievance that had not been squeezed dry. She wished to impress upon Tom that his mother had inconvenienced her that morning, and so, following him into the kitchen to complain of delay, delayed further.

He said mildly, "We'd be lost without you, Audrey." And added, "Shona coming over for lunch?"

Audrey was eyeing a circle of French cakes on a plate. "Cost an arm and a leg."

"Help yourself. Please." Tom was wondering where he had put the empty food containers. In Audrey's codebook, take-away was an offense that compounded profligacy with neglect. Love merited the effort of indifferent home cooking.

"No time, thanks, Tommy. I've got to get my lamb in the oven." She picked up an oval dish, turned it over to check the brand name, replaced it on the table. "You know what Shona's like about her Sunday roast."

Tom spooned tea leaves into a wicker-handled pot.

Audrey observed that there was nothing wrong with bags in her opinion. She lifted the lid of a saucepan. "I knew I smelled curry. That's the thing about curry, isn't it: the smell. Gets into the soft furnishings. I suppose you don't notice if you're born to it."

Still she would not leave. Tom slid pastries filled with vanilla cream into a paper bag and offered them to her, setting off an operetta of surprise, remonstrance, denial, and a final yielding.

Yet at the door she came to a halt. She had remarked the absence of the dog.

MISFORTUNE BROUGHT OUT the best in Audrey, providing scope for pity tempered with common sense. She was twelve years younger than Arthur, and the great regret of her girlhood was having missed the war. Clean gauze bandages, wounded officers wanting to hold her hand: she could have managed all that, she felt. She had trained as a nurse for six months before her marriage, and for the rest of her life would check a pulse against a watch, lips professionally tightened.

Audrey was always quick to extend what she called a helping hand and, finding it grasped, to detect exploitation. Muggins here; a soft touch: so she described herself. Debit and credit were computed with decimal precision, each benign gesture incurring a debt of gratitude that could never be paid in full.

Her brother's death she judged a piece of characteristic foolishness, yet it opened pleasant avenues for dispensing favors. There she might stroll, vigilant and loved as a guardian angel. She was of a generation that had attended Sunday School and the word *raiment* came into her mind. She pictured it as a kind of rayon that cost the earth.

It was decided that Arthur's widow was to stay on in Audrey and Bill's annex; Bill wouldn't hear of Iris moving, said Audrey. In time it would transpire that he would not hear of Iris cooking curry more than once a fortnight, and then only if all the windows were open; would not hear of Tom turning up the volume on the radio, nor of replacing the orange and green paper on the feature wall in the living room with white paint. It was a catalogue dense with prohibitions communicated piecemeal by Audrey. Bill, the silent source of so much nay-saying, took Tom to the cricket every Boxing Day, and slipped him five dollars now and then, with a finger laid along his nose and a music-hall wink.

Charity, as those who have endured it know, is not easily distinguished from control. Audrey gave Iris and Tom a lift to a multi-story shopping center on Friday evenings. Here, everything from cornflakes to flannelette sheets could be acquired with Audrey's approval. Brands were crucial, a novel concept; the Loxleys' vocabulary expanded to take in Arnott's and Onkaparinga. They were grateful for guidance. Iris, fingering pale wool, was informed that cream was not a winter color. Silver escalators carried them to new heights of consumption.

A few of the girls in Filing invited Iris to join them for tea in a coffee lounge in the city after work the following Friday. Audrey asked how Iris was going to get her shopping done; or did she imagine that Bill and Audrey would rearrange their whole time-table to suit her? Iris ventured the notion that she might walk to the shops on Saturday, to a street two blocks distant containing a butcher, a baker, and so on.

Audrey concentrated on economics: the wastefulness of eating out amplified by the extravagance of neighborhood shopping. Did Iris realize the delicatessen was run by Jews? She possessed the despot's talent for representing oppression as benevolence and was herself entirely swayed by the performance. The pain she suffered at the prospect of Iris squandering her resources was genuine, but its source, the bid for independence she sensed in her sister-in-law's plan, exceeded her diagnostic skills.

It was a pattern repeated in Audrey's dealings with all she encountered. In the theater of her mind, as in the classical drama, brutality occurred offstage. What was on view, above all to herself, was only the aftermath of invisible carnage. So Tom observed, with the cold-eyed scrutiny of adolescence. It left him resolved to be clear about motive. Which, admirable when directed inward, strengthened his cynicism about motive in others.

That was the impress his aunt left on the minds around her. Audrey had the inquisitorial approach to innocence: subjected to enough stress, it was bound to crack.

Sixteen-year-old Tom, dazzled by Julie Vogel, who had just started at the newsagent's, discovered in himself the desire for new plumage. He bought a T-shirt: rich blue, trimmed with scarlet at the neck and sleeves. It was a garment pleasing in form and hue. It would in any case have drawn his aunt's eye, for everything the Loxleys acquired was by definition not Audrey's and therefore resented.

"That's a nice T-shirt, Tommy. Looks expensive."

"Four bucks." Tom's thoughts were busy with the golden Vogel, but he knew what was required, Audrey pricing every item that entered the Loxley household.

"That's good value for money. Where'd you get it?"

He told her.

"I might get one for Shona. Did they have other colors?"

"I think. Yeah."

"Do they come in girls' sizes?" Then, with a bright little peal, "Although you could hardly be called manly."

The annex was reached by a path that led past dwarf conifers and a yellow-flecked shrub before turning down the side of Audrey's house. The next day, approaching an open window in soundless sneakers, Tom heard his name.

"...conveniently vague. I could tell at once he was lying. So I took the bus up there this morning, and sure enough they were five dollars. Five, not four. He's been out of the house, avoiding me, all day."

The boy turned and went out again into the street. There was the summer evening smell of barbecued flesh. Minutes before, he had been joyful: for Julie had smiled at him when he bought a green ballpoint from her; and again when the newsagent's closed and she emerged to see him absorbed in a window where teddy bears and booties were displayed. He had made up his mind to speak to her the next day. Now he was trembling. The gulf between his feelings for shining-haired Julie, the image to him of all that was pure and fine, and his aunt's caricature of his soul was hideous. In that chasm he glimpsed the edge of his species' capacity for needless harm.

Anger quivered up through his body, liquid rising to the boil. He raged at his mother in an undertone. "We've got to get out. I can't stand it any longer. She's such a bitch."

"Don't use that language, child."

"It's Audrey's language you should worry about. Calling me a liar. Sneaking around, checking up on me. I don't know why those T-shirts were five dollars today. I paid four. I've had it with her. I'm going to bloody tell her so."

"Don't upset her, Tommy. What will happen if she gets angry with us?"

"We'll be rid of her and this dump for good."

It ended the usual way, with Iris in tears.

Now and then Tom would stand before his aunt, his voice rising in denunciation. There would follow a period of intricate punishment for Iris. Before giving herself over to those slower pleasures, Audrey would observe, with mingled triumph and righteousness, that if, after everything she had done, matters were not to the Loxleys' satisfaction, they were always free to leave. It was, she assured them, no skin off her nose.

But who voluntarily relinquishes a victim? In the wake of an argument, Audrey related stories of perverts who preyed on widows, circled reports of inflationary rents and extortionate landlords in the newspaper she passed on to the Loxleys.

After Iris was made redundant at the department store, Bill found her a job cleaning offices. She rose in black dawns and dressed before a single-bar radiator in a series of muffled clicks and taps, so as not to wake Tommy, a presence sensed rather than seen in musty darkness traversed on her way to the door. At the corner of the street it might occur to her to doubt whether she had switched off the radiator; there followed agonizing indecision over returning to check or missing her tram.

There was fear, and its twin, safety; their relationship was mirrored, fluid. Iris looked out of the window of the tram and saw the compartment in which she sat hovering golden and unfinished in the dark street, inhabited briefly by towers or trees. She shifted on her seat, giving a little expert kick at a nylon or trousered shin in the process. The ensuing interlude of apology and forgiveness confirmed her anchorage in the world.

Her knees held up until the day after Tom was awarded a university scholarship. At least now he was off her hands, as Audrey said, reducing Tom to a stubborn stain.

Iris had been taught to darn by French nuns, but that was scarcely a marketable asset in an economy where the notion of mending rather than replacing was already as quaint as a madrigal.

In India, finding herself in need, she would have had recourse to a web of human relationships. Here goodwill, or at least obligation, was impersonal and administrative, though no less grudged. She was grateful for sickness benefits; later for the pension. A savings account hoarded every spare cent. She did not wish to be a burden. It was one of Audrey's mantras: I wouldn't

want to be a burden. Love was represented as a load; one saw
tiny figures broken-backed under monstrous cargoes.

Iris took comfort in having a roof over her head. It was a
phrase she liked; it brought to mind the plump-thighed cherubim on her father's vaulted ceilings. Beyond it lay Australia:
boundless, open to the sky. "As long as we stay with Audrey, we
have a roof over our heads." "What can go wrong if you have a
roof over your head?"

"It can fall in and crush you," said Tom.

Toward the end of her son's last year at school, Iris spoke now
and then of renting a flat with him after his exams. The idea was
vague and constituted nothing like a plan; it was also what Tom
had urged on her in the past, seeing in his mind a bare space that
was his alone. A compact, neat teenager, he had blundered, again
and again, into the clutter of the annex, his shins encountering varnished wood, his knuckles grazing a long-necked, stoppered bottle
of warty yellow glass, an object both ugly and useless. At night,
when he lay swaddled before the TV's gray eye with the metal
underpinnings of his sofa bed ridging his spine, a room — lofty,
pale-walled, floored with grooved boards — formed in his mind.

In those years all his unadulterated energy was spent on the
captive's instinctive lunge toward light and air. Books furnished
him with a daily, spacious refuge. Later, looking back, he would
see swift water widening, his mother a diminished figure on the
shore.

By the time Tom's university offer came through, Iris had
become part of what he was intent on leaving. Of this small, cata-
clysmic shift in his thinking he was unaware. All the same, a lie
slid polished from his tongue. He told Iris that his scholarship was

conditional on his moving into student housing, "a university reg-
ulation." When he had lifted the last carton of books into a friend's
car and kissed his mother — "So long, Ma!" — he was light-headed
with the sense of having gotten away with something.

On the day before he moved out, Tom waited until he was alone
in the annex. Then he carried the hated yellow bottle into the
kitchen. There he broke its neck. When Iris returned, he told
her he had accidentally smashed the bottle when packing. The
pieces of thick glass, wrapped in newspaper, were already in the
pedal bin. But he had removed the leaf-shaped stopper before
hitting the bottle against the sink and had somehow failed to
dispose of it. Thereafter, whenever he opened a certain drawer
in his mother's kitchen he would see a malicious amber eye loll-
ing among place mats and paper napkins.

   In the last weeks of their shared life, Iris suddenly said, "When
you were small you used to follow me everywhere. In and out of
rooms all day." She must have been to the hairdresser that morning because Tom could still remember the brownish smears of
dye on the tops of her ears. He had refrained from remarking on
them, pleased with this proof of his restraint.

INFORMED AT LAST that the dog was lost, Iris said, "I'm very sorry to
hear that." She spoke formally; the calamity might have befallen
an Australian.

Tom, having dreaded a storm, was goaded by calm. The contrary arithmetic of his relations with Iris converted it at once into lack of feeling and added up to the need for brutishness. So that he paused, in the act of serving out his mother's lunch, and said, "He's probably dead, you realize. Choked to death on his lead. Or run over."

"Ah," said Iris. And with quickened interest, "Don't serve so much."

"Christ! Can't you think of anything but yourself for a minute? And what does it matter if there's too much? Just leave what you don't want."

Her filmy eyes rose to his face. She had the familiar sensation of striving to decipher a riddle in a foreign language; failure meant Tommy would be angry. The small hillock of saffron rice surmounted by curries and surrounded by pickles had brought to mind a white-haired skull protruding from mud-colored rags on a pavement, an image glimpsed and only half understood in childhood. It had floated to the surface of her thoughts buoyed by the word *waste*.

Tom found his tongue stuck to his palate. Lowering it unclenched his jaw. He set his mother's laden plate before her, having thwarted the impulse to do so with force. "I'm just worried about what might have happened," he said. He was accustomed to knowing better than his mother, so apology was not a coin readily available to their commerce.

Iris picked up her spoon and fork and began to eat. Some minutes later, halfway through a mouthful: "I have my unfailing prayer to Saint Anthony," she said.

The Meg Ryan video in front of which his mother was dozing after lunch penetrated Tom's study in irritating little swells. He opened and shut drawers, at last finding the earplugs in a hollow glass cube that held paper clips and stamps.

"The familiar contention that modernity is concerned with the differentiation and autonomisation of the aesthetic sphere..." Tom switched on a lamp, as the afternoon darkened. Light lay obliquely on a page, highlighting dull prose with gold.

He was reading the lectureship application sent in by a recent D.Phil. from Bristol, who had appended a strenuous article on Edith Wharton to her CV. She had only one refereed publication and minimal teaching experience. But she was the student of a famous James scholar, a woman who wielded academic power. Tom thought of his book; of the weight the Englishwoman's endorsement would carry with publishers.

After a while he realized he had stopped reading and was constructing a tale. "Nelly and I go looking for him whenever we go up there. Oh, I know it's hopeless now. Not knowing what happened is the worst thing. But I tell myself he was doing what he loved best, following a scent."

This fiction, queasy with the play of desire and disloyalty, was interrupted by a specific memory: the dog, plumed tail held high, absorbed in tracking a moth around the room, breathing on it.

Internal windows in Tom's study gave onto a narrow sunroom, where a long, gridded window overlooked the yard. The effect, when he looked up from his desk, was of a bright, pictorial glow ruled with black, a Mondrian fashioned from iron and light. The impression of clean modernity carried through to his study, a geometric, dustless space. Here books were ranked like soldiers on dark metal shelving that rose against pale walls. Lamps leaned at acute angles. Surfaces gleamed. There was a rug from Isfahan on the boarded floor, its pink and slaty blues smudged with white, for naturally the dog was in the habit of singling out its sumptuousness, and Tom could not at present bring himself to rid the room of that animal residue.

He was, in any case, habitually tolerant of traces of the dog's passing, of grit, earth, fur, a warm, sweetish reek. His forbearance had called forth the light mockery of his wife; for the streak of dried sauce Karen left on a kitchen counter or the pink-stained toothpaste she neglected to swill from the washbasin were tiny barbs on which Tom's temper quickly unraveled.

His disgust was disproportionate, its blossoming rooted in childhood. In scrubbed Australia children know the causal chain that links dirt and disease as a cautionary tale. In India, the word was made flesh. Skin peeled, or flared with ominous pigmentations, burst to reveal its satiny red lining shot through with gold. Distended or racked bodies were everywhere on public view. Even a child's eye could perceive the fatal, webbed relation between the flies sipping at a sore and the black crust that crawled over sweetmeats at a stall.

Therefore years later Tom recoiled from dishes accumulating in the sink, from the clotted handkerchief his fingers encountered under a pillow.

Around the time of his thirtieth birthday, he grew conscious that the narrowing of his life had begun. Karen and he still took pleasure in each other's company, sought it in each other's flesh. They were working hard, starting to make money. But from time to time there would swim into Tom's mind a page from a book he had owned when very young. Within the book, paper tabs could be pulled or rotated to bring illustrations to life. One of them had stirred the child's imagination with special pungency. It showed a cottage with two front doors set in a garden filled with flowers and birds. A tab on the left flipped open the corresponding door and pushed out an apple-cheeked boy in blue breeches; the right-hand tab produced a girl in a gingham pinafore.

Again and again, the child Tom trundled out the boy, the girl, singly, together. They were Boo and Baby. He conducted complicated conversations with them. Sometimes he punished one or the other, Boo's door or Baby's remaining shut all day. He would stroke the relevant tab, shift it a fraction, then withdraw his hand. The satisfaction he knew at such moments was intense.

But in years to come the page struck Tom as a terrible foreshadowing of his ordered existence. Each day was a sum with a red tick beside it. Intellectual curiosity, love's huge anarchy: he had succeeded in taming even these. There he came, the bright-eyed boy, one arm raised in merry greeting, the plaything of a shuttling machinery.

Into these broodings arrived the dog.

The dog hid blood-threaded bones down the side of a couch. He tore open a pillow and clawed the paint from a door. He sprang into a neighbor's ornamental pond and swallowed a goldfish. There was his ecstatic fondness for rolling in filth. He would dig in his ear with a hind foot, extract the paw, and lick it. Now and then while snuffling along a footpath he would hastily eat a turd. His desires were beastly. At his most docile, he remained an emissary from a kingdom with enigmatic laws.

And slowly, slowly it dawned on Tom that the animal acquired to please his wife spoke to a need that was his alone. All giving is shot with ambiguity, directed at multiple and paradoxical ends. A gift might exceed thought and desire. It might be epiphanic.

The dog was handsome, sweet-natured. It was easy to love such a creature. Nevertheless, his core was wild. In accommodating that unruliness, Tom's life flowed in a broader vein.

Late for work while the dog danced out of reach, following his own imperatives through mud and weeds, Tom was conscious of anger ticking in him like time. It didn't preclude elation. For fleet minutes, a rage for control had been outfoxed.

Matted fur drifted against baseboards. Even as he worked a soft gray clump from the bristles of a dustbrush, Sucks to you, Boo, thought Tom.

It was not the end of disgust, which is an aversion to anything that reminds us that we are animals. But the dog unleashed in Tom a kind of grace; a kind of beastliness.

SUNDAYS WERE RITUALISTIC. Morning tea, lunch, a video, afternoon tea; then Tom would return his mother to Audrey.

He was transferring sugar from packet to bowl that afternoon when he became aware of an unambiguous organic stench.

He lived in what had once been a capacious family house, one that had offered pleasure to the eye in a way that was commonplace before architects discovered their talent for brutality. Later two dentists had run their practice on the ground floor. Later still, the building had served as a rooming house. Finally, it had been converted into flats. This last rearrangement had taken a lavatory situated outside the back door of the original house and placed it between Tom's laundry and sunroom with doors to both. The old-fashioned seat there, marginally higher than the one in the renovated suite, was preferred by Iris.

Tom hovered in the sunroom. Rain had pooled, trembling, in the lower corners of the windowpanes. He raised his voice: "Ma, are you OK?"

"Yes, yes."

He heard her moving about. Water gushed. A ripeness filled his nostrils.

After some minutes, she called, "Tommy?"

"Yes?"

"Can you come?"

On the floor near the seat lay part of a large turd; the rest had been tracked over the linoleum. Feces and wadded paper clung to the sides of the lavatory bowl. The seat, imperfectly wiped, showed pale brown whorls.

Tom's first thought was of a child: of a monstrous infant soiling its pen.

His mother said, "There is a piece of shit."

She said, "Don't be angry, Tommy. I can't pick it up."

She was clinging to the edge of the basin, because the handles of her walker were soiled, realized Tom. He reached around her, ran the tap over a facecloth, used it to wipe the handles clean.

It was difficult to maneuver in the constricted space. With infinite care, he led his mother to the door, trying, with his hands over hers, to steer the walker clear of the filth, trying also to avoid stepping in it.

He was murmuring, "It's OK, don't worry, it's OK."

In the laundry he kneeled and, one at a time, lifted Iris's heels and eased off her ballet slippers. For a small woman, she had broad feet; he had to tug to dislodge the shoes.

All the while, "Wait, wait," shrieked Iris. "I'm falling."

"You're fine. It's OK."

She was wearing nylon knee-highs. "These stockings are slipping." Again she screamed, "I'm falling."

"I'll walk you to your chair, Ma. Just hang on a sec."

Tom checked the wheels on her walker, ran the facecloth over them.

"Have you washed your hands?" he asked, and caught, again, the echo of childhood.

"Yes, yes."

Iris let herself be steered along the passage to the living room. Her chair waited in front of the TV. She lowered herself onto it by degrees, with creaks and sighs. When she looked up she saw a face that had slipped from its bones in the gray depths of the screen. It was a moment before she recognized her reflection.

She said, "Give me my bag."

While she was foraging in it, Tom went into his bathroom. He washed his hands, thinking that it was the first time he had heard the word *shit* from his mother. It was out of place in the realm of the ladylike, which admitted only *big job, kakka, number two.*

When he returned to her, Iris was checking her lipstick in a hand mirror: pressing her lips together, pushing them out. About to snap her bag shut, she said, "Better see that I've got my key."

"You have. You checked before lunch, remember?"

Iris went on pulling pills, spectacle case, tissues, rosary, from her bag. "My God, what'll happen if it's lost?"

"It's not lost, Ma. How could it be?"

"But how will I get in?" Her voice had risen. She was close to tears.

"Your key can't possibly be lost. Think about it. If it is, I've got a spare. And so has Audrey."

"What if she's not there?"

Tom felt he might scream with her. He said, "Ma, I'll be driving you home. I've got a key. And in any —"

"Ah. Found it." Her agitation subsided in an instant. "Thank God for that." Then she said, "These tissues are all wrong now." She began refolding them, all her attention concentrated on the flimsy pink squares.

Tom was reminded of his own intense involvement, as a child, with his immediate surroundings. A segment of a forgotten day came back to him: he was sucking up a fizzy orange drink through a straw, sometimes letting the liquid in the anodized metal tumbler subside before it reached his mouth. While this was going on, the sun moved in and out of clouds, and there was the pleasure of light alternating with shade on the side of his face.

He handed his mother a small, silver-capped bottle.

"What's this?"

"Cologne."

"What for?"

"You might like to put some on."

"What?"

"Put some on!"

Deafness, conducive to imperatives, discouraged nuance. Tom said, "How about a cup of tea?"

Iris, absorbed in perfuming herself, ignored him.

"Tea!" he bellowed.

A tray held a milk jug and sugar bowl, a white cup, a pastry cloud on a blue-glazed plate. The mother inspected these objects. The son braced himself for criticism.

Praise was rare on Iris's tongue. When Tom, as a child, presented her with his school report, she would scan it for deficiencies. "What is this eighty-seven percent in Geography? Why are you second this term?"

She had her father's sixth sense for inadequacy. No servant had lasted long in the de Souza household: Sebastian reached automatically for the smudged tumbler on the credenza; Iris's finger trailed over the undusted ledge. The dhobi's fortnightly bundle of spotless laundry unfailingly lacked a sock or a pillowcase.

But her son overrode Iris's instinct for shortfalls. In the last month of her confinement, gripped by premonition, she had prayed daily that the child would be spared Arthur's nose. Then he arrived, furiously protesting the breach of their union. Iris saw a slimy, dark, curiously elongated organism that was whisked from her at once. She began to cry, because she had beheld perfection.

Her son was healthy; he grew up handsome and clever. Of course she feared for him. There was the evil eye. If a neighbor remarked that the child was looking well, Iris assured her at once that he was sickly. When Arthur heaped praise on the boy, she cut him short and crossed her fingers behind her back. Calamities, like moths, are drawn to the light. To speak glowingly of Tommy was to risk the wrong sort of attention. "Jesus bids us shine with a pure clear light," piped the massed infants of St. Stephen's; and Iris, radiating pride in the front pew, thought how men, even the best intentioned, so often missed the point.

It became her habit to call attention to her son's limitations. Disparagement might mean the opposite of what it says; it might be a form of love. Only it is difficult for the disparaged to construe it as such. How was Tom to distinguish between the flaws his mother discovered in his best efforts and her fault-finding with the world? "She doesn't mean it," Arthur would say, but like so much Arthur said it was easily discounted.

When Tom was older, he might have been capable of unraveling Iris's ruse; but if so, he would have scorned it. "It's superstition, Ma! How can you be so irrational?" Thus he greeted the pinch of salt his mother flung over her shoulder, the pin over which she bent stiffly in the street. It never occurred to Tom that superstition might be an expression of humility: an admission that knowledge is limited and possibility infinite. Rooted in the desire to free his mother from unreasoning fear, his loving impulse flowered as criticism. "Ma, that's totally dumb!" Of course Iris, recognizing her own strategy at work in her son, paid no attention to his belittling. Besides, the devil lurked in spilled salt. Besides, *See a pin and let it lie, / All the day you'll have to cry.*

And so: the tray, the milk and sugar, golden tea in a cup, a miniature éclair on a blue plate.

Tom's breath caught in anticipation.

"That looks absolutely nice," said Iris.

Tom assembled gloves, lavatory brush, disinfectant, cream cleanser, water, mop, wipes, what was left of the roll of paper.

Afterward, while the floor was drying, he took his nailbrush and Iris's shoes into the yard. There he turned on the hose and scrubbed dark, gummy excrement from their soles, using a twig to gouge it free where necessary.

He washed his hands again and soaped his arms all the way to the elbow. There was the tang of lemon verbena. And behind it, the fragrance of feces.

It went on and went on, like a terrible dream. Floor, bowl, seat, toilet brush, paper holder, washbasin, were spotless. The soiled towel had been replaced with a fresh one. His nails gleamed, but to be safe he dug them into the wedge of soap. With his hand on the tap, he saw a few brown grains stuck to the chrome.

AT THE BACK of the deepest drawer in Tom's desk was an object unlike any other he owned. In the Loxleys' last week in India, he had spied a small, lilac-bound book among the rubbish in a wicker wastebasket. It was his mother's old autograph album. He retrieved it straightaway and secreted it under three starched white shirts in his suitcase.

It was an unfathomable action. For weeks Tom had watched the unwitting objects that had furnished his life — dessert spoons, mattresses, a treadle sewing machine, a carom board — sold or given away. This dismantling of the past, which had seemed so solid and was now shown to be as flimsy as a painted backdrop, had caused him no grief. He had known he was witnessing something at once terminal and cathartic. He met it with the grave exhilaration that was its due.

Yet there was his baffling rescue of the autograph album. As a small child he had turned its pastel pages carefully, drawn by their delicate water-ice hues. Later, when he had learned to decipher handwriting, he read the verses the album contained, but only as he read everything that came his way. Years had passed since he had troubled to look inside it. Autograph albums were a girlish amusement. Twelve-year-old Tom Loxley held them in scorn.

From the wreckage of the past he might have salvaged a favorite toy, a book. But these he relinquished with never a pang, pressing them on friends or neighborhood urchins, as munificent as a maharajah. He watched old exercise books curl and blacken in the mali's bonfire with glee. The little album with its dinted spine remained his only souvenir of India. No one knew it was in his possession; or so Tom believed. In fact Karen, for one, had pondered the anomaly it represented with some curiosity.

From time to time Tom flicked through the album. Signatures made him pause. Childhood mythologies uncoiled from certain names; others sank back into the faceless, unimaginable swarm of those who had known his mother when she was young. *Be good, sweet maid, and let who will / Be clever.* So Sebastian de Souza's exquisite copperplate enjoined his daughter.

With time and rereading, Tom knew the autograph album's contents by heart. He didn't wish to retain vows of undying friendship, mildly salacious witticisms, exhortations to virtue and remembrance, but the album had taken possession of him. He could never be rid of it now.

DETAILS OF NELLY'S PICTURES would blend with Tom's dreams, spawning brilliant figments lost to ham-fisted day. When he woke, his eyes looked wider in the mirror, sated with images.

There was a nebulous quality to him in these months. Women were susceptible to it. In strange bedrooms he profited from their interest. He was ghostly; his rapture precise, embodied.

He speculated about the transformation of Nelly's work after Atwood disappeared. The change to showing photographs of her paintings, too radical for evolution, suggested extremity. Tom was inclined to read it as a fable of loss: Atwood as categorically absent and mourned as the paintings Nelly destroyed. Photography was a form of willed remembrance. Tom was wary of it: this spectral medium, tirelessly calling up the past. Sometimes he shrank from a spread of Nelly's photos as from a collection of gravestones, each a loving memorial to her marriage.

He brought up the topic with Brendon. Who said, "I've always figured showing photos is Nelly's way of paying tribute to painting. To that whole inheritance that's been nudged aside by new ways of thinking about art. I'd say it's about photography as a memory of painting."

Nevertheless, Tom divined the play of the erotic in Nelly's choice of medium. In its early years, photography had caused trepidation. The little likenesses it fabricated were so uncannily exact that it was feared they would drain vitality from their subjects; a vestige of the older, Romantic dread of the double who was believed to destroy a man's true self.

The suspicion lingered, in attenuated form, well into the twentieth century. But it was symptomatic of an era in which photographs were few, the power of the copy deriving from its relative rarity. By contrast, the postmodern plethora of images struck Tom as enhancing the particularity of an original. An array of photographs standing in for a subject only accentuated what wasn't there. Desire swelled for the absent flesh, the real elsewhere. In substituting a photograph for a painting, Nelly raised the temperature of interest in her work. There was shrewdness in her method, decided Tom. Her photos tantalized with the promise of *something more* that was always deferred.

The painted landscape he had first seen in Posner's gallery possessed a quality entirely absent from what followed. Trying to identify it, Tom thought of innocence. Then, as his mind played about the little oblong, he realized that its aura was also a lack. It was an image that knew nothing of time.

As the year lengthened, a development escaped Tom's attention. His copious stream of notes was dwindling, growing costive. On a night in October, an hour spent with Nelly's work produced only this spiteful trace: *Photography is a result of the desire to freeze time. A photograph is always a record of a failure.*

One evening, Nelly and he watched an old video of *The Innocents,* which was, they agreed, not nearly as disturbing as *The Turn of the Screw.* Afterward, as Tom walked her back to the Preserve, Nelly kept returning to the standard, unsolvable enigma of James's ghosts. "I mean, you're shown them in the film. When what's so creepy in the book is you can't tell if they're there or just something the governess imagines."

The dog was with them that night, clicking along the pavement. From feathery plots of wild fennel by the railway line, he emerged odorous with aniseed. He cocked his leg at every opportunity, writing his chronicles in urine. He was drawn by unmown grass and the pellety excrement of possums. Ramshackle paperbarks detained him for minutes with their aromatic folds. He was attuned to an invisible world, to the redolent leavings of bodies that had once populated these spaces.

Nelly said, "This is going to sound a little crazy."

"Yeah?"

"About five years ago I was on this tram, and I felt someone watching me." It was delivered in Nelly's usual sporadic style: talk as faulty machinery. "You know that feeling between your shoulder blades?"

On the opposite side of the unlit street, a block of flats rose over a parking garage. Something pale was astir in its darkness. Tom looked away.

"The tram was packed, and I couldn't see anyone I knew, and everyone was just doing that staring-into-space thing. But I was sure Felix was there." Nelly said, "I knew he was watching me. It went on for a couple of blocks, and then it was gone."

A little later: "Another time it happened in the supermarket. He was there, but he wasn't."

Tom glanced across at the garage again, and saw only parked cars.

He summoned reason to the scene. "Wouldn't Felix have tried to get in touch with Rory if he'd come back?"

A cold breeze had arisen. The dog was straining forward on

his leash. Nelly drew a length of knitted wool from her pocket, folded it, placed it about her throat, passed the ends through the loop. It was the first time Tom had noticed this way of tying a scarf, although it was much in evidence that year.

HE SPENT Sunday evening in blessed solitude, putting together his short list for the lectureship. At the last minute he added the British D.Phil., with a question mark beside her name. Afterward, he downed two whiskeys, fast.

When the doorbell rang he was sure it was Nelly. He went swiftly to the door and opened it to Posner.

"There you are." Posner spoke with a trace of impatience, as if Tom had been slow to answer a summons. "Bloody awful weather."

He thrust a crumpled black wing at Tom and glided past. There was an odor of damp cloth from the umbrella; nothing else. Posner had no smell.

In the living room he said, "You're in the phone book," as if it were a breach of taste. Then, without a glance at his surroundings, "Quaint little place."

Tom heard *shoddy* and *cramped*.

The flat was heated by electric radiators, but Posner crossed to the fireplace and stood with his back to the empty hearth. It conjured country weekends, the sense of well-being that comes from killing small animals. Yet Tom realized that his visitor wasn't altogether at ease. It was the hint of contempt; when he was sure of himself, Posner set out to charm.

The umbrella was a wounded thing dripping between them. Tom said, "Whiskey?" and left the room before Posner could reply. When he returned, Posner had shifted to the sofa. He had taken off his leather jacket and sat with one leg cocked, ankle resting on the opposite knee.

In Posner's hand the tumbler looked child-size, the tilting liquid calculated and mean. His moon gaze drifted about until he aimed it at the ceiling.

Tom was thinking of rooms so casually perfect they might have been assembled for the camera, of paintings lining a hall, of polished wood in which a lamp might be reborn as a star. Other images intervened in these remembered frames. Iris's kitchen cupboards, covered with yellow-flowered contact paper, hovered above Posner's mirrored mantelpiece. The accordion door that separated her living area from her bedroom now barred the access to his stairs.

Absurd to blame Posner for the contrast. But the net of Tom's feelings for his mother was not woven with reason. Even as his eye fell on the jacket slung beside Posner, what took shape in his thoughts was Iris's double-handled vinyl bag. It was an object her son could not see without pain.

He sat down, and the pale circle turned to him. A black-clad arm unfolded itself along the sofa, confident as a cat. "A word seemed in order," said Posner.

He might have been addressing an underperforming minion across a desk.

In the silence that followed, some echo of his tone must have communicated itself to the dealer. His manner altered. He uncocked his leg and ran a hand over his silver scalp. "You're a literary man, of course."

A minute earlier, it would have had the ring of accusation. But Posner had hung out his imitation of a smile. "You must know the story of Virginia Woolf's marriage?"

Tom swirled whiskey around in his glass.

"Her family had no illusions about the severity of her illness. They had witnessed the clawing, the howling, every grubby detail of it. But when Leonard wanted to marry her, the Stephens made light of what he was taking on. The merest sketch. Well, he was a godsend, naturally. Most of all to Vanessa, who'd have been stuck with nursing a madwoman if her sister hadn't married." Posner paused. "You know the story?" he asked again.

"The merest sketch."

"You can't help thinking they'd never have had the nerve if they'd been dealing with one of their own. Instead of a Jew boy from Putney."

There crept over Tom the sensation, marvel tinged with awe, that attends the sight of a great painting. It accompanied the realization that Posner might still pass for a handsome man.

"Of course only a Jew boy from Putney would have stuck it out all those years." Posner said, "One of my grandmothers was a Jewess. It makes me sensible to the deception."

His gaze was very intent. But it was apparent to them both that Tom couldn't tell what was wanted of him.

"These headaches of Nelly's." There was a light, feline tread to Posner's words. "They leave her so very...drained. She doesn't always recollect the intensity of an episode, you see."

Minutes passed.

At last Tom said, "Does she know you go around suggesting she's mad?"

"Dear boy! Such vehemence! I would speak," said Posner, "of heightened colors. I would speak of broadened effects." He patted the sofa beside him. When this failed to draw a response, he pulled his jacket across his lap and ran his fingers over the soft black skin.

"There is such pressure on artists to be contemporary. A loathsome notion, frankly risible. But there it is. Painting, landscape, figuration...In certain not uninfluential quarters these choices are condemned as inherently old hat." Posner sighed. "I wonder if you have any idea of the depths of Nelly's self-doubt. Her fear that her work lacks legitimacy. The intolerable *strain*. Nelly is a dear, dear friend," insisted that thin voice. "So marvelous. So moving as well."

"Don't forget mad."

And still Tom could not be sure that he had understood what Posner had come there to say. He had the impression, fleeting but forceful, of something waiting close at hand, something that might yet twitch loose and tear up the room.

"Tom, such willful misconstruction..." But Posner broke off, shaking his large head. He studied the ceiling and said, "I knew this would be a painful conversation. I put it off for as long as I could. But I've known Nelly a long time. Now and then there comes...someone entirely charming." He was folding back the tip of the jacket collar and folding it back again. "Someone who overcomes Nelly's resolution to avoid excitement. And then..." Posner let the leather spring free under his fingers.

"There are so many *aspects* to Nelly." A white hand lifted, fluttered. "There's a painting by Cézanne: *Les Grandes Bai-gneuses*. In the old days I'd go to Philadelphia just to look at it. It's always reminded me of Nelly. Something about the way the figures melt into and out of each other, so that your perception of them keeps shifting. But out of that flurry of muffling and displacement, what emerges is singularity. Oh, it's brilliant, utterly brilliant," said Posner severely, as if the point were in dispute. "Also unsettling. And sad."

"Piss off, Carson."

Posner shifted in his seat. His hand brushed the jacket, sliding it from his knees. It might have been accidental. But Tom thought he could see a swelling in the dealer's crotch.

He couldn't have sworn to it. Posner was wearing black, and his body was in shadow. But Tom shifted his gaze at once. And said, "Tell me: have you shared your opinion of his mother with Rory? Not that I imagine he gives a fuck about you anyway."

He was intent on cruelty. But was unprepared for the stillness that came over Posner's face, rendering the eyes twin caverns in that pallid waste.

He thought, My God, he really loves him.

By the time Posner left, it had stopped raining. In his study, Tom reached for a book.

It was a massive work, *Les Grandes Baigneuses,* its scale and the frontality of its handling closer to mural than easel painting. Tom had once written an essay about it. Had traced its precursors, described the way it vitalized the worn grammar of naked women in a rural setting.

The man leaning over the book had forgotten most of what he had argued.

What he remembered were the bodies. They filled the picture plane: preposterous, lumpish. Nor would they stay still, as Posner had remarked. A woman kneeling at the far right of the canvas was also a striding figure, the torso of one forming the buttocks and legs of the other. Observing this, the mind shimmered between two meanings, as in a dream.

Tom recognized the hurtling sensation: his sense of the duplicity of images. A trace of nausea — stiffened with excitement — worked in him still. The grotesque treatment of the bodies had the effect of rendering flesh itself inorganic. It was a painting in which something mechanistic grated at the heart.

But it was the figure facing out who now held Tom's attention. Or rather, it was the blue line spurting at its groin. He took in heavy breasts, the specific marks of femaleness, and what he was seeing for the first time: a countering, ambiguous penis.

It was what had passed between him and Posner, Tom knew, that had opened his eyes to that doubleness. He thought, It's a painting about him, not Nelly.

The phone shrilled him out of sleep.

"Tom, it's Yelena. Sorry, I —"

"What's wrong?"

"It's Osman." She began to cry. "He's back in hospital."

"Saint V's? Give me ten minutes."

"No, no." He heard her gulp, then a loud, snorting sniff. "They're filling him full of morphine. He will be out of it completely. I'm on my way home. Brendon is with him, and Nelly. He wanted you to know."

"How bad is it?"

"They are doing tests and so forth in the morning." Her

voice was quavery again. "But it looks like it's no longer in remission."

"Oh, God."

"Nelly said to say you should still come and get her at the Preserve tomorrow. And, Tom, this is terrible also about —"

But Yelena couldn't go on.

MONDAY

Into Tom's waking thoughts came fear, those he loved in the world withdrawing from him one by one. The future had the shape of a corridor, empty of everything but time.

He thought of his mother surrounded by shit. Was excrement part of the world or part of the body? It blurred the distinction between inside and outside. Among the things it offended against was the human need for order.

There was a man Tom remembered from India, one of casteless thousands assigned to work with shit. When the sewer in a local tenement clogged, this man lowered himself into the overflowing cesspit, feeling for and removing the obstruction with his toes. He was the humblest of beings and he was charged with transgressive magic. If the Indian dread of contamination was at work, so was a wider taboo. The opposite of what is seen is obscene. The cesspit man embodied the return of the private and unsightly to public view.

Thus Tom's musings rolled about his mother. Was unrestrained shitting the symptom of a deeper unraveling? Language defines humans; and feces are like words, thought Tom sleepily, they both come out of bodies. It carried the irrational, illuminating force of an utterance heard in a dream.

His mind, slipping about, fastened on a terror at once sharper and more manageable. He was afraid his book would never be published. Its premises struck him as ridiculous, its conclusions absurd. He brought his knees to his chest and moaned. He had wasted years on work drained of movement and intelligence. A single sentence in James contained more brilliant breadth.

He moved in and out of sleep. Posner's somber mass was in the room; at cuff and collar, waxen flesh gleamed. What had prompted his visit? Tom cupped his groin, a morning reflex. The blind moved and a rectangle of light shuddered on his wall. An ogre lurching and groaning down the street brought him wide awake, to the accompaniment of running footsteps and slammed bins. Someone shouted, "That was my *good* yellow T-shirt, dickhead."

Now it seemed plain to Tom that Posner's insinuations were a hook baited with slime. *There are so many aspects to Nelly.* The prick'll say anything to get me away from her, show me he's on my side, thought Tom. It was for him, he decided, with a small luxurious shiver, that Posner had come.

But over breakfast he found himself gnawing at another scene. Some weeks earlier, he had arrived at the Preserve just as Rory was leaving with a friend. Consequently Tom entered the building unannounced.

The door to Nelly's studio stood open; a light shone within. Tom followed the corridor, past the fictitious curtained door, to her threshold, and there he remained. What he saw in those few moments would leave its print forever, although it was in no sense shocking or even irregular. Nelly was sprawled on a curious seat she favored, not long enough for a couch but wider than a chair: a *chaise courte* as it were, a distinctive, unyielding contrivance of lacy wood and hard velvet. Beside it loomed the monolith of Posner, his silver skull inclined toward Nelly. He might have been a doctor, listening in his dark jacket. He might have been a courtier attending the levee of a queen.

The tilt of Posner's head hid his face. But a halogen lamp held Nelly in its beam, and the watcher in the doorway saw that she was scratching the side of her head, one hand casually frenzied in her hair, her expression calm with an underglaze of satisfaction. The next instant her aspect altered, as her eyes turned toward the door. And Posner turned also, and the tableau broke up and recomposed itself like a pattern viewed in a child's optical toy.

Nevertheless, Tom was left with an impression. He had observed those two often enough, and in an assortment of contexts: had watched them argue, share a private quip, treat each other with unceremonious disdain. But the stillness of the scene in the studio lent it a force that animation obscured. It stripped sociability from Nelly and Posner's bond, which showed old and iron. That was scarcely a revelation. Yet Tom retained a sense of having come upon something uncovered.

There was surprise in the faces they turned to him; also a hint of alarm. Replaying the episode, freezing each of its elements, Tom could see that his silent apparition might well have been disquieting. And, the first moment past, the occupants of the room showed no sign of discomfiture. Nelly greeted him with her usual ease. Posner gave vent to the piping salutations of a large white bat.

Yet Tom couldn't excise the memory of their communion. It hadn't escaped him — although he had missed the precise moment — that in his presence Nelly had ceased clawing at her scalp. Yet that simple, unhindered act had struck no discord in the scene with Posner. Turning the incident over, Tom

kept reverting to Nelly's expression. The ruminant, private pleasure it projected was suggestive equally of the easing of an irritation or the maturation of a design. Whenever he felt he was
on the verge of decoding it, a shadow intruded on his vision:
Posner bent in command or supplication over that self-sufficient
face.

Tom gathered up what he needed for work and went into the
Monday morning street. Outside the blond-brick flats across the
way, a straggle-locked wizard in velvet slippers and belted gown
was keeping watch over a gathering of empty garbage bins. The
previous evening, Sunday parking had obliged Tom to leave his
car at the far end of the street. It stood beyond a row of thin
white trees belled with silver nuts. Rain and the advent of summer had conspired to put on concertos sustained by the blue
notes of hydrangeas. Behind low wooden fences, the native
thrived beside the exotic, there was a scribble of rose in a fig
tree, the tropics flourished about the Mediterranean. In these
unassuming plots, a nation realized its grandest dream.

   Tom thought, *To look at things in bloom, / Fifty springs are
little room.* But more than Osman would be granted.

IN SEPTEMBER, when spring came, the city had loosened into blossom. On Tom and Nelly's walks, the wind might have been honed
on a strop, but the scent of jasmine swelled from bluestone-

paved lanes designed for the passage of night soil. The football clamor from the MCG was louder now, attendance and passion waxing as the Grand Final approached. Giant toddlers could be seen queuing outside the stadium: wrapped in shapeless, fleecy garments, attached to polystyrene feeding cups.

Tom told Nelly about the headline he had seen soon after arriving in Australia: "Pies Murder Lions." For days it had caused him despair. He was a child at home in words. That too was to be taken from him in this place.

Enlightenment arrived with a conversation overheard while he hung about the locker room at recess, trying to appear solitary by choice. Magpies, Swans, Lions, Demons, were not, after all, escapees from a fabulous bestiary, but the names by which the city's football teams were affectionately known. So began the incident's passage into comedy, where it was now firmly lodged, the mocking of former terrors being one way in which we travesty our younger selves.

Nelly swooped at a gleam underfoot, then displayed the golden coin she had retrieved. It was astonishing how often she found money in the street, fifty cents, a five-dollar bill, a twenty.

Once she picked up a small plastic fish. "Remember when these first appeared? Four, five years ago?"

Suddenly she had begun seeing them everywhere, Nelly said. The little fish were multitudinous. They lay in gutters, on footpaths, in parking lots, on the beach, tiny fish with tapering faces. She had picked one up and unscrewed its red snout. Traces of dark liquid were visible in its scaled belly; its scent was briny. She wondered what purpose it might serve.

The riddle rolled in her mind, until at last she supposed that each fish had contained a single dose of newfangled fish food. Nelly pictured an aquarium and the bodies of fish darting to the thin, nutritive stream dispersing in their pond of glass.

It was a source of amazement to her, said Nelly, that so many of her fellow citizens had taken to keeping fish. She imagined people carrying home plastic bags of water and colored fish, and pausing to feed the fish on the way, and, inadvertently, because spellbound by iridescent life, letting the container of fish food drop.

Then one day she bought take-away sushi, opened the paper bag, and found a plastic fish inside, filled with soy sauce. "I felt like a total idiot."

But Tom was charmed by Nelly's theory of sober men and women deflected from duty by the antics of fish. And there was the fact that she had noticed the discarded containers in the first place. She had a tremendous capacity for appreciating the world's detail. Textures, colors, the casual disposition of forms, were striking to Nelly, extra-ordinary. To spend time with her was to wander through a cabinet of curiosities. She remarked on a shoe jutting *like a muzzle* from a hollow high in a tree. Tom realized that the objects she hoarded were symptomatic of a more profound desire: to drag moments of perception from the gray ooze of oblivion.

When he was an old man, he would still remember a table-tennis ball he had seen in Nelly's company, a sterile egg lying in the weedy rubbish under a nineteenth-century arch. He would remember a terrace opposite an elevated railway line where lit carriages shot past bedroom windows like a ribbon of film. He would remember Nelly in her red jacket on a bridge, entranced by a city assembled in its river.

. . . . .

She owned a selection of glass slides intended for a magic lantern, five colored views of European cities and one of Millet's *Gleaners*. From time to time Nelly would bring out a slide and suspend it in front of a window, so that a diminutive Grand Canal or Brandenburg Gate was a luminous presence in the Preserve. When the sun was at the right slant, a replica of the little cityscape would appear on the opposite wall, a light-painting that hovered there briefly, then vanished.

Tom asked why she didn't keep one or another of the slides up permanently. "You could just rotate them."

She told him about the Japanese practice of keeping a treasured object hidden away and taking it out to look at only now and then. "Because then it seems marvelous each time."

THE SELECTION COMMITTEE was waiting in Kevin Dodd's office when Tom arrived at work on Monday. He muttered an apology, nodded to Vernon, to their colleague Anthea Rendle.

A stranger sprang to his feet and advanced with a purposeful cry of "Tosh!" Tom's hand was seized; squeezed. "Tosh Lindgren. Human Resources. *Great* to meet you."

The center parting in Tosh's hair was a path in a cornfield. His cheeks had kept their boyhood roses above a corporate jaw.

"Right: let's progress this meeting." Professor Dodd coughed in the small, dry way he believed appropriate to his status. "A very satisfactory batch, I must say. There are applications here of the highest standard." He glanced around the room, hoping for dissent. "The highest standard," he repeated.

Kevin Dodd's career, unburdened by intellectual distinction, had attracted sizable research grants and the attention of vice-chancellors. No one could bring himself to read anything he had written, which counted greatly in his favor. Members of the committee responsible for appointing him had assured one another that Dodd was not faddish. His rival for the chair caused offense by being young, female, and brilliant. The dean described Dodd as a numbers man; this was taken up and repeated as praise.

The professor was a study in beige: hair, skin, suit, socks. ("His thoughts are leaking," explained Vernon.) Kevin Dodd believed sincerely, indeed passionately, in his own greatness. It followed that he had to be attracting exceptional talent to the department.

"This fellow from Rotterdam, for instance. An original mind. Thinks outside the box."

"Oh, but originality..." Vernon had taken off his spectacles and was twirling them. "Is that safe?"

"Original in the best sense," said Dodd with a touch of asperity. "Nothing untoward."

Tosh said, "Excuse me, Vernon. If I might make a suggestion?"

"Go ahead, Tosh."

"It's really easy to get sidetracked by subjective descriptors. Like original? That's why at HR we advocate focus on the selection criteria. So that we're thinking neutral instead of personal?"

"I hear what you're saying, Tosh. See, I've made a note: avoid personality, think HR."

Anthea said, "Miriam Beyer's the obvious choice. Gender studies, eighteenth-century, and she gave a great paper on scandal
fiction in Sydney last year. You remember, Vernon?"

"I do. Teutonic. But ironic."

"Excuse me —"

Tom said hastily, "I've got Miriam down, too. And the
Queensland guy — Sims."

"Sims? No way."

"You can't put Sims in front of students, Thomas. Not even
our students."

"Excuse —"

"Not at all right for this department. In the last analysis, it's
about the right kind of person."

"What's wrong with him? It's a pretty convincing application."

"Like for a start, he's got this totally anachronistic great-works
fetish. You know, courses on..." Anthea appeared to be groping after a dim recollection. "Things like Shakespeare," she said
finally.

"Think of a fog, Thomas. An industrious one."

"He chaired my paper on 'The Limits of Poetry.' Claimed I'd
run out of time when I'd barely started." Dodd said, "He was quite
impertinent about it. Definitely the wrong kind of person."

There followed minutes of satisfying gossip about the appli-
cant. (Vernon: "Of course, Sims swears he was only tucking in
his shirt.")

"Excuse me, Professor." For Tosh was not without heroism.
"If a candidate meets the selection criteria, HR would definitely
advocate interviewing him. Or her."

Cheered by the prospect of snubbing an enemy, Dodd was
no worse than avuncular. "At the end of the day, Tosh, it's more

than a matter of a level playing field. Or, to put it less poetically, we can't let mere regulations constrain our—"

"Originality?"

"Freedom. *Academic* freedom," said Dodd, with meaningful emphasis. He leaned back in his chair, knees wide. (Vernon: "It's the kind of crotch that follows you about the room.") On the superior side of the chasm separating academic from administrative mind, professorial teeth came together with a hard little snap.

"There's Helen, of course," said Anthea.

This entirely predictable turn provoked the usual spasm of disquiet. Vernon murmured, "Again?" But it lacked conviction.

There were two grave impediments to Helen Neill's career: she was a conscientious, gifted teacher, and she was bringing up two young children on her own. Years after enrolling in a Ph.D. program, she had yet to complete her thesis. Her scholarship had long run out. She lived on the contract teaching that came her way from tenured staff using research grants to buy themselves out of classroom hours and marking. Their careers prospered; hers did not.

Collective guilt about Helen ran high. It was assuaged by interviewing her for every entry-level lectureship that came up in the department. Afterward, Anthea would take her out to lunch and explain that the panel had been compelled to appoint a candidate with publications and a doctoral degree.

"She's made excellent progress recently." Anthea spoke in the bright, determined tone she reserved for Helen. "I'm sure she'll have a complete draft by the end of summer." It was a topic on which she was a practiced liar.

There hung in her colleagues' minds an image of Helen Neill:

shaggy, overweight, fatally mild. She interviewed badly, lacking sleep and the necessary confidence in her genius.

"We're not obliged to interview her," said Dodd. *"Applicants must have completed a doctoral degree.* There's your bottom line. No reason to start shifting the goalposts."

"Excuse me —"

"It would be grossly inconsiderate not to interview her. Tom? Vernon?"

Tosh said in a rush, "Within context-sensitive parameters, HR strongly advises against unsuccessing in-house candidates." His hair had shaken free in two shining wings. He was an angel who did not fear to tread.

Kevin Dodd would have done very well as a goldfish; it was something about the set of his ears. "Well, if we're pushing the envelope... The young English lass, what's her name now — Felton?"

Tom looked up. Rebecca Finton was the D.Phil. on his list.

"Becky Finton, that's it. She was at the Modern Times conference in Zurich." Dodd cleared his throat. "Very, ah, striking."

Vernon angled his pad toward Tom. "SHAGADELIC! PHWOAR!!"

The meeting went on being progressed.

Anthea held the lift for him. "Can you *believe* Kevin?" She thrust out her lower lip and blew a little puff of air upward. The springy red curls on her forehead shook.

A poster beside them warned of a graduate forum on "Performing Masculinity." *Bruce Lee's body, taught with fury...*

Anthea said, "It's OK for you to laugh. That's one of my students." Then she laughed anyway. "Lunch?"

"Love to, but I've got to dash."

The door pinged open. "We're having a party. I'll e-mail you."
Thirty seconds later she called, "Bring your girlfriend."

When he turned, she was smiling. "So it's true."

He thought, then said, "You've been talking to Esther."

"Three degrees of separation in this town, Tommo."

"Really, that many?"

That Nelly and he were coupled in gossip pleased him. He
walked to the parking lot through light strokes of rain. From the
dome of an umbrella going the other way a voice said, "Yeah, but
will I like philosophy?"

In talk at least he lay enlaced with Nelly. Tom's fingers curved
in his pocket, assuming the round weight of her breast.

On the way to the Preserve, his mood darkened. The premonition of failure returned and spread its wings. Stuck in traffic he
stared past his wipers, seeing his book unpublished, his career
stagnating. The pursuit of knowledge: as a young man he had
thought it honorable, a twentieth-century way to be good.

His faith had wilted when exposed to departmental realpoli-
tik, had shriveled before the academy's wholehearted adoption
of corporate values and the pursuit of profit over larger aims. Yet
a trace of his original reverence had endured, as a vial of scent
perfumes a drawer long after the last subtle drops have evapo-
rated. The constant element in a life is usually the product of
illusion, dreams directing history with surer cunning than any
charter. *Perfection of the life, or of the work.* Tom had never
hesitated, never imagined he might botch both.

There came to him, with graphic intensity, a memory from
his first year of teaching. Lecturing on *Dubliners,* he had looked

up from his notes and seen a student slip from the theater, silhouetted against a bright oblong before the door swung shut behind her. Tom found himself controlling an impulse to shout encouragement, urging her to flee while there was time. Only weeks earlier his appointment had filled him with elation. Now he gripped the lectern and saw the track on which his days would run.

He pressed the button that lowered the car window. Despite the gloom, the air no longer pinched. The mild, rainy afternoon, scented with exhaust, might have been Indian. Another self flickered at the edge of Tom's vision: short-sleeved, subtitled in Hindi. He climbed a grimy stairway, through waftings of urine and mustard seed. On a bus bulging with bodies, he reached past layers of hands that matched his own.

For a period in Tom's adolescence this parallel life had been very real to him. He could still call up a repertoire of scenes rehearsed to perfection. They were not nostalgic, not a revisiting of childish haunts, but sustained visions of an Indian existence. Their function was propitiatory. If he set himself to imagine an Indian life, he would not be returned to one. This bargain with fate involved dropping down the social scale, so that every element of his fictional existence — the clothes he wore, the food he ate, the language he spoke — was borrowed from lives remote from his own. Thus, at the sight of a Friday night treat of fish and chips, Tom pictured himself squatting over a tin plate of spiced lentils. He strolled between the laden shelves of a supermarket while serving glasses of germ-ridden water in a squalid tea shop.

Then, quite abruptly, he had abandoned these dreamy designs. If an inattentive moment found him in their thrall, he would break free through an effort of will. He told himself the practice was frivolous, incommensurate with the gravity of his fifteen years. What he feared, in truth, was more insidious. His life in Australia was rendered superficial by the everyday density of his inventions. Beside his hardy Indian familiar, he appeared cursory and surplus. Even now, after the passage of so many seasons, Tom had no wish to prolong their encounter.

The rain had thinned. There were bundles of light above the river. Tom thought of the life he had led, and the life he had missed, and how he would never see his vague teenage face recycled in a child. A message loomed against the sky: *The More You Spend, the More You Earn;* and Tom, picturing his life, saw the impress left by feet on a beach, as if what mattered had walked away.

At the Preserve, Nelly was putting clothes into a bag for the country. When she got into the car, Tom noticed a wide black band of insulating tape stuck across the toe of her left boot.

They talked about Osman. Nelly turned a pink knitted hat in her hands.

On the freeway, she told Tom she had another piece of bad news. The Preserve had sold at auction in May, but the developers had overstretched their resources. Work on the building had been postponed, and Nelly allowed to stay, for twelve months, she had been assured. But a letter had arrived that morning giving her until the end of January to move out. "I've seen the plans. They're going to squish three apartments onto each floor and put a penthouse on the roof." She folded her hat down the middle, and said, "I'm trying to think of it as a kind of collage. The uses and reuses of a building."

"Where will you go?"

"Brendon's mentioned some place in Footscray we could share. But I don't think he's planning too far ahead right now."

Then she said, "There's a six-month artist's residency in Kyoto coming up. Starting next September."

Kilometers streamed past. Tom said, "That sounds pretty exciting."

"There'll be stacks of people after it. But some guy Carson knows on the board says my chances are good."

In the mid-1990s, Nelly had begun showing photographs of wooden printer's trays of the kind once used to store metal type in compartments of different sizes. She would paint the sides of her trays to resemble elaborate carving. Within these frames, some compartments were left empty; others held an object or image. Tom studied a tray whose sumptuous recesses had been lined with the royal blue velvet of jeweler's cases. Nestled within were banal found objects, one to a niche in reverent display: a pineapple-topped swizzle stick, a barrette, a condom wrapper, two dead matches, a doll's dismembered arm. These items deposited by the human tide passing through its streets bore witness to the city's energy and erosion. Tom was reminded also of the fascination detritus holds for the very young, of the way a small child will pass over a costly toy in favor of absorbed play with bottle tops or a rag or the foil from a toffee, investing the valueless things of the world with joy.

. . . . . .

Nelly was given to recycling images: inserting them into new contexts, reproducing them on different scales. Tom noticed that she kept returning to the skipping girl figure. He came across a series in which a painting of the neon sign had been photographed, then smeared while the paint was still wet, photographed again, smeared again, and so on. The image disintegrated over five paintings, the last showing only billows of gorgeous, violet-tinged reds worthy of Venice. Tom pictured Nelly working with swift concentration, her photographer beside her, stepping back from her canvas with wet red hands.

In a museum's online collection he found a photo of a painted child skipping on the wall of a factory, encircled by the caption "Skipping Girl Pure Malt Vinegar." Nelly had montaged this old black-and-white image over a contemporary streetscape, so that while the painted child remained stranded in two dimensions, her metal twin rose airily above her in the sky.

Tom knew the advertising sign of old. His uncle had pointed it out, on a sightseeing evening drive, when the Loxleys first came to Australia; the sign was one of Tom's earliest memories of the city. The skipping girl wore a scarlet bolero over a snowy blouse, with white socks and strapped black shoes. A neon rope lit up in alternation above her head and at her feet to simulate movement. Her red skirt flared like a night-blooming poppy.

Modern magic was at hand: Tom Googled the sign. He learned that it dated from 1936: the city's first animated neon sign, calculated to imbue dull vinegar with the romance of novelty. Over time it had deteriorated, been dismantled and replaced; the sign he knew as a child was that copy.

When the vinegar factory relocated to a different suburb, the skipping girl was left behind. By then neon was no longer glamorous, no longer a sign of the times. Besides, the skipping girl had become a landmark. There was a local outcry at the suggestion that she might be moved. Eventually, as buildings were demolished and the streetscape altered, she was shifted along the road, to a different rooftop. There she froze in a deathly sleep. It had been years now since her turning rope had lit up the night sky. She had entered the memory of a generation as a spellbound red figure.

Tom could remember the contrary emotions his first encounter with the sign had brought. His instinctive surge of pleasure at the magical sight quickly turned queasy. The big red child's mimicry of the human seemed tainted with malevolence. The boy twisting around in the backseat of the car for a last glimpse of her was reminded of the long, dim mirrors of India that rippled with secret being, objects that shared her strangeness, denizens of a zone somewhere between artifice and life. She called up a personage who had terrified Tom when he was very young, the tall red Scissorman who comes to little boys who suck their thumbs.

There was this too: the sign continued the kingdom of things into the sky. Fresh from a country where giant cutouts and logos and billboards were still rare, Tom was subject to a sentiment he was too young to articulate: that the skipping girl's presence violated something that should have been inviolable. It was a perception that would dim over time, as he grew accustomed, like everyone else in the city, to the invasion of the sky by commerce. Now tiny silver planes routinely inscribed brand names on the atmosphere, as if the blue air itself were a must-have accessory. People stepping out of their houses in the morning lifted up their eyes to hot-air balloons emblazoned with trademarks, hanging from heaven like Christmas tree baubles.

Nelly had a printer's tray called *Own Your Own* that displayed an identical vinegar label, each featuring a skipping girl, in every niche. Tom studied a color reproduction of the construction in *Art & Australia*. There was a depressing hint of the cage and the production line about the imprisoned, endlessly reiterated figure. It was reinforced by the fine white-painted wire mesh fastened down a vertical line of compartments. But closer examination revealed that in all but two recesses, a tiny box camera had been painted in at the girl's feet. Its viewfinder faced out, suggesting that it was for her use.

Tom supposed it was Nelly's way of pointing out that the skipping girl had floated free. In acquiring mythic status she had become more and less than the product she embodied: a servant of the market who exceeded the commodity that bore her name. Once an emblem of modernity, she had fallen out of fashion and into a life of her own.

He walked up to Victoria Street one evening while the light still held, past a glass-walled gym where scantily clad bodies had the stripped look of fish. It was the first time in years he had scrutinized the skipping girl sign. He saw that the building on which it perched had been converted into offices and apartments. A woman came jogging out of the lobby, murmuring "Beat it!" as she adjusted her earphones.

Gazing up at the red figure with a piece of moon at its back, Tom felt his old foreboding flicker. He had just remembered that the skipping girl was double-sided. From the pinnacle of a metal

frame, she stared along the street in a two-faced vigil. Her eeri-
ness was immanent. Nelly's image-making merely drew on that
quality and intensified it.

"A Prime Cut," declared the real estate board adorned with
the picture of a bull in front of a disused warehouse. "You are
everywhere," said the vertical scrawl on a telephone pole beside
it. Across the road, a multistory shopping center was rising from a
hole in the earth. With its empty window sockets and fragmentary
stairs, it might have been archaeological; a ruin from the future.

THE TREMOR usually settled after breakfast, but that morning Iris's
hands went on shaking. She jabbed and jabbed at the remote. It
took both hands to raise it to chest level and aim it at the set,
which made finding the right button awkward.

Iris sat before grainy footage of heads bobbing in water, her
mind taking its own direction. An incident from her department
store years swam up to meet her. She had been on her way to
Hosiery one lunch hour when she heard her name. A stranger
stood in her path, a tremulous form in a checked cap and navy
jacket. "Iris!" he said again. "I say, it *is* Iris, isn't it?" He peered
at her; she saw a brick-red pear packed with teeth. "Frank Saunders." Iris smiled in propitiation, certain he was one of Audrey's
perverts. He said, "We met in India. I was in the Hussars with
Larry Fitch."

What struck Iris was the corrugated column rising from his

collar. The image was overlaid by another, a muscled neck with a little scar at the base. Her hand went to the stranded gilt at her throat.

Saunders was saying, "I say, Iris, you do look tremendously well."

He swayed closer. Stale sweat and fresh beer muddled the fragrant department store air. An officer who gave off an odor of caramel took Iris in his arms; behind his shoulder she glimpsed a presence, sandy hair, a Fair Isle pullover. It was as if a sideboard or a floor lamp should come to life and address her. "Do you remember...?" began Saunders, and Iris said, "No." She said, "My name is Mrs. Arthur Loxley. I don't know you from Adam." In her wake, he called, "I say, I say..."

Iris shook in her chair, and loud farts rolled from her. She was blocked up again. Once she could have turned to milk of magnesia. Lately, however, even a half dose mitigated relief with disaster.

When you could no longer manage the toilet: that was when they put you in a home.

She had reached the age where choice is synonymous with fear. Iris was afraid, in this matter, of an alliance between Tom and Audrey, an ancient animal mistrust of the strong and the young.

She feared soiling herself. She feared the consequences, impressed on her at an early age, of irregularity. Sebastian de Souza had locked himself in the lavatory every morning at twenty-five minutes past seven and remained there until he had extruded a well-formed stool. His wife and child followed him in turn. Thankfully there was a good strong flush, although the slit-windowed cabinet remained pregnant with odors. The implications of the ritual far exceeded hygiene. To fail the daily rendezvous was to fall short of a moral standard. Diarrhea was heathenish; constipation warned of willfulness. If the flesh was disobedient, the spirit was base. Bodies that lacked discipline required control.

Iris's son said, "Stop worrying, Ma." He said it often, with varying degrees of irritation. But Iris's thoughts leaped and raced, skittish with fear.

She worried about Tommy: her clever son without wife or child, his life an accumulation of unwritten pages. She feared he would meet a modern, untimely death: a plane dropping from the clouds, a madman at a service station swiveling a gun. She feared the loneliness that was accruing for his old age.

As a toddler, he had learned to use his china pot only to reject it. The household entered a phase during which a telltale reek would lead Iris to a little mound deposited behind an armchair or under a table. Once a glistening serpent lay coiled inside one of her shoes. The child was visibly excited by these incidents, gleeful even while scolded.

Iris's father detected depravity and counseled thrashing. "Children are animals. The two things they understand are food and pain." It was clear that Tommy knew what was required of him, yet he refused to conform. Iris's anxiety mounted. Arthur advised her to let the boy be, saying he would outgrow the problem. It was no more than his wife expected. That from the sensible English multitude she had managed to acquire a specimen devoid of sense had long been all too plain to her.

With time and observation, she saw that her son's offense had the aspect of a game. If anyone other than Iris happened upon his feces, the child's pleasure was mixed with agitation. But when the discovery fell to her, he chuckled and whooped. Eventually she understood. She had schooled him herself in the use of his pot, praising him as he strained to please her. The habit acquired, she had left him alone; now, when he moved his bowels a servant bore away the aromatic receptacle and returned it scoured. And so the child's ingenuity had contrived a means of continuing to make her the present of his stools.

The foundation of a pattern was laid. The mother fretted; the son provided for her. What neither grasped was that worry, too, might be a form of giving. As Iris aged, her anxieties multiplied to encompass the trivial and the sublime, rational eventuality and wild hypothesis, lost keys, toothache, ATMs, road accidents, seizures, what people would think, the years that had elapsed since her last confession, running out of sugar. To voice anxiety was to risk her son's disapproval. At the same time, he might allay apprehension: find her key, go to the ATM in her place, assure her that the brakes wouldn't fail. Her worrying empowered him. That was part of its value to her.

There was also this: worry, eating away at the present, made room for the future. "For God's sake, Ma: it'll never happen." Thus Tom missed the point. Because worrying was a way of looking forward to something. That it might be a calamity was irrelevant. Fear was Iris's mechanism for allotting herself time. It was a crafty maneuver. She was old and ill and poor. Fear was her best hope.

After Saunders, Iris shunned Hosiery, forgoing her staff discount to buy her tights in a rival establishment. She told no one what had happened. But one morning, years after the encounter, she found herself speaking of it to her son.

Tom pressed for details. At once Iris ended the conversation:

THE LOST DOG   231

"What's the use?" It was her standard response whenever he asked about the years before her marriage.

Fragments of knowledge — photographs, dates, conversations half-heard when he was young — formed a patchwork in Tom's mind. His mother, a beautiful girl, had married late. The strange word *jilted* had snared his attention in childhood. Now he assumed that Iris had run into the suitor who had once betrayed her. He had lately met the woman he would marry, was himself in love. It rendered him susceptible to romantic explanation.

He looked at the lipstick escaping in fine red threads from his mother's mouth; the skin below her chin hung pleated. His own flesh was replete, satiny with consummation. He thought, Nobody touches her. He thought, No wonder she doesn't want to dwell on the past.

How we imagine another person reveals the limits of our understanding. Tom was then not yet thirty. He could not have guessed that Iris, surrounded by artificial limbs encased in nylon, would see Saunders and think, Who's that old man? It was not the past she had recoiled from in their encounter but the future.

Fear had this advantage too: it could sidle up to the future by wiles. There was no need to look what was waiting in the face.

THE WEEKS in 1965 when Indian tanks rolled to within three miles of Lahore had left no impression on the child Tom's mind.

Six years passed in relative peace; then, with Indian troops already moving to support bloodied Dacca, Pakistan declared war on its sibling.

It so happened that Tom had recently read the diary of Anne Frank. With the formalization of hostilities, he sensed the meeting of life and literature. He was a child built by books, and his excitement was boundless.

He couldn't quite settle on his part in the conflict: would he shelter Hindus when Pakistan invaded? To this end, he searched the house for secret places, paying particular attention to cupboards. There was the equally thrilling possibility that he himself would be forced into hiding. He reviewed the Muslim boys he knew: he counted no special friends among them, but trusted that in time the rules of plot would reveal one. What was certain, in any case, was that his role would be heroic. He passed agreeable hours trailing a stick in the dirt, his lips moving soundlessly, imagining the raids he would conduct under cover of night. Sometimes he swung his arms and counted his strides, shouting out numbers as if they were blasphemies. A spindly twig or leaf might enrage him by appearing defenseless, and he would strike it to the ground. His dreams of pursuit and daring were broken into now and then by fear; but like the delicious shiver provoked by a tale of ghosts, it was merely his body's involuntary tribute to art.

This happy state lasted a scant fortnight. Then the war was over, and in the midst of national jubilation Tom tasted the melancholy of those who wake from visions. His reflection in the mirror appeared to have shrunk. For a glorious interval, he had been larger than life. It was his first, dim perception of the power of narrative: war, like love, raising its accomplices to the status of figures in a known story.

. . . . . .

Tom knew that a lucky country was one where history happened to other people. For thirty years after his marginal involvement in its adventure, he had found a place in which to take cover from its reach.

On the September night when he stood in a bar with Nelly watching towers sink to their knees, the fear he felt was an acute version of a child's alarm as the seeker in a hiding game draws near. He had always known it was only a matter of time before it happened. Living in Australia was like being a student at a party that went on and on; he didn't want it to end but couldn't suppress the knowledge that exams were approaching.

Tom Loxley wished what anyone might: that a pleasant life should go on being pleasant. He wished for continuity. He wished for the orderly progression of events. He wished, that is to say, for an end to history. It was incompatible with modern life. It raged over benighted continents and there it should have stayed, ripping up sites already littered with its debris. What was unnerving was the juxtaposition of that ancient face with Power-Point and watercoolers, its eruption in nylon-carpeted cubicles where people were sneaking a look at stuff on eBay.

It was as if the events of that year had set out to demonstrate that history could not be confined to historical places. In the same spring as the destruction of the towers, boats making their way to Australia foundered on the treachery of currents and destiny. People looking for sanctuary drowned. They might have been found; they might have been saved. But what prevailed was the protection of a line drawn in the water.

Night after night, images of the refugees appeared. Tom saw

death flicker in the furtive glow of TV and knew the guilty rage of those who have crossed to safety. Time toppled like a wave. He was a falling thing, spiraling down to wait forever in a room as blue as an ocean. He felt the convergence of public and private dread.

Buried deep in Australian memories was the knowledge that strangers had once sailed to these shores and destroyed what they found. How could that nightmare be remembered? How could it be unselfishly forgotten? A trauma that had never been laid to rest, it went on disturbing a nation's dreams. In the rejection of the latest newcomers, Tom glimpsed the past convulsing like a faulty film. It was a confession coded as a denial. It was as if a fiend had paused in its ravaging to cover its face and howl.

The images he saw on TV brought him out in goose bumps: fear writing its name on his flesh. And since the frightened are often frightening, the pictures on his screen made him grimace and distorted his face.

Bodies flashed up constantly in those weeks: broken, burned, fished lifeless from the sea. He thrust at them with his remote, willing them to disappear. But it was as if the images were imprinted on his retina. They affected everything he saw. In ordinary streets the air turned red with callistemons. Tiny corpses appeared on pavements, nestlings as naked and strange as Martians.

A Rollerblader sped past Tom, fleeing as if from catastrophe; the white stare of the baby strapped to his back following like a curse. A lunatic in flawless linen strode up and down a supermarket aisle, gesticulating, shouting, "What do you mean by a small pumpkin?" Then Tom noticed the wire running into her pocket from her ear.

A municipal collection of unwanted household goods pro-

duced surreal assemblages on footpaths. Tom's route to a protest about the war in Afghanistan took him through dystopian
chambers furnished with soiled carpet squares and disembow-
eled futons. He passed an orange divan stripped of cushions, collapsed vacuum cleaners, torn window screens, a backless TV. A
bicycle wheel leaned against a birdcage. Rusty barbecues might
have strayed from a torturer's repertoire. There were contrap-
tions for improving muscle tone, computer keyboards fanned in a
magazine rack, plastic flowerpots packed with gray earth. It was
like leafing through snapshots of a civilization's unconscious.

Spring came apart under a weight of rain, death-laden spring.
Fear put out live shoots in Tom. Instantly identifiable as foreign
matter, he feared being labeled waste. He feared expulsion from
the body of the nation.

IN THE HILLS, the mild city day was cold and wild. The rain arrived
soon after Tom and Nelly, herding them back to the house, putting an end to their search.

Nelly's pink hat lay on a chair, misty beads tangling its fine
fibers. She built up the fire while Tom set about preparing a
meal. Rain slashed leaves, clawed at the walls. The paddocks
darkened under their leaking roof.

Tom wound spaghetti around his fork, then rested it on his plate.
The wind continued its assault on the trees, pulling their hair. To

think of the dog without shelter in this weather was unbearable. Tom rose, crossed to the window, and drew down the blind.

Nelly had pushed her plate aside and was sketching on the back of one of his flyers. "Look." He saw cross-hatching on a penciled map. "That's where we were today. You can mark where you searched last week. But in any case we'll cover it all, bit by bit."

Approximate, not to scale, unscientific. He sat at the table, and said, "I shouldn't have dragged you up here. I'm sorry."

She was adding to her map: an arrow pointing to the house, the tracks, a compass rose.

"If he's out there, how could he have survived? This rain, this cold," Tom went on.

"The rain'll keep him going. A dog can live three weeks without food. Three days without water."

Her mulish cheer irritated Tom. He sneezed. Once, twice.

Nelly told him that when the house was first built, the interior walls had been covered in burlap pasted over with layers of newspaper. In the tiny second bedroom Tom had previously glanced into but not entered, Atwood's architect had preserved a section of the original decor. Nelly pointed out pages from Christmas color supplements that had been included in the final paper coating. When the house was new, these illustrations must have brought the opulence of icons to the room. Eighty years later, vague figures showed here and there on the wall, faded divas and emperors emerging from a brownish nicotine haze. "They used to spook Rory. He wouldn't sleep in here when he was a kid."

Tom was thinking of the delight colored pictures had once

brought, before the proliferation of images. He remembered a parcel of foodstuffs that had arrived from England when he was five or six. A spoonful of glowing red jam from a tin wrapped in bright scenery: a gift from another world.

They were drinking wine, their socked feet outstretched toward the fire. The planked floor hadn't been polished in years. But it was a living thing by firelight, dark spots swirling on a lemony pelt.

Tom said, fishing, "Denise asked after you the other day."

"Been chatting to her, have you?" Nelly lit a cigarette.

"What?"

She exhaled.

"What?"

"There was all this stuff in the papers when Felix disappeared, about us arguing, things like that." Nelly said, "They got a lot of it from Denise. It's sort of hard to forget."

"Why'd she do that?"

Nelly stared into the fire.

"Was she jealous? I mean, I guessed there was something between her and Felix, the way she's talked about him." Tom could feel his mind laboring, thickened with tiredness.

Nelly giggled. It went on too long. "Sorry," she said eventually. "It's not funny, really. But the idea of Felix and Denise."

When she had dropped what was left of her cigarette into the fire, she said, "Look, I was the one she had a crush on."

"You know how you feel things so much then? When you're seventeen, eighteen?"

Tom said, "I remember."

"We had this party here, loads of people came up, I think it was Australia Day. The year Felix went missing." Nelly shrugged. "Denise had too much champagne, I guess. Like everyone else."

"What happened?"

"Nothing." She said, "It's hard to get over. When you come out with what you feel, and you get nowhere." After a little while: "There was all this other stuff going on in my life at the time. I couldn't really be bothered with Denise. She was just sort of irrelevant."

"Ouch."

"Exactly."

Tom permitted himself a brief fantasy of abstracting some small, odorous item of Nelly's clothing — a sock, the rosy hat. He thought of Herrick delicately sniffing his mistress, declaring that her "*hands, and thighs, and legs are all / Richly aromatical.*"

He glanced covertly at Nelly sitting there beside him on the couch enmeshed in the detail of living: examining a chipped thumbnail, nibbling it, frowning at the result. It was an effort to reconcile the woman he knew, sunk in dailiness, with the Nelly who had existed so thoroughly in the larger-than-life events of Atwood's disappearance.

There was a girl who had been around at parties and clubs when Tom was twenty. She was no older, but seemed stereoscopic: she had starred in a film that had won a prize; her face, smilingly assured below a rakish hat, gazed out from billboards. Then she vanished, summoned by Berlin or LA, and Tom forgot her, until the day, years later, when he and his wife bought a pair of sheets in a department store. On the down escalator, Karen said, "You didn't notice, did you? That was Jo Hutton who served us."

For days Tom was unable to evict her from his thoughts, the saleswoman he had barely noticed as she bleated of thread counts; within minutes of turning away, he would have failed to recognize her if she had materialized before him. While the transaction was being processed, he had grumbled casually to his wife about the time their train had spent in the Jolimont shunting yards before delivering them to Flinders Street Station. The saleswoman looked up: "The exact same thing happened to me this morning. Doesn't it drive you mad?" Then she confided that this was her last day at the city store: she had been transferred to a branch in the suburbs. "I live a five-minute drive away. I can't wait to be shot of public transport." She handed Tom a pen and a credit card slip and shook the two gold bangles on her wrist as he signed: a small, unconscious expression of glee at her victory over time and the railways.

Tom tried to picture the girl in the tilted fedora pausing long enough to fret about train timetables but found the challenge too strenuous.

Now, sitting with Nelly in the drafty kitchen, he thought it was an error to equate authenticity with even tones. Existence was inseparable from tragedy and adventure, horror and romance; realism's quiet hue derived from a blend of dramatic elements, as a child pressing together bright strands of plasticine creates a drab sphere.

Thus Tom reasoned; but some vital component of the case continued to elude him. That *other Nelly* remained a stranger to this one, just as he had not succeeded in matching the two Jo Huttons with each other. The images were not quite congruent, and this was as disconcerting as if a tracing were to lift away from its original and show its own distinctive form.

......

She said, "I'll sleep here," patting the couch.

"No need." To spell it out, Tom might have added. Instead: "I can bunk down in the small room."

"It's warmer here. I prefer it."

Three feet of corded upholstery can assume the dimensions of a continent. Wind tugged at the house. A log shifted and collapsed on the fire.

TUESDAY

It was still raining on Tuesday morning. Nelly turned left onto the ridge road, away from the coast. She had offered to drive, saying she knew the roads better than Tom did.

They meandered about the valley, Nelly steering smoothly around its curves. She had an affinity with engines. Tom recalled seeing her outside the Preserve, her round hands busy with a fan belt under the hood of Yelena's Beetle. The dog had been by his side that afternoon. It seemed a long time ago.

A cemetery with iron gates came into view. Tom thought of the grinning dead in their filthy sheets. On waking he had found a sentence in his mind: *Today it is a week.* He felt the force of it again now, the days piling up, each a fresh clod tamped down over hope. A date over which so many Novembers had flowed without interruption had become an anniversary. Time was thickening around it. He thought of it waiting for him each year.

There was the warm, companionable space of the car. Beyond it, sodden pastures and the sky. Tom scuttled between inside and outside, leaving rain-spotted flyers in mailboxes; every third or fourth farm used a milk can.

It was sharp, slanted rain, a shower of arrows loosed by an archaic battalion.

There were bursts of untuneful humming from Nelly. Then

she remarked on the gleam that potatoes have when freshly dug from the earth.

There would come a day, thought Tom, when he looked back on this one and was envious: because she was there, beside him. His fears for the dog, the news about Osman, everything that at present loomed large, would dwindle to a speck on memory's horizon. What remained would be the floodlit, ecstatic fact of her presence.

At least he had a photograph of her. Mogs, having turned up at the Preserve in Posner's retinue one evening, in due course demonstrated a Japanese camera — "*Isn't* it brilliant!" — that shot out Polaroids no larger than a stamp. The results passed from hand to hand. It was easy to palm the image Tom wanted: Nelly turning toward the camera, snapped before her expression could settle. There was an edge of paisley sleeve in the foreground. Tom thought it belonged to Osman but wasn't sure.

He would have liked to carry the miniature in his wallet but feared it being seen. Instead he kept it in a drawer, slotted between the pages of a square-ruled notebook. It was a form of insurance, a material vestige of Nelly to set against the fickleness of memory. He saw himself in years to come, extracting it from the dimness of his desk. Projecting himself through time, he discovered that he was already moved, affected in advance by that trace of her presence caught in waves of light.

None of it would come to pass. In one of those enigmatic conjuring tricks effected by objects, the Polaroid would vanish within a few months. Tom would turn out his desk, grasp the notebook by its spine and shake, thumb its pages a hundred times. But one day, when years had passed and his need had long withered, he would open a book and discover the photograph within it.

What was strange was that this volume, the collected poems of Christina Rossetti, belonged to his wife. Tom had his own copy somewhere, but this one, a handsome, jacketed edition, was hers. He checked the flyleaf to make sure: *For Becky, Happy Christmas 1992, Love always, Granny.*

On a forested back road, there was a flash of fur in the bush. Nelly said, "Felix hit a wallaby once, have I said?"

Tom shook his head.

"There was nothing he could've done. It came flying out when he was taking that curve near Jack's gate. It wasn't dead. We just stood there, looking at its eyes, with Rory bawling in the car. I went to get Jack, but he was out in the paddocks. So I left Rory with Denise's mum, and Denise came back with me, and put Jack's gun against the wallaby's head, and shot it. This tall, skinny teenager, right, and so *collected.* We go back to the farm, and next thing she's handing 'round these pumpkin scones she's just baked."

Nelly said, "She was sort of amazing in those days, Denise."

They bought coffee from a shop that served a deserted campsite. Nelly drove on to a spot where they could pull off the road. Mountain ash rose before them, superb and desolate. The forest was chilling in the way of ancient landscapes, evoking human insignificance. It suggested eons; vegetable time. This was how the planet had looked before the advent of their kind.

Riddled with time, it was a scene easily emptied of history. The Edenic new world: an image to set against European sophistication and decadence. Tom was unable to contemplate it with equanimity. He said something along these lines to Nelly.

"Yeah, I know what you mean." She lowered her window; lit

one of her spiced cigarettes. "The whole wilderness thing's so loaded in this country. Landscape without figures: we don't like thinking how that came about."

It was not that Tom disagreed. But the forest disturbed him in a way that far exceeded the merely historical. It was wild and latent and old. It addressed an aspect of his nature that had endured, whatever victories cultivation knew elsewhere.

Clove-scented smoke rolled about. Nelly, shooing it away, said she had cut back to five cigarettes a day. "But I've got to give them up, really. They're hardly the best thing for migraine."

"Is that what they are, your headaches?"

She didn't reply at once. Then she glanced at Tom sideways. "I'm painting again."

"Yeah? That's great."

"I seem to get ill more when I'm working. That's one reason I put off starting." Nelly said, "I know a headache's on the way when I start seeing these shapes like doughnuts. With light where the hole should be." Her fingers fluttered beside her left eye. "Also I get these, like, flickers of gold. And the air goes sort of brittle. Like tiny glass wings."

Something about the gesture, these remarks, the way her eyes slipped away. For a moment, it was as if a stranger had entered the car and was sitting beside Tom. A prickle ran over his scalp.

On their way back, as they were passing a cluster of naked sheep, Nelly said, "When Jack's father was a child, none of this land had been cleared. It was still one of the wonders of the world."

Later still: "They have such small arms. Wallabies."

∴∴∴∴∴∴∴∴∴∴∴∴∴∴∴∴∴∴∴∴∴∴∴∴∴∴∴∴∴∴∴∴∴∴∴∴∴

ON A WINDY BLUE EVENING in October, when they were walking past a broad-fronted house near Tom's flat, Nelly spoke of the elderly immigrant who had lived there. He had sold the house and returned to Greece so that his life might loop to a close as it had begun, on a rock in the Aegean.

On another occasion, she halted before a rickety cottage. "That's Dulcie's place. She's in a home now. She used to have these azaleas on her verandah that she watered every morning from a china hot-water bottle."

Nelly talked of the children who had once overflowed this hushed neighborhood. "Even when I first moved to the Preserve, you still saw kids all over the place, walking to school, playing cricket in the street. They've gone now. People with children can't afford to live here anymore."

There was an evening when she stopped in front of a town house. "See that driveway? There used to be freesias there, the kind with the fabulous smell, before they pulled the old place down. I think of them every spring, trying to push through the concrete. Like a hundred little murders."

Talk like this ran counter to Tom's sense of his surroundings. The city as he experienced it was glassily new. That was its allure. In Mangalore, when he walked down a street, his neighbors had beheld Sebastian who begat Iris who begat Thomas. He trailed genealogies. The air around him swarmed with incident and knowledge, faces that had turned to bone shimmered at his shoulder. In Australia, he was free-floating. Architecture expressed the difference in material form, the bricks and beaten earth of childhood exchanged for superstructures of glass and airy steel. At night they turned into giant motherboards, alive with circuitry: advance screenings of the electronic future.

Nelly's version of the city was a palimpsest. A ruin. It was layered like memory. Tom thought of history mummified and dismembered in the official memorials scattered through the streets and of how effortlessly Nelly conjured the living slither of time.

She pointed to the digital clock perched on the Nylex Plastics sign, and said that as a child on family outings she had watched eagerly for it to appear on the skyline. "I wanted to be the first one in the car to read out the time."

Tom had noticed that the clock, glittering on top of the Cremorne silos, turned up now and then in her work. He was affected by Nelly's remark, recalling the potency of urban signs in his own childhood. He could remember the streaming, neon enchantment of an advertisement for Bata shoes that had flashed out at intervals on the side of a building in Mangalore: the utter blackness he feared might last forever, the thrill as each bright letter took shape again, the twinkling, magical whole.

Then there was "Stick No Bills." Learning to read, he had deciphered it as "Strike on Bells," had felt intense satisfaction whenever he saw the stenciled exhortation. It spoke to him of solemn undertakings and powerful, invisible allies, the kind of message in which fairy tales abound: direct yet riddling, a test of resourcefulness.

The Nylex clock drew him closer in spirit to that small girl peering through a car window. At the same time, Nelly's remark underlined one of their essential differences. To possess a city fully, it is necessary to have known it as a child, for children bring their private cartographies to the mapping of public spaces. The chart of Tom's secret emblems was differently plotted. Oceans separated him from the sites featured on it. A block of flats unevenly distempered pink at a junction in India still materialized in his dreams. But the city in which he now lived remained opaque to him. Like a tourist who has memorized a street plan, he navigated by artifice. His gaze stopped at surfaces, slipped off façades that had never been penetrated by his childish imaginings.

Little by little, Tom's thinking about Nelly's work gathered itself around the skipping girl sign. Although, in this connection, thinking was at once too precise and too restrictive a term. What he divined in the skipping girl was a constellation of impressions, metaphors, quicksilver glints.

She led Tom to the *wild objects:* his shorthand for things Nelly depicted that had outlived their purpose or evolved a new one. They included an ancient pillar-box, graffitied and plastered with posters, lurking in the shade of the shining mailbox that had superseded it. There were the wind chimes made from sporks that dangled in a window in a once-industrial street, the CDs strung from the arms of a scarecrow in a housing estate allotment, the leatherette rocker-recliner positioned beside a "Smokers Please" bin at the rear of a discount electrical goods warehouse.

These images reminded Tom of a toy he had owned when very young, a waxy slate he would cover with childish scribbles. When he lifted the plastic sheet on top, the marks disappeared, magically expunged. Yet here and there on the clean overlay the faint imprint of his hand's labor could still be discerned. The toy, which had enchanted him, afforded three pleasures: inscription, erasure, and remembering. It was concerned, like Nelly's work, with what was discarded and ephemeral yet caught in the tatters of memory.

The *wild objects* suggested that time deals unkindly with things. They spoke to Tom of that period between nostalgia and novelty which contained objects once the height of fashion and now out of date. From time to time one or two would wander into the saga of the present: untimely apparitions, humble fragments from the wreck of modernity. No longer new but not yet antique, they were merely old-fashioned, hence in poor taste.

These tiny punctures in the now-scape of the present allowed the past entry into Nelly's images. No one looks twice at a disused pillar-box or old cutlery, thought Tom. But such things were infected with historical memory. Former emblems of progress and style, they functioned as memento mori of the endless rage for the new.

The skipping girl's programmed rope had traced that frenzy in lights. In place of remembrance, it offered repetition. The skipping girl was as dazzling as novelty and, like it, going nowhere. Now, without her neon, she had the air of a sad revenant, a lifeless trace of history.

Over time, it was that sadness that caught at Tom. He found himself intensely moved by a photograph that showed the outlines of vanished rooms on a wall of a house that had been demolished. There were days when he thrust Nelly's photographs out of sight. Things illuminated, seen and surrendered to darkness: he was not always capable of looking at them with composure.

One day, when they were alone at the Preserve, he said as much to Brendon. Who listened, then led Tom to the room Nelly used for storage. There he opened a cupboard. It contained a jumble of hardware and cables. Tom saw a sage-green dial telephone and a cream one. A slide projector. A boxy beige Mac Plus. A Betamax video recorder. A contraption with a built-in keyboard that Brendon identified as a Kaypro.

Brendon drew out a cumbersome black clock radio. "Remember these? With numbers that click over?" He glanced around. "She's got a black-and-white portable telly somewhere."

"But what's it all doing here?"

"You don't know?"

Tom said, "Outdated stuff."

"Not just stuff. Outdated technology: the most dated stuff in the world. Not so long out of date, either. Stuff people aren't yet nostalgic about. Stuff you can't give away."

The little room was icy. Tom, turning a rubber-banded sheaf of 5¼-inch floppy disks in his hands, saw the flesh pimple along his arms. Brendon noticed too: "It's modernity. Walking over your grave."

THEY STOOD by the place where the dog had disappeared. It was Nelly who had spotted it: a three-toed print set in the bank. "That'll be the wallaby."

The rain had stopped, but Nelly, reaching for a handhold among the bushes, set off a small deluge. She hauled herself up, feet scrabbling. Crouched at the top of the bank, she peered into the bush. "I can get a little way, I think."

Soon they were pushing along through undergrowth that kept bouncing back in their faces. Nelly said, "If you could lift me up. To try to get a better view."

She rose past Tom's face, disconcertingly solid. He had Nelly Zhang in his arms and couldn't wait to be rid of her.

He heard her cooee off to his right. It was an unsettling call, syllables that straddled word and sound; an eerie trace of the real and imaginary vanishings in which Australian folk legend abounded, a mythology whose richness betrayed the fragility of European confidence in this place.

Tom never heard it without thinking of a picture that had hung in his first classroom in Australia: a small girl in a landscape of yellow grass and tall, splotched gums, the pretty wildflowers that had led her astray still clutched in her pinafore. Light folded her in its cloth of gold and drew a veil across the distant foliage that blocked her escape. She wept in her shining prison: lost in Australia, a predicament the Indian boy had understood at once.

The plan was to cross the hill from south to north. They had started out on parallel tracks about twenty feet apart, but Nelly now sounded farther away.

Tom came to a log-ridden gully. Halfway down, he knew he couldn't get any farther. He called to the dog. To Nelly.

He followed his yellow tapes back to the path and found her waiting for him. She said, "The gully's too deep here. We should try farther up, where it peters out." There were scratches on her hands and on one side of her face.

"What's that smell?" he asked.

"What smell?"

They sniffed. "There. I keep smelling it."

"Native mint bush."

She snapped off a leafy stalk and passed it to him. The clouds parted. "The *sun*," they said, together.

Every time they set out again, Tom felt a little surge of hope. After about an hour, his spirits sagged.

He checked his watch and saw that all of twenty-eight minutes had passed.

Sometimes he called the dog's name backwards. To shake things up a little.

"What sort of knot was it?"

He told her. Added, "It won't work free."

They were sitting by the side of the track on their jackets, eating apples. Tom said, "There's all this folklore to do with knots."

"Yeah?"

"Knots are supposed to contain power that can be used for good or evil. It's called maleficium. There's a long history of people attributing magical powers to knots. The Romans believed that a wound would heal more quickly if the dressing was bound with a Hercules knot, which was their name for a reef knot."

Nelly ate apples core and all. She twirled the stem of this one in her fingers before letting it drop.

"In Scandinavia the name Knut used to be given to boys whose parents already had as many children as they wanted. People believed that even the word for knot was powerful enough to prevent another pregnancy." Tom said, "You wouldn't think that'd survive too much reality, would you?"

"I don't know. They probably lucked out more often than not. A woman who had as many kids as she wanted would've most likely been older. Less fertile." Nelly had produced a pencil and was unfolding her map.

Flies sizzled past Tom's face. Somehow he began talking about Iris — not the details; he found himself unable to use the words *mother* and *shit* in relation to each other. But that he feared she wouldn't be able to go on living on her own. "My aunt says it's time she went into a home. And she's probably right. But of course Ma hates the idea. She starts crying every time the subject comes up."

He added, "It's not like all nursing homes are terrible. I've offered to drive her around, find a place she likes. But she won't even think about it."

In this way he established Iris's irrationality and his willingness to do everything that might reasonably be expected of him.

Nelly had stopped drawing. She asked, "So what does she want to do?"

Tom was about to say, She wants to stay where she is, of course. But knowledge that had remained hidden within him, so that he had been able to ignore its tenancy, chose that moment to emerge into the light.

"She'd never ask. But she'd like to live with me."

He waited for Nelly to assure him that it was reasonable for the old to be sent away from their families into the care of strangers.

He waited for her to say what any reasonable person would say, what he himself had said to friends beleaguered by the needs of elderly parents. *But that's crazy. You have your own life to lead.*

Nelly said, "Is that possible?"

Tom saw his books dispersed, his study transformed into a lair. He saw pillowcases stained with hair dye and throat lozenges turning sticky in a drawer. He saw his mother in a big pink chair in the sunroom, her flesh warming, the blurry nimbus of her perm.

"Not really." He got to his feet. "I can't imagine it."

MIGRATION HAD ENTAILED so many changes that years went by before Tom remarked a decisive one: in Australia he was no longer the child of the house. The obvious displacement in space had obscured a more subtle dislocation in time. The shift, facilitated by his father's death, was sealed by the proximity of his young cousin, Shona. She was a large, dull child, lightly spotted with malice; their relations were wary but amicable.

That first Christmas, eating roast turkey at Audrey's table, Tom saw his uncle pluck the wishbone from the ruins of the bird. Automatically, he put out his hand. No one noticed, because attention was focused on nine-year-old Shona, who screwed her eyes shut, grasped the other end of the greasy bone, and pulled. Tom's gaze shot to his mother, but Iris was saying, "Tell, darling, did you make a nice wish?" The boy pretended to be reaching for the gravy.

Not long afterward, and in quick succession, he was displaying symptoms of diseases evaded in disease-ridden India. Measles, chicken pox: the classic illnesses of childhood. It was a simple ruse and it failed. His mother had to go out to work. Tom was told to be a big boy, tucked up, and left for the day, with TV, a thermos of Heinz soup, and a stack of Shona's old comics for cheer. Outside the window mynahs called into the huge Australian silence.

After he recovered the second time, Tom remained healthy for years. There was no one to look after him; the message had been received. But it was couched in cipher. What remained vivid from that Christmas was the recollection of looking across the centerpiece of plastic fir cones and seeing his mother speaking with her mouth full. The sight of food that was neither inside nor outside the body, food that had broken down into an indistinct, glutinous mass, was disgusting: an Australian rule clever Tom Loxley had absorbed. He would believe it was the reason he flinched from the memory of that meal. The wishbone he had not been offered vanished under a slime of mashed fowl.

Consider the great cunning of the operation. It enabled the boy to transfer his gaffe to his mother. It demonstrated that he knew better than she did; that in the antipodes their roles were reversed. It aroused his pity. Crucially, it shielded him from pain.

But it was not foolproof. Time passed, and Iris grew frail, and what Tom could not bear to grant her was childlike need. A request that he fasten her clothing or cut up her food might provoke a putrid eruption; at best a spike of rage. It was a disgraceful reaction, and he did his best to master it. He eased his mother's arms into her cardigan and folded a tissue for her sleeve; he wiped her swirled excrement from the floor. With cautious steps, Iris was finding her way back to the kingdom of childhood. One of the emotions it aroused in her son was a terrible envy.

A THIN STREAM of self-pity was decanting itself into Tom. They were climbing the hill for a last foray into the bush, Nelly a few steps ahead.

"It's nothing like you and Rory," he said wordlessly to her back. "We don't *talk*. It's not one of those modern relationships."

His thoughts slid to Karen's parents. The Cliffords were as groomed and athletic as the couples featured on billboards for superannuation funds. They played tennis three times a week and jogged around an artificial lake every morning. Tom had once watched them power walk down a path in twin designer tracksuits with the wind lifting their silver hair. In their dealings with their children, they deployed a brisk, practical brand of affection. One Christmas, Karen and her sisters had been given copies of their parents' wills and invited to choose furniture and other keepsakes from the family home. They were also informed that their parents had inspected a range of what they termed *low- and high-care facilities* and had entered into agreements with suitable establishments. "We don't want you girls bothered with our lifestyle options."

What about deathstyle options, Tom had inquired privately of Karen. "Have they given you the go-ahead to switch off the machines?" He was electric with derision and envy. It was all so

sensible, so sanitary. It was emotional hygiene and it was unavailable to him. He was a giant child engulfed by the unfairness of
life's arrangements.

How was Tom to convey — to Nelly, to anyone — the muffled
dependencies that weighted his relations with Iris? He was
unable to shake off the image of that powder-puff head. His
mother's claim on him was mute, elemental; the animal invitation to feel *with*.

When she had worked as a cleaner, she would tiptoe past
Tom before sunrise, her breath pinched so he could sleep undisturbed. At night she went to bed early. Tom sat at the folding
table in the living room, his books and papers spread before
him. His sleeve, moving across a page, produced a soft swish-
ing. Later he lay in bed reading, or watched TV with the sound
down. During the unwelcome intimacies imposed by school, by
the annexed, he looked forward to these solitary hours.

Iris had been cleaning offices for a few months when Tom,
working through a page of calculus one evening, became aware
of a noise that had been going on for some time. He listened.
Then he knocked. Then he went in.

"Ma? Ma, what's wrong?"

She didn't answer but went on with her soft keening.

Tom switched on the bedside lamp. Iris's eyes were closed,
but she was plainly not asleep. Again he asked what was wrong;
roughly, because he was afraid. Tears went on slipping down
her face, but still she didn't reply.

He asked, "Do you want Audrey?"

After a little while, she said that her back hurt. Rather, she
said it was paining.

He corrected her mechanically. But in fact it was he who was mistaken. Her locution, which had struck him as *sounding Indian,* was not after all geographical but historical. Years later he would come across it in a book of good Edwardian prose.

He asked, "Shall I get an aspirin?"

When he returned, she was propped up against her pillows.

Tom said, "I can leave school. Get a job. You don't have to do it."

Her mouth was full of water and aspirin, but her head shook vigorously.

Later she said, "What's to be done." It was not a question.

Her dressing gown of quilted pink nylon lay across the bed. Its spiritual twin was suspended on a hanger hooked over the wardrobe door: an unlined gray coat trimmed with fake fur, ready for the morning.

Other men came up with strategies that rendered their mothers harmless. Neglect was one solution; so was marrying a woman with a capacity for ruthlessness. There was also comedy. There was Vernon, who had reconfigured his mother as a monstrous buffoon. Her prying, her avarice, her vanity, her hemorrhoid creams, the satisfaction the old despot derived from making children cry: farce drew the poison from it all. Now and then, even as he was laughing, Tom detected a familiar flutter of frustration or despair in Vernon's anecdotes, but it twitched uselessly in a web of comic invention.

Tom had always thought of himself as siding with the defenseless, as most people do when the risk of personal inconvenience is small. But Iris grated on his sensibilities. He thought of abrasions his soul would endure if they were to live together. There would be questions: Where are you going? What time are you coming back? Who is that friend of yours? There would be ritual conversations, stupefying banalities. Laugh tracks crashed through his concentration. His mother inspected the crustless salmon sandwiches he had prepared for her, and said, "That's wrong. You've cut them wrong."

Forebodings rushed to fill the future he might share with her. His best intentions would sour. The example of Audrey was before him. Having risen to the occasion, he would swiftly descend. He heard himself enumerating, for Iris's edification, the sacrifices her presence entailed and the virtues he imagined himself to be displaying.

When he was fourteen, he had turned the corner of a street and seen a figure hesitate at a pedestrian crossing. From the protection of a curved tin awning, he beheld a brassy perm and hectic rouge perched on the body of a slack-bellied sprite. It placed its thumb between its teeth, and peered into the traffic from the prudent curb. The gesture brought recognition without dispelling estrangement: the queerest sensation. It was his first glimpse of his mother as left over from another time. He studied her as though she were a page in an anthropological text, taking in the knowledge that she was no longer essential to him.

At the same time, he was aware of an impulse to dash out diagonally through streaming cars and gather her up in his arms. He would carry her to a place of safety. But where, where?

The sky was solid Australian blue, lightly laminated with cloud near the horizon. Nelly was waiting for him at the top of the track. Lines from a poem about hope came into Tom's mind: *With that I gave a viall full of tears:/But he a few green eares.*

He didn't speak them, for poetry can be alarming. His fingers sought and found the leaves crushed in his pocket.

WHEN THE MAN first appeared, Iris had been afraid. It was true that he was a long way away—beyond gray palings, beyond trees and tiled roofs—and that he did not seem to be coming closer. Still: a man floating in the sky. In all but the most jaded civilization it was a vision to arouse trepidation and wonder.

He was large and shiny, with rounded limbs. When the sun was out, as it was that afternoon, his body ran with light. Then he was dazzling; Iris had to look away. Dull skies enabled her to see him whole, golden against his backdrop of lead.

She was waiting for her electric jug to boil. The tea bag and two spoons of sugar were in the mug, the carton of milk was on the counter. This modest state of affairs took time to engineer. That was, in its way, a blessing. Time is the great wealth of the elderly, and the spending of it, as with any fortune, poses a quandary.

The jug was too heavy for Iris to fill directly. She had to position a plastic beaker under the tap, lift it out of the sink when it held a cupful of water, ease it along the counter, then lift it again to tip its contents into the jug. All manner of daily acts called for guile. Iris lived by contrivance. There were gadgets, provided by her son, designed to twist the lids off jars or manipulate taps. Elsewhere she had arrived at her own arrangements, a cord looped over a handle enabling a drawer to slide open, bras renounced in favor of mercifully hookless vests. Certain objects defeated her: buttons, nail clippers. At the hairdresser's, with a hot helmet clamped to her skull, she looked into a mirror and saw a girl draw a rosy brush over a client's splayed fingers. Iris would have liked a manicure herself, but Audrey could not be kept waiting. There was also the expense.

When her son was small, he had loved to sit beside her whenever she painted her nails at her dressing table. The instant her little finger was done, Tommy would lean forward, lips pursed. Iris made a fan of her hand. The child blew on her nails, moving his head this way and that. His eyes were turned sideways, to the fifteen fingers fluttering in Iris's triple mirror. He called it "doing butterflies": their private game.

Iris found herself thinking about a nail file she had owned. It was made of silver metal and shaped like a stockinged leg. The rough grain of the stocking's weave provided a filing surface, while the smooth, pointed foot served to clean under nails. This object, once unobtrusively part of her days, had slipped from her mind for years. She couldn't remember which part of her life it had belonged to, nor imagine what had become of it; why or how their trajectories had diverged.

In the lavatory, lacking the suppleness required to reach around behind herself, she had devised a method for wiping while holding on to her walking frame and keeping her trousers from collapsing about her ankles. It involved preparing wads of paper in advance. These, when soiled, were placed on her walker until she had adjusted her clothing, twisting her knickers around, and her hands were free to grip the frame and turn herself with it to face the bowl. It was a disgusting practice. But what was Iris to do? It was a question of balance: the need to remain upright measured against animal necessity. Every day on a stage fitted with baby-blue porcelain, she reenacted civilization's elemental struggle.

Iris had raised the subject of the floating man with Audrey, referring to him with calculated nonchalance as "that thing." Later she sought a second opinion from her son. He confirmed Audrey's diagnosis: the man was connected to the car dealership that had opened on the highway. The name of the dealership was written across his chest, Tommy said, while Iris peered through her window. Her sight was much improved since she had had her cataracts done, but the man often had his back to her and she hadn't noticed the lettering. He was "Like a balloon," said Tommy, and offered to drive her past the dealership one day. But he always forgot, making his usual left turn at the Dreamworld showroom instead.

Iris didn't mind. Facts may reassure, even convince, and yet fall short of adequacy. Every time she saw the man, her sense of his power was renewed. Now and then he disappeared for a day or two, which strengthened her impression that their association was not casual. Distance was integral to it. It was akin to her relations with talk-show hosts: an intimacy predicated on detachment. Late afternoon sun, pouring into her kitchen, showed her a man touched with fire, caused her to fold her head, for she was mortal and might not look upon such splendor.

Brought up never to importune the Almighty on her own behalf, Iris sometimes asked him to heed the petitions of those striving to find a cure for arthritis. The safe return of a dog was a more straightforward matter. A dozen times between waking and sleeping, she began, "O holy Saint Anthony, gentlest of saints, your love for God and charity for his creatures made you worthy when on earth to possess miraculous powers."

This was the third day, and she knew the prayer by heart. It was a powerful incantation, to be used in extremis. Iris had never doubted its efficacy. Yet it was only now, in her kitchen with her eyes closed, that she *saw*. She had been granted a sign. Matthew Ho's image had been hung in the sky to show that her prayers were heard in heaven.

TOM SAID, "I'm going to go see Jack. I haven't thanked him for everything he's done."

"Cool. I'll come with you." Then, in response to his silence, "What's wrong?"

"What about Denise?"

"What *about* her?"

As they walked down the track, Nelly was talking about the terrain around her house being unsuited to mechanized farming. "Cows do fine. Machines tip over. That's what finished off the McDermots. Like imagine trying to get a baler around those paddocks." The Feeneys, farming at the bottom of the hill, had fared better. "Also Jack got himself a license to dig tree ferns from the bush and sell them to nurseries. He did pretty well out of that."

Tom asked, "Do you think Denise married Mick just so there'd be someone to help Jack with the farm?"

"Sounds complicated." Nelly said, "He's sort of sexy, Mick."

At the sight of Tom's face, she burst out laughing.

The scrape of the gate sent invisible dogs crazy. Nelly raised her voice: "No hatchback, see? Tuesday evenings she's got clinic."

"We've had no funny buggers with sheep." Mick Corrigan said, "If your dog was alive, he'd be after a feed for sure, eh? Nah, tell you what: he copped it from that wallaby."

"He's a city dog. He wouldn't make the connection between a sheep and food."

"Dog's a dog, mate."

The scent of sausages hung in the room. Nelly and Jack were by the window, which left Tom with sexy Mick. There was soundless boxing on TV; Mick's gaze never left the screen. Now and then he tensed as if anticipating a blow.

Tom caught snatches of farm talk from Jack: "...fatten them up in about four months...picking out the dry ewes."

Mick sat with his arms crossed over his chest. "Best just get a new one, eh?"

But Tom had seen this: as Jack passed his son-in-law's chair on his way across the room, he had picked up the remote and pressed the mute button. He addressed no word to Mick, who made no protest. It was a thirty-second silent film summarizing what Mick Corrigan was up against.

On the porch, Jack said, "The bush was an open place when I was a lad. We'd go running through the trees on the way to school." He turned to Tom. "There were four farms along this road before the war. I'm the only one left now."

The old man spoke with a survivor's pride. But what he was remembering was the sensation of flight. He had emerged from the bush and gone racing down a hillside, unable to stop. He remembered the wind in his face, prickly grass underfoot. He shouted at cows and shocked trees. At the hurtling future.

It was always the worst hour, night coming on, and the dog missing from the circle of firelight. Nothing was said between them, but Nelly lit the lamp and placed candles about the kitchen while a lurid sunset was still smearing itself across the horizon.

With her hand on the blind, she paused. "Cows. I always want to go over and talk to them. It's something about their faces."

"You could tell them how terrific they'll look on a plate."

He had not yet quite forgiven Nelly her assessment of Mick Corrigan.

When they were eating, she said, "It used to be solid dairy country 'round here. Then one day Jack sold off his herd and got sheep in. He'll tell you that all of a sudden he couldn't bear to watch cows he'd known all their lives go off to the yards."

She said, "He didn't sell them all either. One of them, Belle, was still around when I got to know the Feeneys. She ended up with the rest under Jack's old potato paddock."

"So what's that mob doing out there?"

"They're Mick's. He got them in when wool prices were down. Jack doesn't really want anything to do with cattle, which is why they're up here."

"Because sending sheep to the abattoir is a different thing altogether."

"Yeah, I know it doesn't add up. And everyone pointed that out, Jack's wife, the neighbors, everyone. He was a joke throughout the shire. Like it still comes up when people talk about him." Nelly said, "I'm sure he hated being called sentimental. And irrational. But in the end he wasn't ashamed to be those things."

In bed Tom lay thinking about the power of shame.

On learning that he intended to keep searching for the dog, Audrey had said, "There's a limit to how much you can do." She was attuned to limits, especially other people's. Patting the back of her hair, she added, "It's not like losing a kiddie, is it? Count your blessings he's only a dog."

Love without limits was reserved for his own species. To display great affection for an animal invariably provoked censure. Tom felt ashamed to admit to it. It was judged excessive: overflowing a limit that was couched as a philosophical distinction, as the line that divided the rational, human creature from all others. Animals, deemed incapable of reason, did not deserve the same degree of love.

Now Tom wondered if the function of the scorn such love attracted was to preserve a vital source of food: because to love even one animal boundlessly might make it unthinkable to eat any. Bodies craving protein justified their desire as a matter of reason. But perhaps the limit at risk was in fact the material distinction between what was and was not considered fit for consumption.

It was a topic that aroused unease. When eating out with friends, Tom had noticed a fashion for naming the animal that had supplied a dish. *I'll have the cow. Have you tried the minced pig?* An ironic flaunting was at work: I know very well that this food on my plate was once a sentient creature, and that doesn't bother me. Euphemisms are symptomatic of shame; to avoid them was to deny shame, deflecting it with cool.

Another familiar urban scenario: On seeing a beggar, Tom's first impulse was to reach for money. Then he would imagine being observed in the act of placing a coin in a hand; a sentimental act, an act of feeling. The shame this occasioned was so strong that it triumphed over charity. He would walk on, ignoring the beggar.

Now he realized that what he risked in showing empathy was to appear unironic. Irony was the trope of mastery: of seeing through, of knowing better. And it was a reflex with Tom. He had invented himself through the study of modern literature, and it had provided him with a mode; the twentieth-century mode. To be modern was to be ironic. Among the things he was ashamed of was seeming out of date.

He came awake all at once and knew he was alone.

In the kitchen, the fire was out. He went into the passage, where his flashlight showed the yard door ajar.

It was not as cold as the previous night; still, Tom was glad of his jacket. He stood by the water tank and eventually urinated. Then he walked up the drive.

There was a sound; he realized it had been going on for a while, growing fainter all the time, the motorbike heading down into the valley. The stars glittered, fixed as a malediction. After standing at the gate for some minutes, he went back into the house.

In the kitchen, he stumbled over something propped against a chair. Nelly's bag appeared in the wavering circle of his flashlight; and peering from it like temptation, one corner of a small cardboard folder.

Afterward, Tom made himself look at the photographs again, shining his flashlight on each in turn. There were thirteen of them. They lay on the table like an evil tarot. Nelly's Nasties: they were before him at last. Most of all he was aware of wanting to protect his gaze with his hand, to filter the force of what he was seeing through his fingers.

He resisted the instinct. But it trailed an ancient horror. On a long-ago morning, Tom had caught sight of a paperback beside his father's chair as he crossed the verandah on his way to school. So his first view of the book's cover was fleeting, and then, when he looked again, at once he looked away.

That evening he returned to it, and the next day, and the next. On each occasion his methodology was the same: a sidelong approach, followed by flickers of vision. It was seeing and not seeing at the same time. The child felt that to behold that picture in its entirety would be his undoing. But as long as it exceeded him, he was compelled to return to it.

Wholeness was in part what was horrifying about the image. A furry black face filled the cover of the book. Raised by the table, it loomed close to Tom's own face. He was six or seven at the time.

Among the words on the cover was one that was larger than the rest. The child associated it with excretion; with what was at once necessary and repellent. It was spelled out plainly in thick dark letters: P-O-E.

Patterns of light on the verandah shifted with the sun's journey across the sky. Brightness and shade worked their own dissection of the image. Tom took it in in glimpses. A slice of black fur, a sectioned snarl. Perception was jerky, a series of shudders. Straight after the flash, his eye lowered its shutter. If it happened often enough, he might assemble what he had seen, hold it steady in his mind.

On that night in Nelly's kitchen, the trace of an old dread persisted in Tom's desire to place his hand over his eyes: a child's protective gesture.

The fireplace was silent and cold. Tom rocked gently back and forth, and wrapped his arms about himself. Opposite him was the window, with the blind down. After a little while, the notion came to him that something was pressing its face to the glass. The idea gathered strength, swelling to a conviction that kept him nailed to his chair.

At last he tore free. When he turned around, a figure was watching him from the door.

Nelly did practical things: lighting candles, getting the fire going, pouring whiskey into glasses.

"The photos fell out of your bag. I kicked it over and…"

"It's OK." She said, "Obviously, they're not for general view. Nelly's Nasties, like they say."

Tom said quickly, "They're great." But his gaze slipped to the image closest to him. There was something of Fuseli's *Nightmare* behind it, something also of *The Night of the Hunter*. Yet the stance of the man in the photograph might have been protective, and the hat shading his face made it impossible to read. And who could say why the girl, on the edge of the scene, had flung up her head? But there was a carousel horse, gaily colored, with a flaring eye. Situations revolved in the mind. Altogether, it was not an image Tom wished to look at for very long.

Nelly gathered up the photographs and replaced them in their folder. Then she sat at the table. Said, in a matter-of-fact way, "They frightened you."

Tom refilled his glass. "What went on with you and Felix?" he asked.

"I got married so young." She held her glass between finger and thumb, rocking it on the table, and repeated, "I was so young."

Tom waited. She spoke patiently, as to a fool: "That was *it*." For a moment she was frightening again, jaw hard, eyes slitty. "That was what he liked," said Nelly.

It was Posner who introduced her to Atwood, said Nelly. The two men had been at school together. When she realized she was pregnant, "Felix was the one who wanted to get married. He was so happy. Well, we both were."

She said, "It began when I started to show. I didn't for ages, not until about six months. Then I disgusted him."

Tom understood long before she had finished. The old Polaroid pinned up in the Preserve: he remembered thinking how much younger than her age she had looked.

Scraps of what she was saying lodged in his brain. Atwood had liked to buy her clothes. At first it excited Nelly. Her husband dressing her up the better to undress her. But she quickly grew bored with his taste, with pin-tucked frocks of English lawn. "I mean, all the artists I hung out with were in torn black." She began refusing to wear the garments Atwood bought; or wore them incongruously, a baby-doll nightie pulled over a long-sleeved flannel vest, a Peter Pan collar half-hidden under a polyester shift or a safety-pinned T-shirt.

He liked her in pigtails, so she had her hair cropped and gelled into spikes. She dropped a clutch of white cotton panties into a vat of magenta dye.

Her resistance infuriated Atwood. What began as a mild squabble expanded into one of those sour conflicts that leave both sides drained yet resolved not to yield. Nelly's clothes — her appearance, her image — became the site each struggled to control. It was ludicrous and deadly. Sometimes, in the early stages, an argument collapsed because they would catch each other's eye and begin to laugh. She didn't speak of the lovemaking that followed, but Tom guessed its edgy mixture, the desire to punish leaving its tang in the syrup.

Nelly's elastic young flesh sprang back within weeks of giving birth. But her milk-gorged breasts repelled Atwood. "He wanted me to bottle-feed. He'd leave the room as soon as I undid the first button."

It had phases. In one of them he bought concoctions of silk, or lace, or gossamer French chiffons, an armful of extravagant, feminine wisps one or two sizes larger than Nelly required. Slipping from her shoulder, a dress emphasized the slightness of her frame. There was also the dress-up aspect: lipsticked, hung with flashing paste jewels, she was a child essaying a sexual disguise.

They both mustered their weapons. Nelly's income was minimal. Rory left her exhausted, with neither the time nor the stamina needed for painting; in any case, in those days only Posner collected her work. Atwood settled the household bills and did so unstintingly, but no longer paid a fortnightly sum into Nelly's account.

He withheld treats: a line of cocaine, a trip to Venice. In bed he aroused her until she whimpered; at last, pinned beneath him, she would consent to his scheme. Arrayed in whatever elfin costume he required, she acted out his wishes.

She shaved off her hair. "It looked terrible. My skull's that lumpy kind. I'd get around in these old Doc Martens I bought at Camberwell, looking like the love child of Johnny Rotten and a Buddhist nun." She searched thrift shops for matronly castoffs and paraded them at formal dinners. "Those corporate occasions where all the men wear their wives." Atwood told his colleagues she was suffering from postnatal depression. "Anything I did from then on was down to being *hormonal*."

She thought Posner guessed. "Sort of. He was friends with us both. But he'd known Felix for years. And been in love with him from the start. It was really important to him that things worked out between us." She said, "In a way, it was like I was his proxy."

The maneuvers husband and wife practiced on each other were misleading. They lent the thing the aspect of a game. That was one reason Nelly stayed. Besides, there were stretches of calm. There was the delight the child brought into the world. They might be drinking cold wine on daisied grass while he crawled over a rug between them, and she would relish the ordinariness of these pleasures.

There was the eroticism that still reeled her in to Atwood. She said, "He had perfect ears."

Nelly had no aptitude for narrative. But that night it poured from her. Tom was of no account in the spate. There was something unnerving in her indifference to his reception of her tale. She spoke with scarcely a pause. She grew repetitive, elaborating on avowals, coiling back over explanations. She told a pointless story about a mothers' group she had attended with Rory. She was prolix. A draft set the candles flickering and carried the smell of wax around the room. The tiny kitchen filled up with words.

At some point, quite early on, she must have grasped the significance of Atwood's preferences. What she failed to imagine was that they might encompass other beings. Nelly was accustomed to the cluster of fantasies that she drew from men. With the egotism that is a symptom of innocence, she believed it was her singularity that triggered Atwood's response.

In this way, her knowledge of what her husband desired was tempered. It was seeing and not seeing: the perfect mechanism for controlling dread. Nevertheless, what made its way into her paintings was fear.

Atwood began spending longer at work. He was often away. There were meetings in Sydney, in Hong Kong, in Singapore. When he had a free weekend, he would drive to the house in the bush. Usually he went alone. Their skirmishes might have turned wholly vicious but grew routine instead.

At the time, the dwindling of his attention brought Nelly relief. It was only long afterward that she began to imagine what it might have meant. At once the void left by his lack of interest in her filled with childish forms she had never seen. She pictured flesh so immaculate it measured each caress in damages.

In the last months she spent with Atwood, Nelly's headaches were more frequent and more brutal. Between bouts of illness, she shut herself into her studio and worked. Rory had started kindergarten, in addition to which she hired babysitters for him while she painted. She borrowed their wages, as she borrowed money for materials, from Posner. In five months she completed her *Nightingale* series, a lunatic flow.

"The selection in the show, Carson said those seven were no worse than gruesome. I was totally pissed off with him for refusing to show them all, but then..." She shrugged. "I was walking around the gallery after the installation, and I stood in front of those paintings, and it hit me for the first time. Felix had been gone months, and it was only then that I realized what'd been really going on."

Tom asked, "Why carry the photos around?"

But the answer took shape even as he formulated the question. When understanding fails, the consequence is always a haunting.

In the last year of their marriage, Atwood began pressing her to have a second child. The idea, once speculative, took on definition: a print emerging into clarity through the chemistry of talk. Nelly temporized; not while she was working toward a show. In that rationalization of reluctance, she was entirely sincere.

Atwood accepted it without argument. There was an increasingly disengaged quality to his scenarios. "I guess things were hotting up at work." It was a period when more than ever before Nelly was struck by the abstract nature of money, its almost hallucinatory disembodiment. She was hard put to lay her hands on twenty cents for the bag of mixed lollies her son begged for at the convenience store, but luxuries multiplied around her as in a dream. She swigged vintage Krug in her bath and lay every night in a clean linen envelope.

She said, "I can see why Felix lied about that money. It just wasn't real. Even the way he and his mates talked about it. Like they never said 'half a million' — it was always 'half a bar.'"

Once, early on in the marriage, Nelly had visited him at the brokerage on Collins Street. She spoke of the modern, luminous beauty of the green figures on the dealing screens, of the telephones ringing nonstop in the trading room, and the clashing screams of "Buy!" and "Sell!" There was a reverent undertone to Nelly's words. Her eyes were bright as screens in the shadowy kitchen. "Loads of zeros. Unreal money."

Her husband kept returning to the topic of a second child: acquiescing in its deferral but urging it toward reality. A phrase tripped so often from his tongue that she heard it as scarcely more than an arrangement of phonemes. How nice for Rory, he would remark, to have a sister.

That small figure from the future kept them company for a season, was summoned and dismissed, and glided again through their desires. It passed through the *Nightingale* paintings, occasioning unease but withholding clarity; a riddling presence, as apparitions so often are.

Afterward, she would think, A little girl in that house!

WEDNESDAY

They sat on splintery steps in the sun, the last of the fresh milk in their coffee. An artful spray of white clouds had transformed the sky into a screen saver. The odor of cattle, a sweet country stench, arrived, then faded.

Tom's face itched with stubble. It was a discomfort intrinsic to the wretchedness of looking for the dog, one of the small miseries that dissolved in the large one and thickened the brew. He sniffed himself discreetly. Everything that leaked from the body's wrapping, emanations the city defeated in brisk, hygienic routs, was triumphant here.

He drew the back of his hand first one way, then the other, along his jaw. A truck coming down the ridge road changed gears on its way to the trees.

Nelly had been saying something about the apple tree in the cow paddock no longer bearing fruit. Now she scraped her spoon around the remains of her porridge, licked it, set the bowl aside.

The night's revelations lay untouched between them. It was like opening a locked door and stumbling on a bound, swaddled form, thought Tom: the coverings could be peeled back, but who would want to do it?

Something tugged faintly. Something Nelly had said the previous day. But what intervened was a bright, painted horse with a rolling eye. So that he blurted, "Don't they frighten you?"

There was no context to the question. Nelly didn't require

one. She was fastening up her hair with a plastic comb and only nodded, without pausing in her task.

In that way, negligently, she made him an enduring gift. It revealed itself by degrees, a slow enlightenment. Slowly Tom realized that Nelly neither shunned nor welcomed the past. She merely allowed it space. It was a question of accommodation. He saw that sometimes she was afraid of the shape it took. Sometimes fear is a necessary response to ghosts, but room must be found for them, nonetheless.

By midmorning the sun, no longer a novelty, lay across their backs like a load. They were pushing forward through scrub, collecting fresh grazes. *The green plant groweth, menacing / Almighty lovers in the spring.* Only they were not that, thought Tom.

Birds worked and whistled. He cursed the cunning of blue gums, the rapid growth that produced density without shade. "We could pass within feet of him and not see."

Nelly wiped her forehead on her arm. Her T-shirt was navy cotton with a red star on the chest; a long red-and-blue-striped sock with the foot cut off had been sewn onto each sleeve.

One leg of her jeans was filthy. She had stepped knee-deep into the pulpy remains of a log. A thread of sweat made its way down her neck to pool above her collarbone, and Tom saw why the hollows there are known as saltcellars.

They were sitting at the foot of the tall eucalypt eating almonds and dried apricots. Withered branches lay around them like broken limbs. Gum forests so often suggested the aftermath of hostilities, the bark litter of dried bandages, the trees as bony and gray as the remnants of regiments.

Tom's mind drifted, by related channels, to Nelly's story of the wallaby, to the amazing teenager with the shotgun and scones.

He was tired. It took him a little while to get there. Then he said, "The woman Jimmy Morgan saw on the beach. Denise."

"Sure."

"No, listen. You said she was tall, even back then. Morgan said he saw a tall woman, remember?" It was coming together with the thrilling symmetry of an equation. "Could Denise have got hold of that dress? The one she made for you?"

"How come you know about that?" And before Tom could reply, "No, she couldn't have."

"Did the cops ask you about it?"

He thought Nelly was going to ignore the question. But eventually she said, "That dress never fitted me. Felix got Denise to make it because I wouldn't wear stuff he bought. And of course he got her a pattern that was way too big. I wore that dress like maybe once, to please her. Then I put it with a whole bunch of stuff to take to the Salvation Army."

Tom waited.

"Look, when the cops started asking, I couldn't find the dress, OK? So I told them I'd chucked it out in the rubbish weeks before, I didn't know when exactly. I said they could check with Denise that it hadn't fitted me."

"So maybe Felix went through your thrift shop stuff and passed the dress on to Denise."

"Why would he do that?"

But the tone wasn't quite right. Nelly sounded cautious rather than unconvinced.

Tom said, "So that people might take her for you? I don't know. But Morgan said the woman he saw had hitched up her skirt so she could climb the dunes. A dress made for you would be a mini on Denise. And it would be tight. Awkward to get around in. Which would be why Morgan thought there was something weird about her."

Nelly closed her eyes, then opened them wide. She said, "Except none of this fits with Felix and Denise. The way they related to each other."

"Denise had a crush on you. And just then she hated you. And being asked to help Felix would've flattered her. He'd have put some jokey spin on it, and by the time she'd realized what it was all about and that he was going to stay missing, it was too late and she was too scared to say anything."

"How would she have got home from the beach?"

"Maybe he'd rented a car. She could've driven his car to the beach and set up the scene with his clothes, and then he dropped her back in the rental before taking off in it."

"There was no record of Felix renting a car. The cops checked out all that stuff."

"Maybe Denise rented it."

"I don't think she was old enough to have a license."

"Who do you think she was then? The woman on the beach."

"I nearly went crazy trying to figure it all out, you know. And in the end —"

"What?"

"There's all these bits and pieces. Little unconnected facts. Smart guesses. What they add up to..." Nelly said, "It's a puzzle."

"Puzzles have solutions."

"And which is more intriguing? If we knew what happened to Felix, do you think we'd be talking about him?" She said, "Like I think that's what he wanted. To create a mystery, something people would remember."

"Meaning you think it was all a setup?"

"If he killed himself, it wasn't there, not on that beach." Nelly got to her feet. "Somewhere else, somewhere in bush like this would be my guess, somewhere he knew he'd never be found."

Then she said a thing that made Tom's skin crawl. "It's been at the back of my mind all the time we've been searching. What we might come across at the bottom of a gully."

EVERY CHRISTMAS, Iris received a publicity calendar produced by the travel agency where Shona worked. Photographs of unblemished views and merry peasants presided over the feasts that governed her year: birthdays, pension days, medical appointments. Not that Iris, whose memory was excellent, needed to consult this almanac. Its function was purely magical. The shaky inscriptions it displayed were anchored to a submerged set of needs and wishes. One of these was the hope that the future would be like the past. A ringed date warded off ambulances, perverts, glaucoma, the fridge breaking down. It signified life going on as usual.

On Friday, Audrey would be driving Iris to the local health

center. There, on a molded plastic chair, across from the disgusting poster of a man with his red interior on view, Iris would tell her story, while her doctor fingered the coffee mug stamped with the same name as her anti-inflammatories.

Iris had decided that she would refer to "motions." She would take her time: delaying the moment of diagnosis, postponing dread. She would speak of blockages, wind, the treacherous packages that slid from her; she would describe what her body withheld and what it yielded.

What survived of the tea set was a single cup, bold red dragons on a shell-pink background. Iris kept it wrapped in a nylon scarf in the suitcase under her bed. There had been a time, not so many years ago, when she could kneel beside her bed, bend forward, and drag the suitcase out. But that was before verticality began its onslaught on her attention. Now it was vital to keep her feet on the ground, and the rest of herself off it.

As she drowsed after lunch in front of the TV, the improbability of having entered her eighties struck Iris anew. She thought of the long, long string of her life, so many afternoons and Easters and Julys, so many Wednesdays. How many times had she woken up to Wednesday?

There were days when being eighty-two was a terrible thing; bad days, when Iris was subject to small jagged outbursts, the remains of her temper, which had worn down like everything else. On bad days, Iris was afraid: not of what was waiting but of what was past, the arrangements that had seemed as fixed as stars and now shuddered with plastic invitation. On bad days she allowed herself to dream. She dreamed of a childhood unclouded by fear, where a raised voice signaled delight, not anger. She dreamed of a girl who dropped to her knees before a Chinaman kneeling in betel-stained dirt.

It was dangerous reverie. Iris could feel its pull. She rationed it, as she rationed the little liqueur-filled chocolate bottles Tommy brought her, measuring out doses of Cointreau and daring. She sculpted the past according to whim, as a child plays with the future, each having an abundance of material.

Iris had arrived in the world when Sebastian de Souza was twenty-seven years old. Twenty-three years earlier, he had asked for a dolls' tea set for his birthday. It was yet another improbability: no matter how hard she tried, Iris was unable to construct a story that coupled dainty pink china and the man whose rage had filled her childhood; the bony orb of even his smallest knuckle refused the curve of the teacup's handle. Nevertheless, these things were true: her father had once been four years old and wanted a miniature tea set more than anything in the world.

How could you know when something was the last time? wondered Iris. The last time a stranger turned to look at you in the street, the last time you could stand up while putting on your knickers, the last time there was no pain when you tried to turn over in bed, the last time you imagined your life would change for the better. On TV a woman sang about fabric softener, and Iris longed to hold her father's cup, to gaze one last time on fearless red dragons. Her heart stuttered with the marvelous absurdity of it: that blossom-thin porcelain should survive when so much had been smashed or lost or discarded.

Beside that miracle, it was scarcely remarkable that Iris Loxley, née de Souza, who had sausage curls and climbed a banyan in the monsoon, Iris, who had an eighteen-inch waist and rode a pony by a mountain stream, that gardenia-scented Iris, bare-shouldered and straight-spined in the gilt-lace frame beside the telephone, should have mutated into this mound of ruined flesh, which had flouted gravity for eighty-two years and was afraid of falling.

· ·

NELLY HAD HER HEAD BACK, drinking water. When she passed him the bottle, Tom said, "Have you noticed? We've both stopped calling."

"It's the sun, on top of not enough sleep. Making us dopey."

"Or because we know he can't still be alive." Tom said, "Look, I can drive you back this evening. Or drop you at a station. No point us both wasting our time."

"So let's say he's dead. Don't you want to keep looking anyway? We can still take him home."

"Hey, look."

They bent over the wing: bone and cartilage and dusty brown feathers. Tom's toes drew back in his boots.

"Do you think...?"

He sniffed: nothing. "Probably been there for days."

In the clearing nothing seemed to have changed. The smooth tire, an assortment of damp rubbish. Tom had half expected the remains of brutality: smashed bones, slit corpses strung from trees. His foot stirred a set of filthy cardboard corrugations stamped with a brewer's logo and uncovered a condom.

"Did you hear the motorbike? Last night, when you were out?" Tom asked.

"Don't think so."

"I came looking for you. Couldn't see you."

Nelly yawned. Then said indifferently, "I walked up to the top of the hill."

Tom fastened a length of yellow tape to a branch. Nelly was somewhere on the hillside below. He stepped forward, trying to do so soundlessly. For a while now, it had been gaining force, the impression that something was listening to him.

A stick cracked in the distance. Tom peered through the under-growth and caught a glimpse of red between jittery leaves. He was about to call out to Nelly, when he remembered his dream of the previous week, the stumpy child raging over the roof, its face full of fury. Suddenly he was very frightened. Trees he couldn't name pressed about him.

Fear revived the memory of an exchange that had taken place in May, not long after Tom had begun visiting the Preserve. A tiny fat woman he knew by sight, a friend of Yelena's, had been complaining about another student. "It creeps me out, how she never says much. But just hangs about *watching* everything — you know?"

Yelena said amiably, "You are right. It is very powerful this way to be still and observe." Her gaze drifted about the little group drinking Shiraz from a cardboard box. "It is frightening. Like Tom."

People concentrated on the contents of their glasses. The fat girl's eyes met Tom's briefly. A terrified giggle broke from her, and she spoke at once of something else. The conversation slid gratefully away.

Pinned in Nelly's armchair, Tom was returned to a rainy morning when, in the course of a schoolboy discussion about breakfast, a classmate of his, a boy named Sanjeev Swarup, had said, "Boiled eggs make your breath stink. Like Loxley's."

There was the shock, never adequately anticipated, of finding himself, the sovereign subject, an object of conversation. There was the terrible content of the statement, of course. But what had pierced Tom was the casualness of Swarup's remark, a fatal lightness echoed in Yelena's words. Like Sanjeev Swarup, she had intended neither harm nor provocation, had referred merely to a known, accepted fact. Tom thought, So that is how they see me! It was as if he had glanced down and discovered a precipice at his feet.

It was an incident he had dismissed over time, reasoning that as Yelena and the others came to know him their view of him had altered. If he had failed to smother the recollection altogether, nevertheless its power to disturb had grown feeble.

But now a curious notion came after Tom, took hold of him and swiveled him, as he blundered among unfamiliar trees. He had assumed that Posner's hints about Nelly's fragility had been designed to frighten him off. But what if the dealer had been trying to protect her? From me, thought Tom, horrified. The idea was like coming upon something unholy. He fled from it, refusing to look over his shoulder.

He came out of the bush on the southern trail and found Nelly waiting there. She gestured at the shawl of paddocks below them fastened with the bright brooch of a dam. "We should search the farm. Jack — even Mick — would've spotted anything obvious. But they won't have been everywhere. There could be something they've missed that we'd see."

Her eyes were pouchy, the whites stained. Tom looked at her scratched hands and grimy clothes and thought, She wants a break from this.

She was saying, "Like there's this old paddock that's going back to bush with a grassy bit still in the middle. There's so much you can't see from the road or take in at a glance, all these tucked-away places."

"Why don't you go back to the house and have a rest? I can keep going here."

"I think we should check over the farm. And I'm OK. I don't need a break."

Tom could have sworn that the farm track was empty when they first turned on to it. Then he saw that a woman was standing by the bank, in the shade of an overhanging branch. As if released by a Play button, she began moving toward them.

"I was just on my way up to your place." It was the first thing Denise said, as if her presence there required justification. And then, "Hi, Nelly."

"Hi." After a moment, Nelly said, "How you doing?"

"Yeah, good. You?"

"Yeah."

"That's good. You look good."

This was so patently absurd that Nelly smiled. At once, something invisible altered, as if a breeze had found its way into a room.

Denise looked at Tom. "This bloke came into the clinic who's done his hamstring. He said he saw your dog up near Walhalla."

"That's miles away!" But hope sprang open instantly within Tom. "When was this?"

"This morning. Oh—when did he see the dog? Sunday, I think. I gave him one of your flyers so he could call you." Denise was digging in the back pocket of her jeans; embroidered white cotton tightened over her breasts.

"Here you go." She handed Tom a Post-it. "I got his number, in case."

He had his phone out. "Thanks. I'll take this up to the top of the hill."

"You're welcome to call from the farm if it's easier."

"No, it's fine. Thanks. Thanks."

No messages.

He called his landline. Nothing.

He sat on his heels in the grass beside the track. Two magpies swooped low, a third began to sing. A long, greenish beetle lifted one antenna, toiling past Tom's foot while somewhere a phone rang and rang.

"Hello?"

He said, "Could I speak to Trevor, please? My name's Loxley."

"Who?"

"Tom Loxley. I think Trevor saw my dog. Is he there?"

He could hear her breathing while she thought it over. Then she shouted, "Trev, you there? Trev?"

There were indistinct voices. Tom pictured the receiver held against her breast.

A man said, "Yeah, g'day?"

Tom explained.

"Yeah, sorry, mate, I was gunna call, but the day got away?"

In the background, the woman said something. Trev said something. Tom cried, "You're breaking up."

"What?"

"I didn't catch what you said."

"Listen, mate, I dunno —"

The woman said, "It's me. Shirl? What he's trying to say, love, it wasn't your dog."

After a moment, Tom said, "Are you sure?"

"I was the one spotted him, love. By the side of this track coupla hundred yards this side of Walhalla? Cute little tyke."

"Little."

"Yeah, little curly white fella, got a bit of that Malteser in him, I reckon? I didn't get a real good look. Took off into the bush when I slowed down. Like he just vanished?"

"So he definitely wasn't..."

"No, love. Nothing like, except they're both white. Trev just remembered I said I'd seen a white dog."

"Right. OK."

"Sorry, love."

The women's faces were turned to the bend in the track. Tom saw the light go out of them at the sight of his own.

When he explained, Denise said, "That Trevor Opie. Might've known. Guy's a dickhead."

"At least we haven't wasted much time. Back to Plan A."

Tom understood that Nelly's briskness wasn't directed at him alone, that one of the people she was trying to rally was herself. All the same, it set his teeth on edge.

She was saying, "Nees says she'll come with us. Help us search the farm."

Nees! Unreasonably, that grated too.

"Thanks, Denise. But to be honest, the last thing I feel like doing right now is traipsing around a whole lot of paddocks." Tom said, "We could look over the farm tomorrow morning if you like. But let's face it, the whole thing's a waste of time, really."

He saw the two of them exchange glances, adults dealing with a fractious child.

Nelly said, "It's just..." She gestured skyward. "This weather."

"Yeah, you've already made that point. Three weeks without food, three days without water. Wasn't that how it went?"

Nelly started to say something. He cut across her, keeping his tone very level. "Just think it through. If the rope got caught up in some undergrowth, he's been trapped in one spot for nine days without food. If he's still alive, he's already gone twenty-four hours without water. So if we're looking anywhere, it's got to be in the bush. Where you know as well as I do, we'll never find him."

"But the thing is to act like we will. And to try everything we can think of. Like he might've got free at some point. Headed for the farm looking for food and collapsed there."

"Yeah, he might have. And he might have been picked up by someone who dumped him on the freeway, or used him as target practice, or took him home as an early Christmas present for the kiddies. Or he might have been bitten by a snake, or a fox might have waited till he was weak enough and finished him off. We can imagine whatever we like. But believing we'll find him out there is just deluded."

"It's not, it's hoping. It's not like giving up's going to get us anywhere."

Sweaty and furious, the two of them glared at each other.

Afterward, they wouldn't be able to agree on what Denise said. She was looking past them, at the path climbing to the ridge. When she spoke, Tom turned his head. A dog had appeared in the distance, small against the sky.

"Nearest vet's Traralgon." Denise glanced at her watch. "You'll just make it before he closes. I'll call and let them know you're on your way."

Tom said, "The house —"

"Leave everything. I'll lock up and that. Just grab what you need and go." She was turning away, heading downhill toward the farm.

Nelly was already running in the opposite direction. Tom gathered up the dog and followed.

As the car approached the farm, Denise came racing out of the gate. She thrust a bag through Nelly's window. "Thermos. Only instant, but I figured it was better than nothing. Hope you take milk and sugar."

"Denise, you're a goddess."

"There's some honey there as well. Feed him honey," shouted Denise.

Nelly leaned out of her window, waving. The dog was a sack of dull fur on a quilt spread over the backseat. In the mirror, Denise stood with her wrists on her hips, watching them go.

"Getting a bit old for this kind of caper, aren't you, fella?" The vet's long nose was blunt at the tip, as if someone had placed a finger there and pushed. He tickled the dog's chest, examined the gash on his foreleg, the shallower slits above. "Rope cuts. Every time he tugged on it, the rope would've twisted tighter around his leg. See how it's just starting to scab over? I reckon he got free sometime in the last twenty-four hours."

When Tom put his arms around him, the dog squirmed and struggled. His claws scrabbled on the table. An unbearably light bundle, he hated being carried. He had lost eight kilos, a third of his weight. His hips were angle brackets coated with fur.

"He'll need plenty of sleep, plenty of good tucker. Small amounts: four, five meals a day. No meat to begin with, and introduce it gradually. Wouldn't do any harm to have your regular vet check him out in the next few days."

"You know, in a way he looks pretty good," said Nelly. "Look how bright his eyes are."

"That's how fasting works. The toxins go, along with the fat. But I wouldn't like to say how much more he could've taken. You found him pretty much just in time, I reckon."

"It was the other way 'round," said Tom. "He found us."

The dog licked honey from Nelly's fingers. In the waiting room, he strained at a cage of snow-bellied kittens.

On the far side of the clipped pittosporums that separated the clinic from the street, an invisible woman said, "She's good-looking in that really obvious way. You know?"

Tom put his hand over his ear. "What?"

In the city, Iris cried, "You're not coming tonight?"

"Ma, I'm still at the vet's, it's hours away..." Tom broke off. "Not tonight. We'll have dinner tomorrow, OK?"

"What?"

"Dinner *tomorrow!*"

"All right."

He said, "Ma, do you understand? He's very thin, but he's basically OK."

"I know." Iris had greeted the news with the same calm. "It's a miracle. Saint Anthony never fails."

"What I don't get is, if the rope got twisted around something and he chewed through it, or if it wore through somehow, why wasn't the end of it still tied to his collar?"

"Because the knot worked loose," said Nelly.

"I've had that knot on my mind ever since he ran off. There's no way it would've come undone."

They shot past a car on the shoulder of the freeway, its hazard lights flashing. A nun paced beside it, talking into a phone. A little farther on, a billboard floated a lucent female over a city, replacing her entrails with skyscrapers.

"What was it called, that magic in knots? Didn't you say it could work for good?"

"Do you think someone might've found him caught up in the bush?" Tom was hearing a motorbike fading into the night. "Just untied the knot and let him go?"

"You hungry?" she asked.

"Starving."

"Next bypass, OK?"

Tom said, "My mother says it's a miracle. She's been praying to Saint Anthony."

"Well, there you go then."

. . . . . .

Nelly nudged him. "Look."

In the mirror tiles that covered the back wall of the pizza parlor, two wild-eyed grotesques had appeared. Their garments were squalid, their hair feral. They were escapees from an experiment conducted on another planet. Unearthly happiness glimmered in their soiled faces.

ONE EVENING, Nelly was waiting for Tom when he rang her bell. "Come on, come on," she said. "You have to see this while it's still light."

She led him to a street they hadn't visited in weeks. "Look."

It was a flat-faced, two-story house in a street of early-twentieth-century cottages. Just completed: a dumpster containing rubble and crumpled guttering still at the curb, the yard a stretch of trampled earth.

The glass panels that covered the façade of the house contained the life-size image of a low, wooden dwelling with finials and decrepit fretwork.

"It's a photograph of the house that used to be here," said Nelly. "A digital print on laminated glass. Isn't it brilliant? Don't you love it?"

When a building has been demolished, the memory of it seems

to linger awhile, imprinted on the eye. Here, before them, was that phantom rendered material.

The house that was there and also not there might have been a metaphor for what passed between them. Tom thought of what his relations with Nelly lacked: sex, answers. Straightforward things. Instead, she offered ghosts, illusion, imagery, a handful of glass eyes. Nelly offered detail and excess. Things extra and other, oddments left on the pavement when the bins had been emptied, illuminated capitals for a manuscript not written. She offered diversions, discontinuities, impediments to progress. Tom thought of scenes that present themselves to a traveler, in which confusion and brilliance so entrance that scenery itself eludes attention.

The past is not what is over but what we wish to have done with. That year time turned translucent. Old things moved just beneath its surface, familiar and strange as a known face glimpsed underwater.

It was a year of fearful symmetries. There was a fashion for shopping bags made from woven nylon that reminded Tom of the cheap totes found in the markets of India. They had handles formed from skipping rope and were patterned with stylized skipping girls. Tom saw them all over the city, colorful presences signaling from women's hands.

Once he saw a ghost. On a kidney-shaped coffee table in the window of the retro shop on Church Street stood an object Tom recognized with a small, sickening lurch. Knobbly purple glass, an elongated stopper: the amethyst double of the yellow bottle

he had smashed all those years ago, as if smashing were all it
took.

THERE WAS the sea hiss of the freeway in the background. They
sat at a picnic table beside the parking lot, devouring pizza.

The dog was licking around his take-away container, nosing it
over the gravel. When he was sure it held no more spaghetti, he
returned to the car and raised a shaky leg against a tire. Then he
waited by the door.

Nelly opened the door and lifted him onto the seat, placed her
face against his fur. He sighed and fell asleep.

Tom crammed the empty food containers one by one into a slit-
mouthed bin. Night's brilliant little logos were starting to appear
all over the sky.

He was on his way back to Nelly, advancing in a measured
diagonal across the parking lot, when he fell. His foot tripped
over nothing and he went down.

After a moment he registered pain, gravel-scorch on the palms
flung out to protect his face. Also, one knee had hit the ground
hard.

What was overwhelming, however, was the astonishment: the
sheer scandal of falling. Tom was returned, in one swift instant,
to childhood; for children, not having learned to stand on their
dignity, are accustomed to being slapped by the earth.

His first instinct was to scramble to his feet as if nothing had happened. But the dumb machinery of his flesh refused to obey. The rebellion was brief and shocking; then his thoughts took a different course. He stayed where he was, the adult length of him at rest in graveled dirt. Without realizing it, he began to cry.

Later, he leaned his forehead on the steering wheel and cried. He wiped his face on his sodden sleeve and went on crying.

At some point he said, "I'm sorry, I can't help it." He said, "I keep thinking how the rope would've cut into him whenever he tried to struggle free or lie down. That he'd have had to choose between pain and exhaustion."

What Tom meant also was that while the dog had persisted in his painful effort to rejoin him, he had persuaded himself that the dog was dead. What he meant was that he was unworthy of grace.

He thought of Iris doing what she could to help, adding her prayers to the world's cargo of trust. He remembered the receptionist at the health center who had told him about her grandfather's dog, the ranger who had spoken kindly on the phone. He recalled the gifts of hope and reassurance he had been offered, and cried with his hands over his face.

Nelly kept saying, "It's OK, it's OK." Tom lifted his head and saw her hands opening and shutting. They made passes in the air as if essaying spells once familiar but long forgotten.

Grace, rocking along Tom's fibers, murmured of wonders that exceed reason. It whispered of the miracle of patient, flawed endeavor. It butted and nuzzled him, blindly purposeful as a beast.

On the freeway, Nelly slid a CD into the player. "This'll keep us awake."

The Beastie Boys were blasting through their first track when he glanced across and saw that she was asleep.

Tom took the exit ramp. In the rearview mirror, the dog raised his head.

At the Swan Street lights, Nelly woke up. The dog staggered to his feet and put his nose out of the window.

"How come you're turning right?"

"Something I've remembered."

The dog swayed on the backseat as they approached the bend in the empty road. Tom pulled in opposite the disused tram depot. In the sudden silence the engine ticked like a heart.

Nelly peered out at the orange-brick relic of a stubborn, unmodern need. The huge, ugly façade of the church was wrapped in forgiving darkness. But it was possible to pick out the pale figure of the saint with the child in his arms.

Tom said, "Perry's Pebbles."

She looked around. "What?"

"Another time."

And still the endless day had not used up its store of wonders. With sublime unhaste, the tip of Nelly's finger began to trace a circle on Tom's knee.

The tears that had filled his eyes started rolling down his face.

He was still crying soundlessly, unable to stop, when the dog tottered through the flat, tail waving gently, and into the laundry. There, he stepped into his basket, turned around three times while sniffing his bedding, folded his limbs, drew tail and nose together as neatly as a knot.

. . . . . .

Tom washed his hands, his face. He breathed in the merciful scent of a clean cotton towel.

Nelly wasn't in the kitchen. He poured warm water onto oats for the dog and placed a cloth serially stamped with the Mona Lisa over the dish.

Across the passage a light gleamed, but there was no one in the living room.

Then he noticed a piece of paper lying on the TV. He went closer and saw a hand-drawn map. It was stained and much creased. But it had been updated with the addition of a tiny stylized dog, tail jauntily aloft.

Tom switched off the lamp and went to Nelly.

THURSDAY

They had gone to bed late and not slept until later still. But Nelly roused him early, while it was still dark. The bedside candle she had lit lay in a shallow cup of red glass. It was the ruby and gold illumination of Tom's solitary performances. What he desired, on the instant, was her direction. His hand passed across his hip, glided over hers, and drew her fingers toward him.

"Hang on." She said, "Something I want to tell you."

She had twisted up her hair, secured it with the comb he had taken from it some hours earlier. Now she retrieved his bedspread from the floor and arranged it about her shoulders. Its loose blue folds, in which tiny mirrors glittered, lay open at her breasts. The soft indigo cotton flowed like a kimono. This brazen orientalism achieved, she was ready to begin.

"What you said yesterday about Felix taking my dress."

Propped on one elbow, Tom waited.

Nelly said it was what she herself had suspected when she heard Jimmy Morgan's story.

"So I was right about Denise. Why didn't you say?"

"I don't think he took it for Denise."

Nelly was silent for so long that Tom slid his free hand into blue shadows. At which she said, "I think Felix took it for himself."

I didn't want to see her face. Jimmy Morgan's unease slid into Tom's mind as female flesh parted unambiguously at his touch.

Nelly murmured, "Like you said about Denise. If someone saw my dress, they might think they'd seen me. And also —"

"What?"

"Felix knew I would know." A little later: "It was his message to me. The note he didn't leave."

Scented molecules were being released into the air; a flower was opening, thick-petaled, sweetly reeking. The man's flesh fluttered and thrilled in response. *Silently fly the birds / all through us,* he thought.

But Nelly went on talking. "It's like he turned himself into a letter only I could read."

Tom tried to concentrate. "Wouldn't he have looked weird? People would have noticed for sure."

"It was mostly dark. And just to get to the beach and away."

She spoke hurriedly; Tom realized she was impatient for him to continue. He rearranged blue pleats, the better to observe her.

"Jimmy Morgan thought the woman he saw was carrying a bag," Nelly said. "Felix could've had other stuff in there, clothes that fitted him."

"It sounds... I don't know, incredible. Not to mention risky."

"He didn't have a lot of time to plan it. And he was good at risks."

While she was speaking, the flame in the red glass dipped and died, and a great wing of shadow reared against the wall.

In the blind dark, Nelly said, "It would explain why he's never been found."

She said, "He might have gone on doing it. Cross-dressing, I mean."

Tom was conscious of her body's heat, of her quick blood under his fingers. At the same time, she seemed mechanical in a way he hadn't noticed the previous night; a pulse jumping at a stroked wrist suggested not so much life as animation. He had created this staccato, but it was not susceptible to rule.

Afterward, it would occur to him that her narrative too might have soared beyond control. Replaying the scene, listening yet again to the increasing urgency of Nelly's whisper, he would ask himself whether her tale was only a by-product of bodily imperative, a device for ensuring his interest and her consummation.

Even at the time, as his sight adjusted itself to the dark, he was aware of her possession by an antique demon. He watched her gaze turn glassy and inward, and thought, She'll say anything now.

When she spoke, it was Tom who shivered. "A child would be more frightened of a man."

It was his cell phone that woke him the second time. He traced it to the kitchen table, answered it standing naked in radiant light.

"It's joy."

It chimed, for a moment, like magic, like a message from the universe. "Yes!" he cried. Thinking, Such joy!

"I gave out your flyers to our drivers."

"Oh — *Joy.*"

She said, "Sorry I haven't got any news"; and Tom recalled, vividly, her grave, well-mannered air. "I was just hoping he might've turned up? So I thought I'd give you a call."

He was still smiling when he carried the dish of oats into the laundry. The dog's tail beat in his basket. He lifted his head to quiver his nostrils about the man's hand.

Tom said, "What went on out there, eh? What a story you could tell." The animal's coat was dry under his fingers, leached of its natural oils.

Having bolted his food, the dog scratched at the back door. Tom left it open. Sunlight and the scent of mock orange blossom from the bush by the gully trap poured into the laundry. It was a perfect day.

In the shower, there was the bliss of massaging shampoo into his scalp. The sun slipped under a cloud, and the frosted shower door turned into a miniature alpine landscape under a dull sky. Then the sun came out again and touched the small glass peaks with gold.

He was thinking about what Nelly had said, picturing Felix Atwood assuming femininity with a dress. It was possible, of course. But above all it was fantastic. In the bright light of day, it was the extravagance of Nelly's conjecture that prevailed. Tom, turning his face up to steamy water, thought, She can't really believe that stuff! And following the path that was opening before him, he found he had arrived at the theatrical. The recent cabaret in his bedroom, with its drapery and candlelight, now struck him as supremely contrived.

But why?

It took shape all at once, as infused with design as a flower. From the press of motives that might have inspired Nelly, one sprang vigorously forth. Tom made himself consider it, the better to thrust it from him, but that only strengthened its hold. It carried the conviction of a thing half-known and dreaded, and seen for the first time.

He stepped out onto the bath mat and into a cube of vaporous light: a man strung with breaking beads of water. Posner's visit came back to him in a new guise, his hints masking a confession Tom had not allowed himself to unveil. He remembered the dealer's eyes, leveled at him like a gun. Posner knew what had happened to Atwood; Tom was sure of it. There had been something else in the room when Posner had called on him that night, something invisible and potent. Something Tom hadn't wished to hear and so willed Posner to leave unsaid. A tiny noise burst from him — if only he hadn't missed it!

At once the whole edifice collapsed like a pricked bubble. It was air and absurdity. It was contested at every turn by his sense of the woman in his bed, by all that was intangible in her makeup, and yet resisted, as if densely material, being modeled into a repulsive form.

And still doubt twisted in Tom's mind; flashed like a fish. Almost, almost, he let it go. But the world chose that moment to break in on his hesitations. A labored breathing close at hand had been growing steadily louder. Now the exhaust fan screamed, shuddered a long moment, and died. Tom flicked the switch but failed to bring about a resurrection.

The death rattle of that fan: it would turn up in dreams for the rest of his life.

The air in the bathroom was dense with misty wreaths. Tom went to the window and tilted it open. When he turned around, it was to the likeness of an incurably benign face. The next instant the haze thinned and Arthur was gone — if he had ever been present, dispersed like steam, before his son had confronted him, a sweetly ineffectual ghost.

Afterward, Tom would ask himself if it had not in fact been a form of counsel: the silent advocacy of kindness that asked nothing in return. But at the time, in that scented room, he was seized by a live impatience. What he required was resolution, not the ambiguity of visions.

The mutiny of the fan played its part in what followed. As things do, needling us with the fickleness of our inventions, provoking displays of mastery.

The draft from the window was feathering Tom's damp skin. He drew his towel close.

In his bedroom he raised the blind by fractions, so that light crawled across the floor.

She didn't stir.

He bent over her.

Nelly's eyes flipped open, and what they held was alarm. Then she smiled, and said, "Hi."

He was thinking, I can't start —

"What's wrong?"

He sat on the bed.

"*What?*"

"Just...oh, you know, that stuff about Felix, what you said before, it's sort of hard to credit."

She half sat up. There was a small, faintly shiny smear where something had dried near her mouth.

She went on looking at Tom, who said in a rush, "If that was you Morgan saw on the beach, if you were there, you have to say. Whatever it was, whatever happened. I'd understand. But I need to know."

The bedspread had long since returned to the floor. After a

moment, Nelly pushed back the sheet under which she lay, one leg folded at the knee. For a long minute she displayed herself to him. Her throat was fibrous, her breasts lolled. There were creases on her thighs, a silver filament of scar tissue below her navel, a roll of flesh at her waist. She was one of Balthus's flagrant little models grown into imperfection. She was a timeless, female arrangement of ovals and planes, of triangles and molded curves.

What Tom desired was a different clarity. Nevertheless, the luminous sight of her, falling across the question in his mind, somewhat altered it. He heard himself saying, "Swear it. Please. Swear by Rory that you had nothing to do with helping his father that night."

Like most triteness, it was fed by genuine emotion. So he was unprepared for what came next.

Nelly began to laugh. Her head tipped back, her pelvis rocked forward, and she laughed. It went on and on, the noise rolling and crashing about the frowsy room. It was like witnessing the materialization of something uncharted, as if that indecorous cascade arrived independently of the figure convulsing against his pillows.

Yet Tom could have vowed the phenomenon was sane. And eventually, he was able to smile. One of the things he knew he was being was ridiculous.

"I swear it." She held up her right hand. "By Rory."

"I'm sorry." He lowered his head and kissed the springy, delicate center of her.

It set her off laughing again.

THREE OR FOUR TIMES a year, when Tom was still at school, Audrey would invite the Loxleys to join her on Saturday for afternoon tea. Bill was always out on these occasions, playing golf. "A man needs an interest to take him out of himself," said Audrey. Her eyes flickered over Tom, embedded in unmanly selfhood on the far side of her third-best tablecloth.

Tom would rather not have been there but was at that stage of ravenous adolescence where he could not forgo the sponges, tarts, and sliced ham that marked the ritual. There was always a plate of triangular sandwiches, another of tinned asparagus. A proper English tea: it was a ceremony dear to Audrey, setting her apart from mere Australians.

Shona, driven by the same sullen need as Tom, would slouch from her room. Silently they competed for butternut crackles.

It soon became apparent to Tom that these afternoons served an unvoiced purpose. Newcomers to the area, extravagantly welcomed by Audrey, in time always merited a good talking-to. Shop assistants, bank tellers, tradesmen: Audrey assured the Loxleys that she stood no nonsense from any of them. Nothing cleared the air like a good talking-to, she said; unless it was giving the offender a piece of her mind.

A summons to tea invariably followed one of these showdowns, from which Audrey emerged energized and triumphant. Over chocolate ripple cake and Scotch fingers, she went over the score: the kindness offered, the advantage taken, the forbearance shown, the treachery exposed. From time to time Iris murmured, "No!" or "What a thing!" but these contributions were redundant. Her sister-in-law's presence was all that Audrey required. An audience justified reenactment, doubling the pleasures of victory. And then, Iris and Tom had a particular value to Audrey. Occasionally an adversary fought back, accusing her of malice or worse. But Audrey put these charges down to spite. She knew she was a good person. The Loxleys proved it. Here they were even now at her table, grateful recipients of her bounty. If now and then a wrinkle of self-doubt threatened her composure, it vanished under the glare of her benevolence. *To give and not count the cost,* remembered Audrey, while making a mental note that a cheaper brand of biscuit would do very well. The quantity Tommy ate while remaining bone thin! Worms, thought Audrey, a diagnosis that amplified her contentment.

She grew expansive. She grew vivacious. It should have been horrible but was in fact funny. Audrey was a good mimic: she could do Liberace, Kenneth Williams, old Mrs. Godfrey next door. She hoarded jokes and brought them out with inventive, straight-faced embellishments. Even Shona stopped eating long enough to snicker.

Overnight Tom lost his taste for sweets. He was in his last year at school, and there was homework to excuse him from Audrey's teas. Now the thought of them disgusted him, his aunt's zestful detailing of her coups as sickening as spray-can cream, as the chemical sweetness of supermarket Swiss roll.

When Audrey's next summons arrived, Tom pleaded his case. He remained in the annex, bent over his books. Slowly light squeezed its way across the room. After a while there came the

mutter of TV on the other side of the wall. Tom knew what it signified: his aunt was not ready to dispel the cozy fumes generated
by goodwill and self-satisfaction. Tea had given way to sherry
and reruns of *Benny Hill* or *On the Buses.*

Tom went into the kitchen to make another mug of Maxwell
House. It could not go on forever, he reminded himself. With his
palms flat on the bench top while the jug boiled, he looked out at
the low evening sun. A nylon half-curtain was strung across the
window. He noticed that the play of light magnified the weave
and overlaid the fabric with a faint moiré sheen.

He had returned to his essay when a sound filtered through
his concentration. After a moment he carried his mug across
the room and stood close to the wall. He could hear the canned
merriment that greeted each quip, but what had captured his
attention was the loose, round noise of his mother's laughter.
It was the rarity of the phenomenon that was striking. Tom
couldn't remember the last time he had heard her laugh like that
with him.

With the ad break, the volume went up and Iris fell silent. Still
her son stayed where he was, resting the side of his head against
the wall. From time to time he blew lightly on his coffee. When
it was cool enough to drink, he went back to his work.

TOM HAD LEFT NELLY at the Preserve and was walking home,
attended by a dwarf double shadow-printed on walls, when

he thought of the skipping girl. She had seemed corpselike, deprived of animating light. Now it occurred to him that her neon had served to cloak the grubby relationship between buyer and seller with obscuring magic. With it switched off, she no longer dazzled her observers but displayed herself for what she was.

A silky, elongated column came into view on the opposite side of the road. It wavered before a window that was sprayed with stars of frost and promised Gift Solutions; Tom watched it rise and sway.

He dodged cars and a grim, spandexed cyclist. "Mogs!" he called. "Mogs!"

"Tom! What a *super* surprise!" Under the brim of her pale straw hat, Mogs was gold-dusted across the nose.

She was saying, "I must say you do look well."

Tom said, "A wonderful thing happened yesterday." He said, "Coffee?"

"Well, I *ought* to be getting back to the gallery —"

But he had seized her arm, above its cuff of shining bracelets. "There's a place just past the lights." A story has no meaning until it is told, and Tom was an Ancient Mariner, brimful of narrative. It overflowed and merged with the changeful kaleidoscope of the street, the cyclist's turquoise rump poised above his saddle, a six-foot koala jangling a bucket of coins, the silver loop glinting on the lid of the manhole at Mogs's sandaled feet. "Come *on*," said Tom. He considered reaching up and licking her freckles.

"That's the most amazing story." Mogs's eyes were glittery. "It's just so *Incredible Journey,* plus *plus.*"

She asked, "And he's all right?"

"Seems to be. Exhausted, of course. And frighteningly thin."

"Oh, the poor love."

"He was walking so slowly. Barely moving." Tom said, "We could have missed him so easily. A few minutes later, and we'd have been gone. I'm not sure he'd have had the strength to follow."

"Don't, no. That's so what you *mustn't* do." Mogs raised her voice over the industrial gargling of the espresso machine. "Once you start thinking what might have happened, there's no end to the horror. He *did* find you, the brave old thing." She blew her nose resolutely on a paper napkin. The green jewel flashed on her finger.

A waitress asked, "You guys right there? More coffee? Another wheatgrass?"

"Oh, no thank you. That was just great."

"Just the bill, please."

Mogs, gathering up bag and hat and sunglasses, said, "You know, I've always meant to try this place. Isn't that clock perfect? And these butterfly coasters. *Brilliant.*"

The bill arrived on a hexagonal plastic saucer, khaki with narrow orange triangles around the rim.

"Carson comes here," went on Mogs. "Rory likes it." She fitted her hat over her glossy crimson head. "It's so sweet, him and Rory, don't you think?"

"I guess." Tom was thinking, *Sweet!*

"Oh, awfully sad, too, of course. You're *absolutely* right." Mogs said, "I mean, I simply can't imagine it, can you? Not being able to acknowledge your child?"

Tom had his wallet out. He went through the business of fishing out some cash and placing it on the saucer, actions he accomplished with the slow deliberation of a dream. Then he said, "Mogs, what are you talking about?"

Moments passed. Then, "Oh, Lord. Oh, how frightful. I mean, I just *assumed*..." Mogs tugged on a pigtail. Her long cheeks were very pink. Tom realized that he had before him one of those rare specimens not enlivened by the dissemination of scandal.

He said, "Just tell me."

"It's only talk. Nothing at *all* certain," wailed Mogs.

Tom waited.

"I've heard...well, one or two people seem to have this notion that Carson is Rory's father. Not that Rory has the *least* idea."

The waitress picked up the saucer. Mogs said, "You know, I'd love a glass of water."

"Still or sparkling?"

"*Tap* would be super."

When she had drunk it, Tom said, "Why would they be keeping it under wraps? Who'd care now?"

"Rory's coming into money. Quite a *lot,* apparently." Mogs's tone was apologetic, as if the sheer size of the sum made for questionable taste. "One of those inheritance trust things. From his father's peop— No, gosh, *isn't* it a muddle? What I mean is, from the Atwoods."

In the street she said again, "It's *really* only speculation. I mean, I always just sort of put it together with the way Carson is about Rory. But that could so easily be Carson. *Such* a sweet man. And if *you* know nothing about it...well, that tips it quite the other way."

She stooped; pressed her cheek to Tom's. "*Lots* of love to darling Nelly. And hug that brave dog for me." Her skin smelled of childhood: ironing and wooden rulers. "The love we have for them," said Mogs. "Sometimes it's almost *frightening*."

IN INDIA, the Loxleys had lived half a mile from a large Hindu temple. It was neither ancient nor celebrated, but its tall gopurams, garishly painted and ornately carved, delighted the child Tom's eye. Pilgrims and sadhus and tricksters passed through its gates, generating noise and emotion. Now and then an elephant would sway forth from its fastness.

If Tom happened to pass the temple in the company of his grandfather, the old man would speak of primitivism and barbaric rites. Sebastian de Souza pointed out men with iron hooks in their flesh, described a reeking stone block where goats were sacrificed. If he caught his grandson looking toward the temple, he would slap him. He referred to filth, meaning the celestial and animal couplings depicted in the carvings as well as the rosettes of dung in the street, when it was in fact the busy little stalls selling coconuts and holy images and garlands of marigolds that had attracted the child's interest. In this way Tom's pleasure in the place was smudged, and the temple became associated in his mind with fear.

In his tenth year, the stories of Catholic missions he heard at school inspired in Tom an evangelizing fervor. He longed to save a soul. He selected Madhu, a six-year-old whose family occupied a modest room in the de Souza mansion. In her gapped smile, he detected malleability. There was also the consideration, only half formulated but nevertheless present, that her low social status would protect him from serious repercussions should the enterprise go awry.

Screened by lush plantains, he spoke to Madhu of miracles. The child listened attentively and repeated the prayers he taught her. But what zealotry fears is not resistance but duplicity. Tom sensed that his pupil was more interested in him than in the substance of his discourse. He felt, at the end of a week, that language alone was inadequate to his purpose. It came to him that if Madhu were to behold its images, the splendor and force of his faith could not fail to impress itself upon her heart.

Conveniently at hand, on the edge of a district that was now a slum but had once housed imperial adventurers, stood a grimy Portuguese church. Madhu trotted there after Tom willingly enough the next morning, although she faltered an instant on entering the high, dim premises. The boy took her by the wrist and led her intuitively toward light, to the great window glowing at the eastern end of the transept.

Madhu looked where he pointed and saw a sublime flowering of the glassmaker's art, commissioned from a French master by a belatedly pious Iberian pirate and shipped east at ruinous expense. She, however, had no means of understanding these things, let alone the allegory of suffering and redemption portrayed before her. And so she screamed and, covering her head with her arms, dashed in terror from the place.

Days passed, days in which Madhu did not come out to play and slipped behind a purple fold of her mother's sari when Tom ambushed her by the gate. That he grasped, eventually, what his convert had perceived was a tribute to the boy's intelligence and the range of his imagination. In his mind he stood once again before the window. He beheld the sacrifice that illustrated his god's infinite compassion; and saw, also, a man whose broken white body and crimsoned wounds the light endowed with awful verisimilitude.

That a sign might proclaim a truth as well as its opposite was in itself a disturbing magic. Further reflection brought a more profound revelation: for if Madhu saw violence and cruelty at the heart of his religion, might there not be loving kindness in the barbarism attributed to hers?

It was an insight both liberating and shocking. Tom Loxley, dusty-toed, felt the foundations of his world tremble. It would always be possible to stroll around to the back of knowledge and look at it from the other side.

MOGS'S LONG STRIDE carried her away, past the ringleted Goth, buckled into black, texting at the tram stop; "Death to Moonlight" read the legend on his T-shirt. A girl emerged from a juice bar and pranced across the street, a golden ring winking in her brown belly. A courier astride a motorcycle turned his glass face to watch her.

On a car radio, children sang, *Christmas in Australia's hot,/Cold and frosty is what it's not*. Two boys with clipboards and ballpoints closed in on a woman trying to slip into the supermarket. Tom put on his sunglasses against the gaudy day.

Listening to Mogs deny it, he had known he had been duped; now he was no longer certain. His mind was running with what Nelly might say, with assurances she might offer or withhold. On a suburban pavement he was privy to the interrogator's exquisite dilemma: nothing less than the truth could satisfy, but when was satisfaction ever a guarantee of truth?

But even as he framed the problem, Tom rejected its terms. If he had got everything wrong, a mistake, levering open prospects, can reveal far more than mere precision. He saw that knowledge, which had sheltered him for so long, had been allowed to shrink to a constraint. Over the clanking of a green tram, he was aware of unruly starlings making mock.

The lights changed. The traffic coursed forward. A skateboarder crossing the other way said, "I wouldn't call it a Kodak moment, dude." Nelly's laughter rolled through Tom again.

On the far pavement, iron railings clasped a municipal gum tree. A window held a crayoned image of a red-cloaked child and a grinning beast. Tom went slowly past uphill. Of where he was heading, he had no clear sense. But what he wished, with all the force of imperial afternoon, was that he might yet be graced with courage and loving conduct in the face of everything that can never be known.

There came, at that moment, a soft vibration against his hip. He took out his phone and found he was reading a message he had sent himself. It was time to feed the dog.

IRIS'S FINGERS tightened on the handles of her walker as it approached the step. The front wheels tilted into space; and, "I'm falling!" screamed Iris. "I'm falling!"

Tom said, "I won't let you fall."

Dear Iris,

By hook or by crook
I'm the last in this book

Your affectionate friend
Dorothy Gomez

2/19 Sea street, Mangalore, India, The world

By ham or by bacon
Your sadly mistaken !! Ha Ha Ho!

ACKNOWLEDGMENTS

I had the good fortune to benefit from the editorial guidance of Pat Strachan, Jane Palfreyman, and Alison Samuel. Sarah Lutyens did what she does brilliantly, and it was a pleasure to work with Caren Florance and Ali Lavau.

Ian Britain, Glenn D'Cruz, Gail Jones, Anna Schwartz, and Chris Wallace-Crabbe advised me on the manuscript. Jan Nelson offered conversation about art and artists, while John Chambers enlightened me about bond trading in the 1980s. Kate Darian-Smith and Glenda Sluga facilitated my research by offering me a fellowship at the Australian Centre in the School of Historical Studies at the University of Melbourne. I am grateful to them all.

Thank you also to Émilie Asselineau, Alexandre Asselineau, and Ned Lutyens for their hand in this work.

Chris Andrews read every draft of the manuscript, and was always insightful and encouraging; which is a wholly inadequate acknowledgment of the extent of my debt to him.

The following books were particularly useful in the writing of this one: *Illuminations* (Fontana, 1973) and *One-Way Street and Other Writings* (NLB, 1979) by Walter Benjamin; *The Lie of the Land* (Faber, 1996) by Paul Carter; *Farewell to an Idea: Episodes in the History of Modernism* (Yale University Press, 1999) by T. J. Clark; *The Practice of Everyday Life* (University of Minnesota Press, 1988) by Michel de Certeau; *The Oxford Book of Australian Ghost Stories* (Oxford University Press, 1994), edited by Ken Gelder; *A Private Life of Henry James: Two Women and His Art* (Chatto & Windus, 1998) by Lyndall Gordon; and *The Country of Lost Children: An Australian Anxiety* (Cambridge University Press, 1999) by Peter Pierce.

The Lost Dog also draws directly and obliquely on various works by Henry James.

The lines quoted on page 34 are from "The Lost Man" by Judith Wright in *A Human Pattern: Selected Poems* (ETT Imprint, Sydney, 1996). Reprinted by permission of ETT Imprint.

The line quoted on page 220 is from "The Choice" by W. B. Yeats in *The Complete Works of W. B. Yeats, Volume I: The Poems, Revised,* edited by Richard J. Finneran. Copyright © 1933 by The Macmillan Company; copyright renewed © 1961 by Bertha Georgie Yeats. All rights reserved. Reprinted in the USA and its territories with the permission of Scribner, an imprint of Simon & Schuster Adult Publishing Group. Reprinted elsewhere by permission of A. P. Watt Ltd. on behalf of Gráinne Yeats.

The lyrics quoted on page 321 are from *Christmas Where the Gum Trees Grow* by Lesley Davies. Reprinted by permission of Lesley Davies.

ABOUT THE AUTHOR

MICHELLE DE KRETSER was born in Sri Lanka and immigrated to Australia when she was fourteen. She was educated in Melbourne and Paris and has worked as an editor and a book reviewer. Her first novel, *The Rose Grower,* won international acclaim.

The Hamilton Case, her second novel, received the Commonwealth Writers' Prize (South East Asia and South Pacific region) and the Society of Authors Encore Award (UK) for best second novel of the year. It was also first runner-up for Barnes & Noble's Discover Award in fiction and a *New York Times* Notable Book of the Year.

The Lost Dog, De Kretser's third novel, received Australia's "Book of the Year" Award, the Christina Stead Prize for Fiction, and the Gold Medal from the Australian Literary Society. It was a finalist for the Commonwealth Writers' Prize and was longlisted for the Man Booker Prize and the Orange Broadband Prize.

Reading Group Guide

THE
LOST
DOG

A Novel by

MICHELLE
DE KRETSER

A CONVERSATION WITH THE AUTHOR OF *THE LOST DOG*

Michelle de Kretser talks with Boyd Tonkin
of *The Independent*

The best stories lodge in the memory and return to haunt their readers. Michelle de Kretser, whose fiction often dwells on the ghostly afterglow of narrative, spooked my summer holiday last year. On a showery, late-monsoon August day in Sri Lanka, I took a cab through swamp to jungle to the lovingly preserved home of Bevis Bawa. A soldier, lawyer, and aesthete, Bawa carved a beautifully unlikely landscape garden out of the tropical profusion. I found myself viewing every classical statue, flowering tree, and oddly displaced lawn through the lens of *The Hamilton Case*. In that novel, de Kretser captured a doomed clan's rage for order as colonial Ceylon was engulfed and smothered by a history that not even the most manic cultivation could resist.

The author has never been to Bawa's "Brief Garden." In fact, she has rarely revisited the island where, the daughter of a judge, she lived for fourteen years until the family migrated to Australia. "I deliberately didn't go back when I was writing

The Hamilton Case," she says over coffee atop a high-rise West End hotel, the hubbub of London reduced to a silent diagram. "Memory is good filter. You remember what is striking. Fiction is about selection — it's about leaving out — and memory does that for you." Besides, she grew up in Ceylon: "It's a lost country, a ghost country. The name changed the week I left.... Modern Sri Lanka has been shaped, sadly, by the war [between the state and Tamil Tigers]. I, luckily, have not been part of that."

All the same, a Colombo paper recently greeted her new novel's triumph in a Sydney fiction award as: "Sri Lankan author wins prize." "I was extremely touched," says a writer who avoids the stale protocols of "migrant identity" fiction and, "most of the time," feels "terribly Australian. It's a successful multicultural model in that sense. When multiculturalism is working well, you're not aware of it."

After a debut, *The Rose Grower,* set in revolutionary France, *The Hamilton Case* proved a breakthrough book. Here was a dazzlingly accomplished author who commanded all the strokes. Her repertoire stretched from a hallucinatory sense of place to a mastery of suspense, sophisticated verbal artistry, and a formidable skill in navigating those twisty paths where history and psychology entwine. De Kretser, for years an editor at the Lonely Planet travel group, came to fiction relatively late. Indeed, the sole quality that I missed in *The Hamilton Case* was a feeling of intimate investment in an island story that, after all, was hers as well. Yet it did lurk there, somehow buried in the rampant foliage.

"Going to Australia was an awfully big adventure," she recalls. "There was no sense that this was anything but gain. And I always had that sense that I never said goodbye properly. I think that, completely unconsciously, that novel was my way of going back and taking my leave in a more considered and, I hope, honoring way than I was capable of when I was young."

Leave-taking, loss, and the fragile gifts of memory propel Michelle de Kretser's third novel. In *The Lost Dog*, the Anglo-Indian academic Tom Loxley — who himself left Asia for Australia at age twelve, and now writes on Henry James — spends eight days searching for a beloved mongrel who goes missing in the bush. Day by anxious day, we learn of his insecure childhood in the "aromatic streets" of south India; of his delphic, seductive artist friend Nelly Zhang, the queen of a bohemian tribe; and of the unburied secrets that return to "ghost" his life and hers. Behind their troubled affections lies the "ghost story" of Australia itself, "this country with a haunted past, which we don't want to think about too much. Yet it comes and visits us when we're least expecting it."

The mutt comes back, as did de Kretser's own — late — dog, Gus, after a longer absence. "We never knew how he got free. So there was real-life story with a mystery at the heart of it." As for the family riddles that crowd around the disappearance of Nelly's banker husband, they remain as tantalizing as the semi-occult tales of Henry James — which do the literary haunting here. De Kretser praises the "fantastic undecidability" of James's open-ended plots. "James is so endlessly quotable," she says, "but one of his great mots is 'Never say you know the last word about any human heart.'" William Boyd, she notes, liked the idea so much he took it for a title. "People always exceed your understanding of them. People are endlessly surprising." And so, "No one is beyond redemption."

The Lost Dog springs its own surprises. Many British readers still expect a literary Australia of broad vistas and open hearts. Yet de Kretser depicts an arch and arty Melbourne, so steeped in coterie in-jokes and post-modern ironies that it could make Shoreditch feel like Saskatchewan.

As she evokes Nelly's deadpan art of urban collage and kitschy bricolage, de Kretser becomes a psychogeographer to match London's Iain Sinclair or Will Self. "More than 80 per cent of the country's population lives in big cities," she says, "not different from London or Berlin or Paris or LA. They are Australian, but they are also global." Even out in the soggy wilderness, when Tom looks for his little beast in the jungle, man-made forests have replaced first growths: "The wilderness is not as wild as it seems."

The novel unleashes plenty of hyper-conscious irony, but finally muzzles it. Tom, a dark and timid migrant boy, has learned to flourish as an ironist: "the trope of mastery; of seeing through, of knowing better." Nelly, with her parodic, thrift-shop Chinoiserie, at first seems to trump even him in a taste for masquerade. But need, and curiosity, will get the better of both.

Tom's love for his wayward hound trumps every cool boho pose. "Dogs don't do irony," de Kretser points out. Above all, his relationship with his ailing mother, Iris, deepens his "affiliation" to others. Divorced and childless, Tom must learn to act as "parent to his own mother." He has to clear up the mess of a mutinous body and a wandering mind. "Sex is something written about so endlessly," says de Kretser. "Now, the bedroom door is so wide open. But bodily functions are still slightly taboo in literature. I wanted to write about it in a way that was neither prudish nor sensational." Although "in the West, there's a tendency to privilege mind over body," ageing means "that is reversed.... In the end, the body will triumph over all of us."

De Kretser had her own warning foretaste of debility when a slipped disc plunged her into pain and immobility. "If you've got any kind of debilitating illness, it is like a flash-forward into dependent old age. And what you fear...is that you will be treated as an object. I was very lucky: I had a very loving partner who looked after me. But I couldn't walk." Later, she even came to think of her affliction as "one of those weird gifts, in very unwelcome packaging. It did give me...a glimpse of what it is like when the circumference of your life shrinks to the constraints of the body. I've always been someone who considered myself an intellectual — the mind, the mind, the mind. But it was a reminder that you are a body."

Some critics have saluted de Kretser's almost flagrant virtuosity while worrying that she might come over as — well, too clever by half. That strikes me as unjust. *The Lost Dog* showcases not only a writer as subtly perceptive about feelings as ideas, but one who, via Tom, traces a thinker's quest to overcome cerebral detachment. What is true is that the novel loads much of its emotional charge not into talk but into things — from Iris's tatty ornaments to Nelly's artfully mounted detritus of condom wrappers or mutilated dolls. Both women seek to invest "the valueless things of the world with joy." De Kretser connects this urge to curate ephemera with the migrant's separation from a cherished past.

When her mother died, in 2006, "I was just struck by how little she owned that was hers, apart from her jewelry. So much had to be just left behind. This is the story of so many people's lives in a century of migration." In contrast, "If you were to come to my house you would notice that I don't do minimalism. It is extremely cluttered." She admits that "I do haunt flea-markets." In the novel, bric-a-brac and kitsch stand for oceans of unspoken passion or yearning. As Henry James himself advised, de Kretser's fiction shows rather than tells. And the story that it shows, just as she hopes, "goes on haunting you, after you have finished reading it." The artful beasts in this jungle never go to sleep.

Boyd Tonkin's profile of Michelle de Kretser originally appeared in *The Independent* on June 20, 2008. Reprinted with permission.

QUESTIONS AND TOPICS
FOR DISCUSSION

1. Suspense is a crucial element in this novel: Will Tom's dog be found? What happened to Nelly's husband? Are Tom and Nelly destined to be together? Which mystery in the plot did you most long to solve and why? Did Michelle de Kretser provide answers to all of your questions?

2. *The Lost Dog* is set in Melbourne, Australia, where Michelle de Kretser has lived for many years. She has said, "I loved picking out little random bits of the world around me — a house with a photograph on its façade, an overheard sentence, a derelict advertising sign." What are some memorable sights and characteristics of your own town or neighborhood? How do they bring your environment to life and make it unique? How do these touchstones speak to the passage of time?

3. Tom Loxley immigrated to Australia from India when he was twelve, and Michelle de Kretser moved to Australia from Sri Lanka when she was fourteen. How do you think the author's personal experience may have enriched her portrait of Tom? What differences might they both see between

their homelands and modern Melbourne? How does materialism figure in?

4. Nelly Zhang is a high-spirited visual artist and Tom Loxley is a relatively somber, analytic scholar. How do these differences in temperament and vocation serve to bring them together? Do you think these dichotomies influence the outcome of their relationship? Is it true in your own experience that opposites attract?

5. "The past is not what is over but what we wish to have done with" (page 297). Do you agree? Would Tom agree? How can you reconcile this statement with Tom's rescue of his mother's old autograph album (page 195)?

6. Michelle de Kretser's gifts as a prose stylist have won consistent praise from reviewers of *The Lost Dog*. In what ways, if any, did the author's use of the language enhance your reading experience? Identify some metaphors used in the novel — e.g., "He was an umbrella tightly furled" — that seem to you particularly apt.

7. Instances of loss permeate this novel. Tom and his mother's loss of their father and husband, and of their aromatic, warm, and spiritual birthplace; Nelly's inclination to collect objects from the past; and, of course, the missing dog. How does de Kretser prevent her novel from being excessively elegiac? What do you see as the future for Tom and Nelly?

8. De Kretser writes that "the dog unleashed in Tom a kind of grace; a kind of beastliness" (page 189). In what ways do Nelly and Tom's mother, Iris, serve as similar catalysts?

Throughout *The Lost Dog* human physicality is acknowledged as frequently as our cerebral nature. How did you respond to this juxtaposition? Where have you read before, if ever, such intimate accounts of caretaking?

9. Discuss the failure of Tom's first marriage. Was Karen being disingenuous when she claimed not to want children? Was Tom? In what sense does the dog's disappearance stir regret in Tom about how his life has turned out?

10. It is a Jamesian idea that what is seen depends on who is seeing it. How does this idea color *The Lost Dog*? Do you believe, as Mogs did, that Carson Posner is Nelly's son's father? Do you think that Felix Atwood, Nelly's vanished husband, was a pedophile? Do you believe Denise Corrigan's theory that Nelly killed her husband? Is clear evidence for any of these suppositions given in *The Lost Dog*?

11. *The Lost Dog* takes place in 2001 and encompasses the attack of September 11. How does this event cause Tom to reflect on Australia's colonial past and inhospitable present? In what ways can Americans identify with his thought that "buried deep in Australian memories was the knowledge that strangers had once sailed to these shores and destroyed what they found" (page 234)?

12. Sitting with Nelly in her drafty kitchen, Tom thinks, "Existence was inseparable from tragedy and adventure, horror and romance; realism's quiet hue derived from a blend of dramatic elements" (page 239). In what ways, if any, can you relate this sentiment to your own life, however seemingly uneventful or conventional it is?

Also by Michelle De Kretser

The Hamilton Case

"A dazzling performance....It is impossible to describe de Kretser's prose as anything but rich, luxuriant, intense, and gorgeous." — Anita Desai, *New York Review of Books*

"A mini-masterpiece of a mystery....De Kretser's prose is stunning...evoking the glittering excesses of colonial life and the tropical fecundity of Ceylon with equally irresistible power." — Lev Grossman, *Time*

"Multilayered and beguiling....The rackety lives of the Obeysekere family eloquently illustrate the fundamental messiness and illogic of the human condition....*The Hamilton Case* does enchant, certainly, but — more important — the book admirably and resolutely sees the world as it really is." — William Boyd, *New York Times Book Review*

"Prose as lush as a tropical jungle....A poignant meditation on colonialism, family ties, race, and national identity." — Adam Woog, *Seattle Times*

"I devoured this book. De Kretser misses nothing." — Christopher Ondaatje, *Literary Review*

"Elegant, seductive....A novel that charms and beguiles....De Kretser has pulled off something remarkable." — Laura Miller, *Salon*

"Simply put, *The Hamilton Case* is one of the most extraordinary novels I have ever read....It makes the English language sing." — Kenneth Champeon, BookPage

Back Bay Books
Available wherever paperbacks are sold

Now in paperback • Great for reading groups

Say You're One of Them
Stories by Uwem Akpan

"One of the year's most exhilarating reads....Awe is the only appropriate response to Uwem Akpan's stunning debut, a collection of five stories so ravishing and sad that I regret ever wasting superlatives on fiction that was merely very good."
— Jennifer Reese, *Entertainment Weekly*

Stand the Storm
A novel by Breena Clarke

"A passionate, dramatic, and uplifting story of the African American aspiration for true freedom....*Stand the Storm* reads like a great nineteenth-century page-turner....Breena Clarke writes in a deceptively simple and subtle style, with an almost perfect sense of period and history."
— Gail Buckley, *Washington Post Book World*

Beginner's Greek
A novel by James Collins

"While the title of James Collins's comedy of manners might cause Jane Austen to raise an eyebrow, were she to crack it she'd discover a debut novel worthy of her own book club....A satire of modern love that will charm both sexes equally."
— Elissa Schappell, *Vanity Fair*

Back Bay Books
Available wherever paperbacks are sold

Now in paperback • Great for reading groups

The Blue Star
A novel by Tony Earley

"I galloped through the novel and relished every page.... Tony Earley's simple prose is always informed by Jim's good heart.... *The Blue Star,* like its hero, is irresistible."

— Scott Turow, *New York Times Book Review*

Testimony
A novel by Anita Shreve

"Contrasting the sweetness of young love with the primal recklessness of lust, Shreve paints a chilling portrait of how bad decisions in brief moments can ruin lives."

— Joanna Powell, *People*

The Road Home
A novel by Rose Tremain

"At once timeless and bitingly contemporary, *The Road Home* explores the life now lived by millions — when one's hope lies in one country and one's heart in another."

— *The New Yorker*

Back Bay Books
Available wherever paperbacks are sold